OLD AND NEW

THE MACLELLAN SISTERS TRILOGY

LUCINDA RACE

MC TWO PRESS

BOOK ONE OF THE MACLELLAN SISTERS

The MacLellan Sisters

Old and New

By

Lucinda Race

Edited by Mackenzie Walton

Cover design by Jade Webb www.meetcutecreative.com

Manufactured in the United States of America
First Edition June 2019

Print Edition ISBN 978-0-9986647-5-0
E-book Edition ISBN 978-0-9986647-6-7

ACKNOWLEDGMENTS

For my readers, who encourage me to keep writing.
Thank you.
To Caroline, a Scottish lass who shared her love of Scotland with me.
To Suzanne, for sharing the love of romance writing. You're awesome!

There's a bit of magic everywhere.

1

Thud. Jamie slammed the door behind her, shutting out the biting cold. The silence embraced her as she entered the quaint cottage. A familiar ache wrapped around her heart, this was home but she was alone. Kicking off black high-heeled boots she walked in stocking feet to the mantle, flipping a switch the gas fireplace whooshed to life. She held her hands out towards the fire and rubbed them together absorbing the warmth. *Welcome home, Jamie.*

She wandered into her bedroom and changed into yoga pants, a well-worn fisherman-knit sweater and plush heavy socks, perfect for hanging out in the house. The back door chimed. *Must be the girls.*

"Come in," she called down the hallway.

"Jamie, where are you hiding?" Kenzie shouted.

"In the bedroom. Be right out. Is Grace with you?"

"She's right behind me."

Jamie walked into the hallway, her smile tugging at the corners of her mouth.

"What's going on?" Grace came bopping through the door, clear blue eyes dancing.

Jamie tugged at a curl that had escaped from Grace's bun. "I'm happy to see my sisters."

The sisters were exactly eleven months apart, Scottish triplets. Each sister was born on the eleventh of the month, Jamie in May, Kenzie in April and Grace in March. They had the same crystal-blue eyes and chestnut hair, but that was where the similarity ended. Jamie was tall and willowy, and her long hair fell in thick waves around her shoulders. Kenzie was vertically challenged and athletic, her short, spiky hair suiting an active life. Grace, the baby, was average height and her figure was curvy like her bouncy curls.

"It's about time you got here, Grace, I'm starving." Kenzie grabbed two paper bags out of Grace's arms and hurried into the kitchen. Over her shoulder, she said, "Hey, I thought Jamie was buying tonight."

Grace shrugged off her long tailored black coat and tucked the butter-soft pink leather gloves and pink beret into a side pocket, and hung it next to Kenzie's deep blue pea coat. She tugged on the bobby pins holding her hair secured in a bun, letting her curls bounce free. Closing her eyes, she sighed, "Oh that feels so good." She tousled the curls into place. "I volunteered to pick it up." Glancing at the counter, and then at Jamie she smirked, "Is there wine?"

Jamie's eyebrow arched. She smiled in response—"But of course"—and pointed to the kitchen. "Help yourself, there's white in the fridge."

Kenzie rummaged through the wine rack. Victoriously, she thrust the bottle in the air. "I'm opening the merlot."

"Pour me a glass too?" Jamie asked, and Grace echoed the request.

Jamie sniffed appreciatively. "My gosh, the lo mein's making my mouth water." She rummaged in the second bag. "I hope you got extra dumplings."

The sisters quickly filled their plates and the wineglasses. Settling into the deep cushions in front of the crackling fire, plates resting on the square wooden coffee table, the girls held up their glasses—cheers!

Kenzie twirled noodles around her fork and shifted her gaze to Jamie. "Your text said a box from Scotland arrived?"

Jamie's shoulders slumped and she munched on a slice of bread. "I got an email from Mom. She and Dad are cleaning out some of Gran's things and found it. I guess it was addressed to us. I thought it would be better to open it together."

Kenzie looked between her sisters, her smile pained. "It's hard to believe she's gone."

Jamie wiped away a lone tear. "I keep expecting the phone to ring and hear Gran asking when we're hopping on the next plane."

"Guys"—fighting back tears, Grace's face sagged—"can we concentrate on what's in the box? It hurts too much to talk about Gran's death."

Kenzie wiped away the tears that had slipped down her cheeks. "Grace is right. Let's open the box and see what's inside, after we finish this amazing lo mein."

The girls bounced ideas around over what might be in the box until dinner was finished. Grace stood up and whisked away the empty plates. She called over her shoulder, "I'll grab the wine if someone can get the box. You know how much I hate waiting to open any kind of box."

Jamie went in search of scissors and pointed to the closet. "Kenz, the box is in there." Kenzie opened the door and carefully carried the box to the coffee table, as if it contained something irreplaceable.

Jamie returned, and said, her hand hovering over the tape, "Here goes nothing."

Grace came in holding a bottle of wine. "Be careful, Sissy," she whispered reverently. "It was Gran's, so it's really old."

Jamie held her breath as she cautiously sliced through the layers of packing tape and eased back the cardboard flaps.

Standing on tiptoes, Kenzie peered over her shoulder. "What is it?"

Jamie withdrew a cream-colored envelope. "It's a letter." Grace reached out to pull back the bubble wrap when Jamie touched her hand. "Wait. We should read it first and then we'll see what's inside."

Kenzie stretched out her hand. "I'll read it." She slit open the wax seal and pulled out several pieces of stationery. Glancing down, she said, "I don't remember Gran's handwriting so spider web like, so it might take a while."

Grace leaned in and studied the page. "I don't think its Gran's. What if it's Great-gran's? You know Dad's grandmother."

Jamie admonished, "If we stop talking and let Kenz read, I'll bet we find out." She picked up her wineglass and settled back on the sofa cushions.

My dearest granddaughters,

This is your father's grandmother writing to you long before you were even a gleam in his eye or even before he had any interest in lassies. If you have received this box, it means that I've had the joy of seeing my beloved daughter, your grandmother, again. I'm sorry for your loss and hope your memories of her will sustain you through the years to come and her wisdom will guide you. I will assume you have a box from your Gran. Have you looked inside? If not, carefully unwrap the contents and lay the three items I chose for you on a table.

Jamie's eyes grew wide as she looked at her sisters. "What the hell, is she psychic or something?"

Grace clapped a hand over her mouth. "Remember, Gran

said the women in our family were special. Maybe that's what she was talking about."

Kenzie's eyebrow shot up. "That would explain a few things about Gran. She always seemed to have eyes on us all the time."

Absentmindedly Jamie tapped her glass with her finger. "Do you remember the time…I must have been around ten. We decided to get up early and go fishing, and when we got to the bottom of the stairs Gran was dressed and waiting for us? I know we never talked about sneaking off while we were in the house where she could hear us."

"You're right." Grace let out a rush of breath. "Our sneaky plans were always hatched underneath that old willow tree near the creek."

Kenzie gasped. "Oh, wow. That does make me wonder about all kinds of things."

Jamie waved her hands toward the box. "Enough speculating about Gran being able to read our minds—let's see what's inside."

Taking care not to rush, Grace took a small package wrapped in plain brown paper. She pulled back the paper and cut the bubble wrap inside, to discover a carved wooden box. Her voice was barely above a whisper. "Should I open it?"

"Hold on, let's see what Kenzie has."

Kenzie withdrew a large floppy package wrapped in white tissue paper tied with the deep green satin ribbon. She pulled back the paper, revealing a large piece of wool, a Scottish tartan. "Isn't this the MacLellan plaid?" She carefully placed it on the back of the sofa.

Jamie and Grace nodded, eager to see the third item.

"One item left, Jamie, your turn." Kenzie slid the box in front of her older sister.

Jamie pulled out an identical-looking package tied with

the same ribbon. "Do you think it's another plaid, maybe a cape?" She tugged the bow and eased back the tissue paper.

"Oh my gosh! It's a wedding dress." Awestruck, Grace reached out and fingered the silky fabric. "Do you think it was Great-gran's?"

Jamie's voice softened. "It must have been—look at the style. The simplicity of the cut is definitely vintage. The fabric feels like silk," she turned the dress over, "and look at the laces on the back, that must have been how it was secured." Jamie held it up to look closer. "This eyelet looks to be hand-sewn. It must have taken hours and the needle work is exquisite."

Kenzie picked up the letter. "Let's see what Great-gran has to say about it."

"Wait! What's in the little box?" Grace pried off the top and unfolded a square of the same silky fabric as the dress. Nestled inside was a large brooch. She held it up in the fire-light. "Look, it's a thistle, and I wonder if the stone is an amethyst." Grace turned it over in her hand. "It's stunning," she said breathlessly.

Kenzie's eyes were drawn back to the letter. She began to read.

Now that you have the plaid, the dress and the brooch unpacked, it's time for you to know what this means.

When I was a young woman I was convinced I would never marry. I was rapidly approaching spinsterhood. I was fine with not having a husband or a family, for a while. But there did come a day when I longed to have a man to share my life with and raise a family.

One day while I was preparing a meal for my parents I had a vision of three lovely young women—Jamie, Kenzie and Grace. I didn't tell anyone, but I knew deep in my heart that you were my legacy.

. . .

Grace hit her hand on the table with a thud. "I knew it, Gran was a psychic."

Jamie felt goose bumps crawl over her arms.

Annoyed, Kenzie looked over the top of the page. "Can I continue?"

Grace sank back into the pillows and sulked. "Sure. Don't let me stop you."

After my vision I wondered would I marry and have a family. The next day I went to an old wise woman who lived in our village. I told her what I had seen and asked, how can my blood flow in the veins of these young women I saw when I'm not betrothed?

The old woman asked me to fetch her sewing basket. Of course, I did. When I handed it to her, she dug to the very bottom and pulled out a large spool of ivory silk thread. She handed it to me and told me to purchase the finest fabric I could find and make a wedding dress, but only use this thread. Once it was complete, put the dress on and look into a mirror. If I did as she instructed, the man meant to be my husband would find me.

I was skeptical. However, the image of three lovely young women began to appear in my dreams. I made the dress you have in your possession. I followed the instructions exactly. I wore the dress one time after it was complete, as a woman without a man to marry.

My parents thought I was touched with fever, but I was compelled to do this. Our family legacy depended on it. I guess by now you've figured out I did marry—his name was James Mackenzie. He was a good man and a good father, and we were blessed with one daughter.

Your gran, Arabel, was hesitant to marry. She felt there wasn't a man to live up to her standards. On her eighteenth birthday, I implored her to don my wedding dress. She did, and later that year she fell in love with and married Rory MacLellan. As you know, he was your Grandfather MacLellan.

Kenzie looked over the top of the page. "Did you know any this, Jamie?"

Shaking her head, Jamie fought to keep her voice steady. "I know some of the names, but nothing about the dress. Keep reading."

That leads me to you, my beautiful Great-granddaughters, and your current situation. Each of you is unmarried.

Grace sucked in a breath. "What is she, a witch?"

Jamie laughed, breaking the tension. "Remember she said she could see the future. But I don't think she was a witch."

Kenzie's voice cut through the giggles. "Hey, you two, let me finish."

As my last request to my daughter Arabel, I had her take the brooch my dear husband gave me on our wedding day, the MacLellan family plaid from Rory MacLellan, and the wedding dress that has been worn by two of your ancestors, and store it in a chest with instructions the items be sent to you upon Arabel's death.

It is time for each of you to try on this dress. As long as the original seams are untouched, this dress will continue to hold the magic of love and hope for the future in each stitch. Although we have never met, I have great love for you, daughters of my beloved grandson James.

Be brave, my lovelies. I am with you always.

Your Great-grandmother Ann

. . .

Kenzie leaned back in the chair, clutching the sheaf of papers to her chest. "I never gave it much thought, but I was named after our Great-grandfather's surname."

Jamie shook her head in disbelief. "I always thought I was named for Dad, but it seems like he was named after Great-grandfather. I never knew."

Sadness filled Grace's eyes as she looked at her sisters. "So where did they come up with the name Grace? I'm not named after anyone."

Jamie hopped up and grinned. "Hold on, I have an idea. Give me a second." She returned with her laptop. After flipping it open, she struck a few keys. "Just as I suspected. Ann means 'graceful one.'"

Grace beamed. "So, in some small way each of us is connected to our Great-grandmother Ann."

"It would seem so. But why do we need to get married?" Kenzie gingerly touched the dress. "Aren't we all fine just as we are? We're successful in our careers, financially stable, and what do we need men for? We've made a choice to be single thirty-somethings. So there's no need to try the dress on, right?"

Jamie closed her laptop. "Of course we're happily single." Her eyes grew misty. "You do have to admit it is kind of cool to get a letter from Great-grandmother Ann and have the brooch Great-grandad gave her, a dress she made, along with the plaid."

"It is, but weird at the same time. But don't you think it's a little creepy that Great-grandmother Ann seems to know so much about us?" Grace stood up and stretched.

Kenzie mused, tapping her chin. "You know I never really thought about psychic ability, but it would explain why we seem to know what each other is thinking."

Jamie rubbed her eyes and shook her head in disbelief. "I really don't think we're psychic...but well, it does leave a lot of unanswered questions."

Kenzie yawned. "I'm beat—it's time for me to head home." She pulled herself up from the couch and handed the letter to Jamie. "Before we head out, we should toast to our family. It's a Jameson kind of night."

The girls walked over to the granite-topped island. Jamie lined up three shot glasses and poured in splashes of whiskey. Holding her glass aloft, she waited until Grace and Kenzie joined her.

Jamie said, "To all the women who came before us."

The girls downed the smooth liquid and set their glasses down.

Kenzie broke the silence. "I guess, since you're the oldest, it's your responsibility to store everything."

Jamie trailed her sisters to the back door. Hugging them tight, she said, "I'll put everything away for safe keeping, and if you get the urge to try the dress on, let me know."

Kenzie smirked. "Yeah, right, like any of us wants to try on a wedding dress."

Grace stifled a yawn and patted Jamie on the arm, "Talk to you tomorrow, sis."

Jamie watched her sisters' cars drive down the deserted, snow-covered street. Shivering, she closed the door and flipped the lock. She wandered into the empty living room and tenderly folded the soft wool fabric, and laid it in the box, adding the wedding dress on top. She ran her hand over the lace and wondering how long it took her Great-grandmother to make it. She touched the brooch. "I need to get this appraised and then insured. I would hate for something to happen to this antique pin."

She replaced the top on the wooden box and carried them into her bedroom. She laid the large one on the cedar chest and the small box, which held the brooch, on her dresser, and she started to leave the room. Hesitating, she turned on her heel. It was as if the dress was calling to her.

With a shake of her head, she pulled the dress and plaid out. "These are far too beautiful to be hidden away."

Jamie draped the plaid over her reading chair and dug around in her closet for a padded hanger. She slipped the hanger in from the bottom of the dress and hung it on her closet door. After propping the bedroom door open, she went back to the kitchen to clean up before calling it a night.

When she was done, Jamie returned to her bedroom feeling wide awake. She curled up in her reading chair and picked up the novel she was reading when a chill came over her. She grabbed the blanket behind her, and tucked an afghan around her feet, and she got lost in her book.

2

Jamie stopped short before closing the bedroom door. The wedding dress looked lovelier in the early morning light than it had the night before. Jamie was inexplicably drawn to cross the room and run her hand down the length of the dress.

She sighed. "It is beautiful. Ann was a talented seamstress."

Without another thought, Jamie hurried from the house and drove off to her office, ready to face testy clients and a desk full of paperwork.

Grace was dressed and waiting for a change when Jamie came out of the locker room. Kenzie's face lit up when her sisters walked in the weight room.

"'Bout time you two showed up. I just finished setting out mats and free weights. Are you ready to sweat?"

Grace groaned and rolled her eyes. "For once, take it easy on your tired, stressed-out, overworked sisters. Today was brutal. I was on the run from the moment I walked through the door—it was a never-ending parade of patients."

Kenzie tipped her head in Jamie's direction. "I can guess your lower half never got out of your cushy chair today. Right?"

Jamie shrugged and held up her hands. "What can I say, I push papers for a living. And might I remind you,' she razzed, "I take care of both your company and personal finances, so taking it easy on me might be a good idea too. It is tax time, you know."

"If I did, neither of you would ever break a sweat." Tossing them each a small clean towel, Kenzie said, "Let's get down to business. If you work hard, I'll buy dinner tonight." A mischievous gleam lit up her blue eyes. "How often do I voluntarily open my wallet?"

"Ya know, Jamie," Grace snickered, "I don't remember the last time Kenzie bought dinner."

Jamie smiled, enjoying the camaraderie she shared with her sisters. It wasn't often that siblings had such an intense bond. Maybe it was being so close in age, but from the time they were small, right through school, they were the best of friends.

Kenzie encouraged and cajoled one more repetition, through abs, upper and lower body exercises, pushing them to the point of exhaustion. "Okay, last one rep and then we stretch," Kenzie wheezed.

Grace plunked the weight down in the rack and flopped onto her mat. Jamie melted into the floor with a little more poise, pushing stray locks of chestnut hair out of her eyes. She eyed Kenzie and panted, "Are you trying to kill us so you don't have to buy dinner? I've never sweated this much."

With a mischievous look, Kenzie said, "Nope, I just want to make sure you work up an appetite for Italian. I've had a hankering, and who better to share pasta with than my favorite sisters?"

Straight-faced, Grace said dryly, "We're your only sisters." She sat up from stretching her hamstrings and scrambled to her feet. "I'm going to take a quick shower. I can't possibly be seen in public looking or smelling like this."

Jamie said, "I think we all could freshen up. Kenz, are you ready to lock up?"

Kenzie bounced up from the floor. "Just give me a few minutes. I need to make sure the main room is covered and Robbie will close up when he's done."

Grace elbowed Kenzie and teased, "There is one good-looking, one-hundred-percent male. Tall, soft brown wavy hair, and those eyes. Yummy."

"He *is* attractive." Kenzie stepped back and looked through the glass separating the two rooms.

"Well, most girls would be taking a good long look at him. Remind me again, how come you two haven't seriously dated?" Grace wore a sweet, innocent expression.

"If you recall we did, the summer between high school and college, but we came to our senses and decided we were better as best friends."

Jamie rolled her eyes. "Gracie, you never mix business with pleasure, and besides they've been best friends since our moms pushed them in baby carriages."

"I think it's a darn shame. He's smokin' hot."

Kenzie's laughter followed Grace and Jamie to the women's locker room as she went in search of her right-hand man.

The girls walked into their favorite Italian joint, the Pasta Bowl. Joey Romano, one of the brothers who owned the place, greeted them with a peck on each cheek and escorted them to a table. "How are the lovely MacLellan sisters tonight?"

"We're ravenous, Joey. Kenzie put us through our paces, and for the record"—Jamie grinned and jerked her thumb towards Kenzie—"she gets the check."

Joey rubbed his hands together and smiled. "Ah, I remember the first time Kenzie bought dinner for your family. I think she emptied her piggy bank of every penny she had."

"Good news, Joey—tonight I'm using plastic." Kenzie laughed "Boy, that sure takes me back to, what, almost twenty years ago?"

Joey poured their water and placed the pitcher on the table. "I've been enjoying your family dining here for years. In fact, your parents celebrated their very first wedding anniversary in this restaurant. I guess you could say we're *la famiglia*." He handed the girls their menus. "I'll be back for your order."

Jamie sank deeper into the deep-red fabric-covered cushions and sighed. "It feels good to relax."

Joey returned to the table with a bottle and three wine-glasses. "I hope I'm not being presumptuous, but I have a new red I'd like to get your opinion about, if you don't mind?"

"Sure." Jamie took one of the glasses and held it out. Joey poured in a small amount. She swirled it around, inhaled the bouquet and swallowed a sip. "Oh, this is nice. It goes down like velvet."

Joey grinned and poured wine into the remaining glasses. "Are you ready to order?"

Kenzie handed him the menus. "Can we have an Italian pasta pu-pu platter for three and a large tossed salad with cheesy garlic bread?"

"Excellent choice. I'll put that right in for you." Joey hurried to the host station and greeted a new arrival.

Jamie's gaze followed their old friend and fixated on a man waiting in the vestibule. Her eyes roamed his tall, lean frame. He wore a suit coat over what looked to be a white shirt. Somehow the semi-casual dress suited him perfectly. His dark brown hair dipped down over one eye. Casually, he pushed it back, and his eyes locked with Jamie's.

She dropped her eyes but seconds later found her gaze drifting back in the newcomer's direction. He was *very* good looking. She kicked Grace's foot under the table and whispered, "Hey, have you ever seen that guy before?"

Grace cranked her head around.

"Don't make it obvious you're looking!" Jamie hissed.

"Who are we looking at?" Kenzie's head swiveled from side to side. "Oh, that guy." She grinned and poked her sister. "Jamie, blink."

Grace sniggered. Jamie wanted to sink under the table. "You are both impossible."

The newcomer's steady gaze never left Jamie's. He gave her a slight nod as Joey ushered him to a table out of Jamie's line of sight.

"You've never seen him before?" Jamie peeked around Kenzie to catch another glimpse.

Grace crunched on a dried breadstick. "Nope, he's probably just on his way through town to destinations unknown."

"Gracie, I think he's tickled her fancy," Kenzie teased.

Jamie was spared having to answer as Joey set a bowl of salad on the table and a basket of cheesy garlic bread.

As the girls crunched on the greens, Jamie tried to see where he was sitting, taking care her sisters didn't catch her in the act.

"So, what's up with springing for dinner tonight?" Grace probed.

Kenzie leaned back in her chair and took a sip of wine. "Well, I've been thinking about the letter from our Great-grandmother and what she said. Do you think the dress holds some kind of magic?"

"Kenzie, really? I would have expected Grace to say something like that, not you."

"Hey." Grace's mouth formed a tiny pout. "What do you mean by that, Jamie?"

"Ever since you were a baby you always thought fairy-tales would come true, whereas Kenzie's levelheaded and logical and *I'm* the ultra-practical sister."

"We're all pretty grounded, but I do love a happily ever after." Grace groaned, "I can't resist this garlic bread." She helped herself to a crusty slice.

Joey hurried over with steaming platters and bowls for the girls. After offering fresh grated parmesan cheese, he backed away, leaving the girls to dig in.

"So anyway..." Kenzie dished up pasta and meatballs from a platter. "As I started to say, do you think the dress does help the women in our family find love?"

"I doubt it." Jamie laid down her fork. "But?"

Kenzie's eyes locked on Jamie. "Maybe one of us should try it on and see what happens?"

Jamie's fork hovered in mid-air. "Do you want to pick it up from my house and give it a spin? I didn't know you were looking for a husband."

Kenzie sputtered and blinked hard. "I'm not. You're the oldest—it might be better for you to take the plunge."

"Ha. Fat chance. Besides, it looks more like Grace's size, not mine."

The girls ate in silence as they were lost in their own thoughts of the dress.

Jamie leaned back, her plate almost empty and patted her mid-section. She looked at her sister's plate and waved three fingers to Joey and did the sign for to-go containers.

"I'm going to assume since we went hog wild with pasta, we're skipping dessert?" Grace looked at her sisters with a glimmer of hope on her face. "You know, I could split a slice of cheesecake or have a bite or two of tiramisu."

Kenzie patted her belly. "Pass."

Jamie shook her head. "Sorry, sis, I'm stuffed."

Joey stopped over with containers and a small piece of paper. Kenzie handed him a credit card. Before he could leave, Jamie asked, "Joey, who was that guy you were talking to earlier?"

Joey's brow arched, and said. "I'm sorry, Jamie, I'm not sure who you mean."

Casually, she continued, "The tall guy who came in by himself."

"I don't know, and unfortunately I can't ask him as he's already left." He winked. "And he paid with cash. Not that I could tell you his name if he used a credit card."

Jamie smiled, avoiding his obvious curiosity. "No biggie. I thought he looked familiar."

Joey left with Kenzie's card and the check.

"I thought you said you didn't know him." Grace leaned forward. "Oh, that was a ruse to get Joey to spill the beans."

Jamie smoothed back a lock of hair. "A passing interest is all, baby sister."

Joey set the credit card and a slip of paper on the table. Kenzie took a look, dropped some cash down for the tip and signed the check. "Ready?"

Once outside the girls hugged each other and went their separate ways. Jamie pulled the collar of her wool coat tightly around her throat. She felt around for her scarf, but it was gone. She retraced her steps back to the restaurant when she saw the mystery man from the restaurant walking toward her holding the scarf in his hands. Her heart quickened.

"Excuse me." His voice was smooth like good coffee, rich and stimulating at the same time. "Is this yours?"

Jamie nodded, at a loss for words, and held out her hands. "Yes," she stuttered, "I must have dropped it." He handed it to her. She noticed his hand was warm as his fingers grazed hers. "Thank you."

"My pleasure," he responded with a curt nod, and walked away.

Jamie opened her mouth but closed it. What would she say to the handsome stranger? She looped the scarf around her neck and secured it. Walking to her car, she turned to look over her shoulder at the retreating figure of the man.

"Why didn't I ask for his name? I'm such a dope."

3

Jamie flipped over and buried her pounding head under the covers. Sleep eluded her.

Her sock-covered feet slowly shuffled across the floor to the medicine cabinet. After fumbling to unscrew the top of the aspirin bottle, she shook out three. She turned on the tap and filled a glass, tossed back the pills with water, and studied her reflection in the brightly lit mirror. She'd like to blame heavy food and wine on her lack of sleep, but if she was being brutally honest, dinner wasn't the reason for the lack of Z's. It was the wedding dress.

Dressed in her standard business suit, she stepped into the tidy office. She saw her note about calling an estate attorney for her parents. She called and left her attorney a voicemail asking for a referral. Next, Jamie prepped for a meeting with one of her larger clients, which consumed the next several hours.

Her office phone rang. Jamie glanced at the caller ID. She picked it up on the third ring. "Hello, Ralph, thanks for calling." Not giving him a chance to respond, she rambled on, "Do you have someone who could help my family untangle a couple of issues with my grandmother's estate in Scotland?"

"Well, hello, Jamie. You're one of my favorite clients and I'm happy to help." She could hear the smile in his voice. "I do have someone in mind. He's in high demand and people usually have to wait months for an initial consultation. After I listened to your message, I gave him a call."

"And did he say he'd meet with me?" Jamie dared to hope she'd get this meeting behind her quickly.

"As a matter of fact, he's free on Friday at three. Can you meet him at his office in Rutland?"

Jamie looked at her appointment book. "That's perfect."

Rattling off the phone number he said, "His name is Steven Sullivan, and I said you'd call to confirm."

Jamie jotted down the number. "Thanks, Ralph. I appreciate you setting this up for me. I need to run. We'll talk soon." She poked her head out of the office as her client took a seat and held up a finger. "Be right with you."

Jamie looked at the pad and dialed the number. She got a prerecorded message with the standard electronic voice.

"Hello, this is Jamie MacLellan, I wanted to confirm our appointment for Friday at three. If there is a change, please email me at Jamie dot MacLellan at MacLellan Accounting dot com. Thank you." She replaced the phone. *I'm surprised a hot-shot estate lawyer isn't in Burlington. Maybe he's not as good as Ralph thinks.*

Turning her attention back to the file folder on her desk, she left it open as she crossed to the door and escorted her client inside. All thoughts of her appointment with Steven Sullivan were on the back burner.

Every time Jamie worked with numbers and balanced endless columns of figures, her adrenaline hummed. She double-checked the calculations one last time before she clicked to the next screen on the tax return. Some would think this was a boring job, but she thrived on the predictability of the results. One and one always added up to two.

Her days were filled with meetings and clients, lunch at her desk, and other than chatting with her sisters, most nights were spent alone in front of the fireplace while she watched television and surfed the Internet.

For the next few nights, before drifting off to sleep, she lay staring at the wedding dress hanging on the closet door. Four days had come and gone with Jamie contemplating why she had never seriously considered marriage. She came to the stunning conclusion that she was terrified of letting herself fall in love. Most people she knew weren't as lucky as her parents, married for over thirty years and not only best of friends but respectful and appreciative of each other's individuality. It was easier to face life alone than be devastated by a shattered heart.

In the gray morning light she flipped back the covers and got out of bed. As her feet touched the cold floor, she sighed. "All right, Great-grandma Ann, I give up. Since you went to all the trouble of writing the letter and Gran arranged to have the dress sent to us, I'll try it on. Not because it will find a husband for me, but so at least one member of this generation can say she wore it."

She turned the dress around and looked at the delicate hand-sewn eyelet holes. Laughing to herself, she carefully loosened the laces. *Of course they didn't have zippers back then. This must be a two-person job, but I can get the idea of what it should look like.*

She shed her pajamas and stepped into the full sweeping skirt, then slipped the short lace-capped sleeves up her bare arms. The dress flowed in soft draping folds—she was happy to see her ample cleavage was adequately covered with a modest round neckline. Gathering the sash, she secured the lightly boned bodice in place.

Turning, she studied her reflection in the mirror from different angles. She grabbed a clip from her dresser and secured her hair, exposing her neck. Color stained her cheeks and her blue eyes were bright. The dress fit to perfection. The underlayment fabric was soft and silky. She looked closely at the lace. *It's handmade; heather and thistle are part of the pattern.* As she moved around the room the soft *swish, swish* filled the room. *So this is what it feels like to be a bride wearing a gorgeous dress ready to walk down the aisle to the man she loves.*

Jamie gazed into the mirror; a pang of longing filled her heart. "Did I decide too quickly that I didn't want to have a traditional life?" The woman looking back didn't have an answer.

A shadow flickered in the mirror. She turned quickly. Who was behind her?

"Is there someone there?" Fear clenched her chest like a vise. Her breathing was short and shallow.

Her answer—a shutter rattling against the window. She sagged against the doorjamb. She gasped. Was that a trick of shadows, or was a man hovering on the edge of the reflection? She looked over her shoulder, confirming she was alone. What was going on? "Am I going crazy?" Her pulse raced. She looked closer, unable to make out his face, but he was very tall…

"Great-gran, is this a nudge from beyond the grave?"

Freaked out, she quickly shed the dress and carefully hung it up. She pulled her pajamas on and sat on the edge of the bed. Holding her cell phone, hands shaking, she hesitated. She wanted to tell her sisters about the dress but was afraid of being seen as foolish.

After setting the phone down on the bed, she crossed the

room. Jamie pulled back the chair and sat down at the desk. She picked up a pen and grabbed a fresh legal-size pad of paper. Taking a deep calming breath, she thought, *I'll focus on my meeting with Mr. Sullivan.*

Father inherited working sheep farm in Scotland.

Is there a requirement of residence to keep everything running as is?

Manager on site for business.

Taxes in United States.

Could Dad work with lawyer, Sullivan, to determine path forward?

She chewed on the end of the pen, then added,

Plan for the MacLellan sisters as the next heirs?

Jamie reread that sentence and then crossed it out with a double line. "That's morbid."

The clock chimed the hour and relief coursed through her. Drained, she tucked the pad into her briefcase. "Time to get ready for work."

Jamie flung open the heavy glass door to Mac's Gym and stepped inside. Kenzie was perched on a stool behind the front desk.

"Hey, sis, I'm here to work off some of the office stress." Jamie's smile didn't reach her eyes. "Care to join me for some cardio?"

Kenzie tilted her head toward the clock. "I'm on desk until close. I wish you had called. I would have gotten coverage."

"That's okay—a little treadmill and bike with headphones will work just as well."

Kenzie's eyebrow arched. "You're going to do both?" She leaned forward. "What's wrong?"

"Nothing. I finished my notes for the meeting with the estate lawyer and I realized you, Grace and I don't have plans for the next generation of little Scots, and it's made me kinda sad."

Kenzie asked, direct and to the point, "Do you want to have a baby?"

Jamie shrugged, attempting to look nonchalant. "I don't know. Do you ever think about it? Having kids?"

"I used to, but since I opened this place it's taken up every free moment. I don't have time to date, find someone I wanted to have a kid with and actually do it."

"Yeah, I hear ya." Jamie hitched her gym bag on her shoulder. "I'm going to get changed. I'll catch you later."

Adjusting her headphones, she cranked up the driving beat of the music and pushed up the speed and incline on the treadmill, finding her rhythm. Halfway through the workout, Grace walked in and waved. She stepped onto the elliptical. Jamie acknowledged her with a thumbs-up and let her thoughts wander.

Who was the man she'd seen in the mirror? A shiver raced down her spine, despite the sweat soaking her shirt. She stopped the treadmill and hopped on the bike. Ramping up her speed, she thought it had to be stress playing tricks on her.

Feeling someone watching her, Jamie's eyes focused. Grace was tapping her wrist where normally her watch would be. Jamie nodded and slowed the pedals until she came to a stop. Mopping her face with a towel, she plunked down a mat.

Grace did the same. "Good workout?"

Jamie's face was beet red. She grinned and gulped in oxygen. "It's torture. Music keeps me in the groove."

"As far as I'm concerned, nothing helps. I don't understand Kenzie—she thrives on sweating."

"Did I hear my name taken in vain?" Kenzie walked in the room, and gracefully sat on the mat. "Good workout, Jamie?"

"Why does everyone keep asking me that?" Jamie

frowned. "It's not like this is the first day I've hit the gym after work."

Kenzie took the opportunity to point out the obvious. "True, but typically you don't beat the hell out of the treadmill *and* bike unless you're trying to work out a problem or avoid talking because one of us has ticked you off."

Grace's head bobbed. "So, 'fess up."

"I give everything my all, so sorry, this time you're barking up the wrong tree."

"Jamie, you have that same face when we were kids and Mom would ask who broke one of her favorite glasses. You wouldn't answer so you didn't have to tell her the truth or a lie. Which is it?"

Jamie avoided her pointed look and held her hamstring stretch a little longer. "Grace, you should just let it go. It's nothing, really."

Kenzie winked at Grace. "You're on to something."

"Will you both just stop?" Jamie jumped up. Irritation flashed across her face.

"Mac…" Kenzie used her childhood nickname. "Before you storm off in a huff, ask yourself one question—if you suspected something was weighing heavy on either of us, would you let it go?"

Jamie stomped into the locker room, leaving her nosy sisters in the cardio room. She stripped off her sweat-drenched clothes, flipped the shower lever to hot and let the spray pummel her fatigued muscles. *What are you afraid of? You should tell them you tried on the dress. You're making it a much bigger deal than it is.*

Toweling off, she did a quick job of blow-drying her hair and secured it up in a high ponytail. Grabbing her tote bag, she pushed open the locker room door, not surprised to see her sisters lounging on the floor mats where she left them.

Standing with hands on her hips, she looked at the ceiling

and announced, "If you must know, I tried on the wedding dress."

Kenzie and Grace were slack-jawed.

"You did?" Grace's voice dropped to a whisper. "Why?"

Jamie sat down on a bench along the wall and rested her elbows on her knees. "Last night I was having trouble sleeping. The moonlight was falling across the dress and I wondered what it would feel like to try on something our grandmother and Great-grandmother wore. I finally drifted off, and when I woke up that's when it hit me—we don't plan on getting married. We're too busy with our careers. No one will ever wear the dress again, unless we decided to donate it."

Grace gasped, horrified. "We can't donate the dress—it's a family heirloom."

Kenzie said, exasperated, "I can't believe you didn't wait for us. I would love to have seen it on you."

Grace said in a hushed tone, "Aren't you worried? You know what Gran's letter said. If an unmarried Mackenzie woman or her descendant wears the dress, she will find love."

Jamie admonished, "Gracie, I don't believe in such superstitious nonsense. A dress can't make the perfect man materialize from thin air."

Grace's lower lip jutted out. "Then how do you explain both grandmothers finding love after wearing it?"

Kenzie snorted. "Coincidence."

Grace sniffed and leaned back on her hands, her legs outstretched. "Think what you want, but I happen to believe the dress is enchanted. All the stories Gran told us about Scotland were *filled* with magic."

Jamie stretched her arms above her head, letting them drop. "It doesn't matter. Magic is for fairytales."

"Jamie, you still need to tell us about the dress!" Kenzie reminded her. "How did it fit?"

"That's the odd part of the story—it was a perfect fit. The style is simple and old-fashioned, but timeless at the same time. And the skirt made that *swishing* sound when I walked." She sighed and, looking wistful, said, "I felt like a princess."

Grace nudged Kenzie, "Yeah, it sounds like something we should have seen with our own eyes."

Jamie scowled and flicked off a piece of fuzz from her leggings. "Knock it off. If you're that curious about how it looks, you're welcome to take it off my hands."

Kenzie held up her hands. "Not on your life. You're the oldest—you need to see this through until the end."

"There's nothing to see through, as you so eloquently put it." Jamie stood and grabbed her wool hat from her bag. She tugged it firmly onto her head. "If you two are done torturing me tonight, I'm going to head home." She slipped into her coat.

Kenzie asked, "Before you take off, Jamie, when are you going to see the estate lawyer for Dad?"

"I have an appointment tomorrow with Steven Sullivan. Want to get together for dinner when I get back? I'll fill you in on the details."

Kenzie and Grace quickly agreed. "We'll bring dinner," Grace said.

Jamie hugged them and went outside in the cold air. She looked up at the inky night sky. The stars were just starting to twinkle. Leaning back, the old childhood wish rushed through her thoughts. *Star light, star bright, hear this wish I wish tonight.*

Jamie whispered, "I'd like to wear Gran's dress again, on my wedding day."

4

The directions to Mr. Sullivan's office were straightforward. Jamie parked in front of a beautifully restored Victorian, complete with deep green house trim with accents of burgundy. An expansive porch screamed for hanging flower baskets, rocking chairs and maybe even a porch swing. She shook off the fanciful images and walked up the wide slate steps.

The ornate brass door handle turned easily in her hand. The heavy wood door, with etched glass inserts, groaned as she eased it open. In the entrance, the dark mahogany wood floors gleamed. On either side of the hall were two sets of what Jamie guessed were original pocket doors. She assumed they would led to offices or a conference room. The oak reception desk was vacant, but there was a small bell with a sign sitting next to it that said *Shake me.*

Jamie's hand hovered over the handle. After looking around and not seeing a soul, she tentatively picked it up and gave it a quick jiggle. The tinkling was barely audible in the expansive space.

"If you want someone to hear you, shake it like you mean it."

Jamie dropped the bell and did a double take. Standing before her was the tall, dark-haired man from the Pasta Bowl. A smirk hovered on his mouth and his eyes twinkled.

Reaching the bottom stairs, he held out his right hand. "Allow me to introduce myself." She could feel the flush rise in her cheeks. "Steven Sullivan, Attorney at Law."

Stammering, she said, "Jamie MacLellan, CPA." She withdrew her hand and stuck it in her coat pocket.

"Now that we have informed each other of our credentials, shall we go into my office and talk about what brings you in today?" Steven slid open one set of pocket doors. "Come in."

Jamie walked into the spacious room and took in her surroundings. The windows overlooked a snow-covered side yard and the room was dominated by a large oak table, hard-backed chairs and bookshelves lined two walls. The only open wall space was painted a deep tan. She noticed the law degree hanging on the wall. That settled one question—he'd graduated from Yale.

Steven pulled out a chair. "Please, have a seat."

Jamie retrieved a pad from her laptop bag. "I'm not sure where to start."

A smile slowly crept across his face. "At the beginning is always the best."

She tilted her head and fidgeted in her chair. "All right. My father inherited a farm in the Scottish Highlands from his mother. We'd like to get advice on dealing with the estate. When I spoke with my lawyer, he recommended you. I'm really just the spokesperson for my family." She played with her scarf, twisting it in her hands and prattled on. "Dad wants to make sure we do everything correctly."

Steven leaned way back in his chair, and Jamie wondered if he would topple over.

"Is this something you could take on for us, untangling the paperwork so the farm can continue to operate? It provides several local families their livelihood and we don't want to take that away from them." She stopped talking, waiting for him to ask a question or two.

Taking his time, he took a white legal pad from the middle of the table. "Ms. MacLellan, please continue."

"That's pretty much it, and please, call me Jamie." She smiled warmly.

Steven's face was transformed into what Jamie assumed was his attorney posture. "Why don't you give me an overview of the property, how the ownership was transferred and how you think I can help your family?"

"The farm has been in our family for over four generations."

Steven jotted down cryptic notes. "I am assuming your father resides in the States?"

"Yes, he met my mother after she had finished college when she was traveling in the United Kingdom. They fell in love and he followed her to Vermont." A tentative smile graced her lips. "Sorry, I tend to over-explain everything."

He responded with a curt nod. "Has he had anything to do with running the farm since leaving Scotland?"

"My parents go back each year for an extended trip to check in with Gran. Of course, Dad would fly over at any time he was needed, but the manager is quite capable and he's been with the farm for many years."

"What does your mother do for work?"

"She was a teacher but has recently retired."

Steven made a few more notes. He looked directly into Jamie's eyes, and her heart skipped a beat. "What is your dad's profession?"

"He was a banker." Unsure why she was so nervous, Jamie rolled her shoulders in an attempt to relax.

Steven paused, his pen hovered over the paper. "Does he plan to spend more time in Scotland?"

She bobbed her head. "He retired a few months ago. I'm

not sure what their plans are long term. I don't think Mom will want to move there permanently, but I couldn't say for certain."

"Tell me about the property and by chance do you have copy of your grandmother's will?"

Jamie picked her bag up from the floor and pulled out a large manila envelope. "Steven—"

"Everyone calls me Sully. My mother is the only person to call me Steven."

"Well, um." Taken aback, she looked at the floor. "I'd prefer to maintain a business relationship and I just thought, well, you know, in your professional life you wouldn't be so casual."

"I'm on the low-key side of professionalism. I don't wear suits unless I absolutely must. Most days it's jeans and a shirt. I keep a sport coat handy to slip on if a client seems like I'm too laidback, but hey, this is who I am."

"I thought all lawyers worth their salt were born to wear a suit and tie."

Steven chuckled. "We don't have a 'must wear suit' clause we sign after passing the bar."

She gestured to the diploma on the wall. "I see you graduated from Yale. Isn't that one of the toughest law schools in the country?"

He shrugged, nonchalantly. "Something like ten percent of applicants are accepted."

Jamie's eyes widened. "I'm impressed."

"It's not that big of a deal. But we shouldn't be talking about me, since we're on billable hours. I'd like to hear a little more about what I can do for your family."

Her chin jutted up. "It's a working farm. Sheep to be exact, and there are a couple of small cottages on the property Gran occasionally rented out for weddings and such. But I was doing some research on the web and I read that full-time residence is a requirement for the family to maintain ownership."

Steven opened the envelope and pulled out a sheaf of papers. He scanned them. "Is this the firm in Edinburgh?"

Jamie walked around the table and peered over his shoulder. She could smell the clean scent of his cologne and decided it suited him. Anything else would have been overkill. She pointed to the name at the bottom on the first page. "According to Dad, this is the man he spoke with."

"Is this my copy?"

"Yes, it is. Dad has the original and I have another copy in my office." Jamie sat back down. "How long do you think it will take before we know what is required?"

Steven laid down his pen and rocked back in the chair. "A few weeks, maybe? It depends on what I learn after contacting the solicitor who was handling your grandmother's affairs."

"Do you need to speak with Dad? I'm not sure when they'll be back from Scotland, but I can give you his number and email. They went over when Gran was asking for him. He got there before she passed." Her heart twisted in her chest, the grief still raw. "She lived an amazing life."

"I'm sorry for your loss." Steven got up and grabbed a box of tissues. He set it down in front of her. "Were you very close?"

She took a tissue and dabbed the corner of her eyes. "As children, my sisters and I spent every summer there. We'd fly over with Mom, and Dad would join us for a couple of weeks. When we got older we'd go without our parents—they'd show up at the tail end of the visit. Mostly we'd hike with Gran in the hills, go fly-fishing in the creeks and rivers, and of course play with the sheep. Scotland has always been our second home."

"It sounds like a wonderful way to grow up, between the two countries and cultures."

Jamie blinked the tears away and wiped her nose. She felt empty inside. Talking about everything reminded her just how much life had changed. "If we're done, I need to be on my way."

Steven's chair scraped over the wooden floor, oblivious as Jamie cringed at the harsh sound of wood on wood. "I'll give you a call if I have any questions, and of course once I have answers we can talk."

She extended her hand and shook his with a firm but distinctly feminine grip. "Thank you, Steven. My family appreciates you looking into this matter. I'm sure you understand we don't want to jeopardize the farm or anyone who works for us."

"Of course." He escorted her into the hallway. "I'll walk you out."

A door banged somewhere in the house and Jamie turned just as sock-covered feet attached to incredibly long legs and a well-toned, jaw-dropping man, raced down the stairs.

Steve frowned and said, "Jamie, this is my brother Caleb."

Jamie clasped her right hand in his. Her brain fizzled as a low hum warmed her blood. "Hello, it's nice to meet you," she murmured.

She couldn't read the expression on his face. Seconds ticked as Jamie stared into his captivating sea-green eyes.

Caleb chuckled. "Can I have my hand back?"

An unfamiliar scarlet heat warmed her cheeks. "Um, I was meeting with your brother on a legal matter. For my family." She lowered her eyes and then met Caleb's. She itched to let her finger trace the scar above his eye and brush back his dark brown hair. Giving herself a mental shake, she reluctantly withdrew her hand. The loss of contact left her feeling unsettled. "I was just leaving."

She turned to Steve. "Thank you for your time."

With a curt nod he said, "You're welcome."

Jamie fumbled with the doorknob. Caleb reached around her and pushed it open. She mumbled thanks and hurried out into the cold air, thankful it would reduce the heat in her cheeks. Without a backward glance, she hurried to the car.

5

Jamie's hands hovered over the keyboard, but her eyes checked the wall clock and then were drawn to the window. *Maybe I could steal a couple of hours this afternoon and go riding.* She looked at her appointment book and sighed. She had an appointment to meet with Steve Sullivan.

Tap, tap, tap. Her pen clicked on the desk. "What will one afternoon hurt?" She mused. "The trail's better than the gym for putting life into perspective."

Jamie made a hasty decision. She punched in a few numbers. Prepared to leave a voicemail, she was taken aback when a deep voice answered. "Hello?"

"Hello, Mr. Sullivan. This is Jamie MacLellan."

"Jamie." His voice was low and smooth. "What can I do for you?"

"We have a meeting scheduled for this afternoon and I was wondering if we could meet later this week?"

"Sure," he drawled.

She continued in a rush. "I don't normally ask people to rearrange their schedules. I hate it when clients do that to me, but it's such a beautiful afternoon I want to play hooky." She hit her forehead with her hand. Why was she blabbing on about canceling the appointment?

"Playing hooky sounds like fun. What did you have in mind?"

Flustered, Jamie said, "What...well, I'm going horseback riding. There's a stable about a half hour from here. I'm friends with the owner—we went to school together—so I don't need to book time. I can just show up."

"Care for some company?" Steve suggested.

"You ride?" Jamie tried to make her response sound more like a question than a smart retort.

He chuckled on the other end of the line. "Yes, I've been known to. But I haven't had the opportunity recently. You'd be doing me a favor. You know, helping someone new in town, so to speak."

"Uh, well, yeah. If you want." Jamie rattled off the address.

"Great, I'll meet you there in an hour?"

"Yeah, sure. See you later." She sank back in her chair. "How did my nice quiet afternoon turn into a guided tour?"

She pushed back the office chair and swept the papers on her desk into her briefcase. Glancing at her watch, she dashed out the door. *Maybe I'll get lucky and he won't show up. I really need some time to clear my head.*

The trip to Racing Brook Stables was typical for spring in Vermont. Mud season was in full swing and it was inevitable her car would make the drive back into town caked in brown globs of muck.

Jamie tucked her key fob into her jeans front pocket. She zipped up her bright pink down jacket against the light breeze and tugged a magenta knit hat over her ears. Before locking the car, she grabbed carrots from the back seat deliberately leaving the green tops peeking out from her coat pocket, a certain horse she knew loved them. Adjusting her sunglasses against the glare from the snow banks, she scanned the muddy parking lot and grinned. He was late.

She jogged over to the office and pushed open the red barn-style door. "Hey, Jo." Her perky smile was contagious. "Is it okay if I take Chloe out today?"

Jo pushed back from the desk, her smile sunny. "I wondered how long it would take for you to show up now that spring has finally arrived."

Jamie grinned. "It's been a long few months—tax season, you know?"

Jo's bright red curls bobbed, and she pointed to the stack of papers on the desk. "Speaking of which, I need to set up an appointment to go over the books. Maybe next week, if that works for you?"

"Of course. I almost forgot to mention..." Jamie's voice trailed off as Jo stood up and peered out the small window overlooking the parking area.

She gave a low, appreciative whistle. "Whoa nelly."

"What?" Jamie looked over her shoulder. "Oh. That's what I wanted to tell you. I'm meeting my lawyer here. He wants to ride."

Jo gave her a sideways look and smirked. "Your lawyer? Nice try, Jamie. My lawyer doesn't look like that. In fact, if memory serves, we have the same lawyer, Ralph, who is overweight and balding."

Jamie shook her head, laughing. "I stand corrected—he's really Dad's lawyer for Gran's estate. Ralph claims Steve's some hot shot in international law stuff. We were supposed to meet this afternoon and go over things, but I got the itch and when I tried to cancel he asked me what I was doing. Before I knew it, he was tagging along, so here we are." She frowned. "I really hope he knows how to ride. I don't have the patience to coddle someone, at least not today."

Jo snorted. "It doesn't matter if he can ride. Just look at how those jeans fit his backside. Yummy!"

Jamie slapped her playfully on the arm. "Stop ogling the attorney."

"It's just an observation, nothing more." With a flip of her curls, Jo turned. "Don't look now, but he's about to walk through the door."

Steve closed it with a thud. "Hello." He stuck out his hand. "I'm Steve Sullivan. I'm meeting…" He caught sight of Jamie hovering near the window. A smiled tipped the corner of his mouth. "Jamie."

Jo looked from Steve to Jamie and beamed. "I hear you're interested in going on a trail ride. Have you ridden before?"

He nodded, but his eyes met Jamie's. "Yes, I grew up around horses and have great respect for them."

"Excellent, then why don't we head out to the barn and pick out a mount for you?" Jo coughed to cover her snicker. "Jamie, are you ready?"

Jamie trailed behind Jo and Steve down the rutted lane to the barn, listening to Jo chatter about the age of the farm and her family's deep roots in the Vermont soil. She trudged through the mud, wishing she hadn't tried to cancel her appointment. Then she would have had a peaceful ride, even if it had been delayed a day or two.

"Here's Chloe, Jamie's favorite. She's been riding this paint for, what, six years now?"

"Yeah." Jamie reached out to stroke the mare's velvety-soft nose. It quivered in her palm, and she cooed, "Hi, girl, sorry it's been so long."

Chloe nickered. Her long brown nose nudged the young woman's side, sniffing and then tugging the tips of the carrots from Jamie's pocket. After Chloe munched the last of the treat, she nudged Jamie's shoulder.

Kissing her nose, Jamie murmurred, "Does this mean I'm

forgiven?" The horse shuffled closer and leaned into Jamie. "I love you too, Chloe."

Jamie could feel Steve's eyes on her. She patted Chloe and grabbed the blanket, laying it on the mare's back. The saddle came next. She made quick work of cinching the girth, and lastly took the bridle and slipped the bit between the mare's teeth and over the ears, securing everything with practiced ease all while Chloe waited patiently. It was a routine Jamie had done countless times.

When she was ready to mount, she looked for Steve, half expecting him to still be gawking at her. She cocked her head. "I can see you're ready."

"This isn't my first rodeo," he said in an amused tone.

Jamie raised an eyebrow. She hated to admit it, even to herself, but he looked damn good on horseback, and his mount, Pirate, was black as midnight and full of spirit. He was one of Chloe's best buddies. "We shall see. We haven't left the barn yet. The trails around here can be tricky, especially at this time of year."

"Is that a challenge I hear, Ms. MacLellan?" Steve sat up a little straighter in the saddle. "If that's the case, care to put a little wager on the ride?"

Jamie snorted. "You want to bet on a trail ride?"

"Sure, why not?" He grinned. "The loser buys dinner and the winner picks the place."

Jamie flipped him a semi-annoyed look. "Loser of what?"

Steve looked at Jo, who threw up her hands and smiled as she took one step backwards. "Don't look at me, this is between you and Jamie. All I ask is you don't put my horses in any sort of jeopardy." She wagged her finger. "No racing—there are icy spots on some of the trails."

"Jo, you don't have to worry. I'm never reckless." Jamie leaned over Chloe's neck and whispered in her twitching ear.

"All right then," Steve said. "Our wager should be on who

has the most normal walk when we dismount. It sounds like it's been a while for both of us."

Jamie tossed her head and nudged Chloe forward. "You've got yourself a bet." Steve and Pirate fell in step beside them.

Jo called after them, "Watch out for wildlife! The bears are waking up."

Jamie gave a salute and nudged Chloe to quicken their pace to a slow trot with Pirate matching her gait. The crisp breeze stung her nose and cheeks. She pulled her collar up around her neck and pulled gloves from her coat. Slipping them on, she looked him up and down. "Glad to see you dressed for Vermont weather."

"I do know how to dress for this time of year. I may be a city boy, but even I know the sun is warm for the moment, but as it dips toward the horizon, the temperature will drop." Steve eased Pirate into a slow walk as they swayed down the trail. "Jo was right, there are some bad spots."

Jamie let Chloe move at her own pace, much as she usually did. The horse was smarter than Jamie, and on more than one occasion letting her take the lead kept them out of some bad storms. "It's typical weather. During the day, the snow melts and at night the temps still dip below freezing. It's good for sugaring season."

Her mind raced. *What the heck am I doing, talking about the weather? I'm a better conversationalist—he'll think I'm boring. Well, this isn't a date. Just introducing a newcomer to the area and to this stable.*

"So, tell me, have you lived in Vermont your whole life?" Steve looked at her, squinting.

"Born and raised. Except for college."

"Your dad is Scottish, right?"

What was he, a dense lawyer? "Well, yeah. That kind of goes without saying since he grew up in Scotland."

"That was a duh moment." Steve grinned. "I know your

parents are retired and they want to get more involved in the farm your grandmother left to them, but what about your sisters?"

"We live in pretty close proximity to each other. Kenzie owns and runs Mac's Gym in town, and Grace is a physician's assistant and works at a local hospital. Enough about me—what about you?"

He shrugged. "Not much to tell. I'm from a typical family with one brother, Caleb, who you met. He's working his way around the globe. My parents live in Boston and I moved to Rutland about a year ago to get away from the craziness of the city."

Pirate headed down a trail littered with downed tree limbs.

"Whoa." Jamie pulled up on her reins. "Steve, let's skip that trail and go to the left." She prodded Chloe forward. She hesitated. Jamie nudged her sides with the heel of her boots. "Come on, girl."

Steve turned Pirate in the new direction.

Chloe plodded along the trail. Jamie picked up the thread of their conversation. "Why Rutland?"

"I love the outdoors. The lifestyle is slower paced and the people seem friendly."

"Aren't you concerned about your career?" She glanced at him and saw he was taking in the scenery.

"No. If need be I can fly anywhere, and virtual meetings are common."

"Anyone special in your life?" Jamie said, keeping her tone casual.

Steve shook his head, his face blank. "Nope."

She exhaled and waited for him to keep talking, but a heavy blanket of silence wrapped around them. Her focus was diverted. Chloe jerked her head back and forth and stamped her front hooves. She tried to back step and collided with Pirate. She whinnied and gave a short snort. The underlying shrillness caused Jamie's blood to run cold. Chloe was on the verge of panic.

Jamie leaned over and patted her neck. "Shh, it's okay, girl, we're fine. We'll go the other way."

Chloe reared and Jamie struggled to keep her seat, but it was no use. Falling out of the saddle, she hit the semi-frozen ground with a thud, her head snapping back.

Somewhere in the distance, she could hear Steve calling to her, urging her to lie still. She could feel he was beside her. Chloe closed ranks with Pirate around the couple; she could hear them stamping their feet and snorting.

Steve's fingers gently probed the back of her head. "Does your head hurt?"

Jamie struggled to sit up. "Ouch!" she cried. She squeezed her eyes shut as a wave of stars danced in front of them. Slowly opening them, she could see the look of concern on his face.

"Hold on for a minute, let me make sure you're not bleeding or have any broken bones." He looked at the back of her head and his hands roamed down her arms and legs while doing his best to keep one eye on the woods.

"What spooked Chloe—did you see anything?" Tears clung to Jamie's dark lashes.

"I heard something rustling in the underbrush, but it's moved on."

Jamie clung to his arm, her voice shaky. "It might have been a bear. Jo did say there's been a few sightings."

Steve helped her into a sitting position. "Do you think you can stand?"

She grabbed his hand for support and pulled herself from the ground, then grimaced. "I must have whacked my head pretty hard." She looked around. "Do you know where my hat is?"

"It's over there." He pointed to a muddy pile of snow. "If you can stand I'll get it for you."

She waved him off. "I'm fine."

He scooped the hat from the ground and tried to wipe the mud off on his pants. "You're going to need to wash this before you wear it again." He handed it to her. "I think Chloe trampled it."

Jamie shoved the hat in her pocket and grabbed the reins trailing on the ground. "It's okay, girl," She caressed the mare's neck, slipping her arm under it. She pulled Chloe close, whispering, "We're safe."

She put her boot in the stirrup and swung her leg over the saddle. Ignoring the fogginess in her brain, she glanced around, worry creased her brow. "We might want to get out of here and get back to the barn before whatever it was comes back."

Holding Chloe reins, Steve questioned, "Are you sure you can ride?"

She caught the hesitation in his voice. "It'll take more than a little tumble to keep me out of the saddle. Vermont girls are made of pretty tough stuff."

His face serious, he glanced around and announced, "I see that." Steve mounted his horse. "Take the lead."

She was happy to oblige. "I'm going to take a hot bath when I get home."

"What about our bet? I think you owe me a dinner," he joked.

She furrowed her brow. "Why do you think I lost the bet? We haven't gotten back to the paddock yet."

He chuckled. "I'm not the one who fell off her horse, which means you'll be the one hobbling."

"We'll see about that. We'll ask Jo to be the judge."

He suppressed a laugh, and Jamie glared at him. Steve said, "Can I ask you a question?"

With a sharp retort, she said, "You just did."

"Snappy. I like that in a woman. Seriously, why don't you call me Sully? All my friends do."

She looked at him sideways. "I didn't know we were friends. I thought we were lawyer and client."

"Nah, we're going to be good friends."

"Well, I think you're presumptuous, but on the off chance we do become any kind of friends, I would prefer to call you Steve. I happen to think it suits you."

The horses saw the barn up ahead and broke into a light canter. Jamie bit her lip to suppress the stars swimming in front of her eyes. They came to a smooth stop at the large barn doors, and she slid off, holding onto the saddle horn to keep from stumbling.

Steve grinned and said, "Dinner's on you. That is, if you still want to go."

Jamie said, "On one condition."

"Name it."

"We stop at my place so I can change clothes. I don't want to be seen in public looking like this."

Steve hopped down and grabbed Chloe's reins. "I'll do one better. I'll take care of the horses and see you at your place in about an hour?"

"You've got yourself a deal. Hand me your phone and I'll type in my address."

Steve swiped the screen and entered the security code. He handed it to her. "You're listed under Princess."

Jamie couldn't help but laugh. "I should have guessed." She looked Steve square in the eye. "You might be right—we just might become friends."

6

Jamie threw open the cottage door and light spilled from the interior, washing over the front step. "Please come in. You're right on time. I just need my gloves."

She went into the back hallway and returned within moments. "Shall I drive since dinner's my treat?"

"My car is already warmed up, so I'm happy to be your chauffeur."

She pulled the door closed behind them and then jiggled the door handle. "Have you given any thought to where you'd like to eat?"

"I don't know what's in town, so lady's choice." Steve held the car door as Jamie tucked herself into the toasty-warm luxury SUV. Slipping behind the wheel, he turned the key. "Which direction?"

She grinned. "There's a charming little bistro downtown. The food is great, but the menu is limited and it changes based on the whim of the chef, who happens to be the owner."

"Sounds intriguing." The car picked up speed.

Jamie stole a glance at Steve. *He does seem like a nice guy,* she mused. "At the end of this street, bear right and take another right. We'll be there in under five minutes."

Steve clicked on the radio. The driving beat of heavy metal blared. He quickly turned the volume down. "Sorry." He chuckled. "I like my music loud."

Jamie giggled. "Me too. But I can't say I care for metal bands. I'm more into traditional rock, or country."

"My love of hard rock is the direct result of rebelling against violin lessons—the classics, you know. My brother Caleb loves country, old and new."

Jamie's head bobbed, grateful the aspirin had kicked in. "I hear ya. My sisters and I played instruments all through school. My parents felt it would make us well-rounded or something." She pointed to a sign. "That's it. There is parking behind the building."

Steve drove cautiously into the parking lot. "Black ice." He pulled into a space and looked around. "Only a couple of cars. It doesn't seem to be crowded tonight."

"Typical. Mid-week and all." Jamie pushed open her door. "Come on, slowpoke."

Steve gave a low chuckle. "I was waiting on you to lead the way."

Her laughter rang out and she slammed the car door. Shrieking, she hopped away from the SUV.

"What's the matter?" Steve's brow wrinkled. "Are you all right?"

"I stepped in a wicked cold puddle." Jamie stamped her feet and grimaced. "Be warned—when we get seated, I'm taking my boots off. Otherwise my feet will be ice cubes. These boots aren't made for warmth, just looks."

He cocked his head and looked at her feet. "I didn't know anyone in the state had boots that were just pretty. I thought everyone was always prepared for the harsh Vermont winter."

Her eyebrow arched. "I'm prepared to go out to dinner a

very short distance from home. It's not like we planned to hike a mountain range."

Steve smirked.

With hands on her hips, Jamie continued, "Are we going to stand out here debating the merits of my choice in footwear or have dinner, where hopefully we can get a table by the fireplace?"

"Dinner by a crackling wood fire does sound appealing." He bent low and swept his arm toward the door. "After you, miss."

Jamie rolled her eyes and stalked to the door with Steve's laughter following.

He helped Jamie take her coat off and hung it on the rack just inside the door. He scanned the small dining room. All the tables were empty. Then he looked through the archway into the bar area. A few people were perched on stools and one couple sat at a small table. "Are you sure the food's good?"

Exasperated, Jamie rolled her eyes. "Trust me."

The bartender was headed in their direction. "Table for two?"

Steve nodded. "Yes, can we sit next to the fire?"

"Sure thing." His eyes caught Jamie's. "Are your sisters joining you tonight?"

She shook her head. "Not tonight, Mark."

His brow shot up and looked at Steve out of the corner of his eye.

"This is my attorney, Steve Sullivan. He lives over in Rutland and we're going over some things about my gran's estate."

Mark escorted them to a table and waited for them to sit before taking their drink order. "Take a look at the menu and I'll be right back."

"Are you embarrassed to be seen with me, Jamie?" Steve teased. His cell phone buzzed in his jacket pocket. He stole a look at the screen and said, "Sorry business call. It'll go to voicemail."

Her eyes widened as she slipped off her boots. "Not at all, but I don't like everyone knowing my personal business, especially that I lost a bet." She flipped over the hand-lettered menu and studied the short list of dinner specials.

Steve put his hand in front of the page, capturing her attention and chuckled. "You don't like losing, do you?"

She brushed back a stray lock of hair and said, "Not really. Now, if you don't mind"—she pushed his hand away—"I'd like to order. I'm starving."

Steve smothered a laugh by taking a sip of water. She could feel him looking at her.

Mark returned with their drinks and a bread basket, and took their dinner order. They ordered the vegetable soup and shepherd's pie.

Jamie flipped the napkin from the bread basket. "You have to try one of these biscuits. It will melt in your mouth, and don't forget to slather on lots of butter." She used a generous smear and took a tiny bite. Closing her eyes, she said, "Mm. Just like always. The bomb."

"I don't think I've ever seen anyone enjoy a biscuit quite like you."

Jamie's eyes popped open. "Sorry. I try to stay away from rolls, biscuits and bread. It's one of my weaknesses."

"What?" he ribbed her. "*You* have a weakness?"

Jamie leaned in and glanced around the room in mock secrecy. "I have a few others, but only my closest friends and family know for sure what they are."

Steve laughed again. "I have to confess I don't remember when I have laughed so much in a single day."

Jamie leaned back and took another bite of her biscuit. "That's sad." She pointed to the basket. "You'd better grab one before I eat all three of them."

Steve grinned. "Surely you wouldn't deprive me of what is rightfully mine?"

"All's fair when it comes to bread. At least it does in my family."

He stretched out and dabbed her chin with his napkin.

Her eyes grew wide. "What did you do that for?"

"Butter." He held up the evidence. "I didn't mean to startle you, but I didn't think you'd want it to drip on your top."

"Oh," she stammered. "Thanks." Using her napkin, she wiped her chin again.

Mark entered the dining room carrying two shallow soup bowls. "Would either of you like fresh pepper?"

They both nodded. After a few cranks over each bowl, he left them.

Jamie held the spoon to her lips and blew. The broth made tiny ripples around chunks of carrots and celery. Gingerly her tongue touched the edge of the spoon. "Oh, be careful, that's hot."

Steve swirled his spoon through the bowl and then tasted it. "This is pretty good."

Jamie toyed with the veggies, pushing then around the bowl, and asked, "Why did you bet me a dinner? Did you feel sorry for me or something?"

"No. Not at all. In fact, it's quite the opposite."

"What do you mean?"

"When you walked into my office, I wanted to ask you out on the spot. But you were a client. But now that I've finished the review of your grandmother's estate and I have a full report for your father, I felt this was the best way to get you to agree. It didn't seem to be as awkward."

"Hm." She cocked an eyebrow. "You could have just asked me after our meeting."

"Would you have said yes?" The spoon hovered in front of his mouth.

Jamie set down her spoon. "I don't date much. It's not that I don't enjoy going out and having fun, but I don't like the complications that can come with dating."

"What complications?"

"You know, expectations of having to spend all your free time with the person you're dating, losing your friendships. And frankly I love spending time with my sisters. We're the female version of the Three Musketeers, all for one and one for all kind of thing."

Steve kept eating while Jamie's hands fluttered as she clarified. He remarked, "Who says you have to merge with someone you date? Why can't you enjoy each other's company but still have autonomy?"

Jamie lightly slapped the table. "That's exactly how I feel."

"Dating should enhance your life, not take anything away from it." He scraped the bottom of the bowl and picked up what was left of his biscuit, using it to soak up the last bit of broth. "Well, since we share the same view on dating, does this mean you might be open to sharing an occasional meal or movie with me? Heck, maybe even another trip to Roaring Brook Stables?"

Jamie's smile filled her face. "I think that might be accomplished. I've had fun today despite Chloe dumping me on my butt."

"About that. I didn't want to tell you at the time, but I did see the backside of a bear waddling away into the underbrush."

Anger bubbled up. "Why didn't you tell me? I wouldn't have lain about on the ground. We could have gotten into some serious trouble."

Steve held up his hand. "Hold on, you don't need to get testy. I never go into the woods without bear spray. If it had come closer, I would have used it and gotten us out of there."

"Who says I'm testy?" Jamie demanded.

In a controlled tone of voice, he said, "Listen to yourself, your voice ratcheted up a few notches."

Jamie sniffed. "It would have been nice to know at the time." She set her soup bowl aside as Mark approached with dinner plates. "Next time tell me immediately."

Steve's hand formed the scout signal and smirked. "I promise. And I'm going to hold you to the 'next time'."

"I didn't know you were a Boy Scout."

Steve winked. "There's a lot you don't know about me, and won't it be fun finding out?"

7

Jamie pulled her collar close to her chin and dashed to the car, sliding on ice she made contact with the door. She used the back of her glove to wipe the fog off the windshield while waiting for the defrost to work. Her cell rang.

"Hi Dad. How's the weather in Scotland?"

"The days are cool and wet, and the nights even cooler."

"Our weather's about the same. How's Mom?"

"She's great. Loving retirement. Is there any news on Gran's will?"

Jamie could hear the joy in his voice. "Steve Sullivan looked over the papers. He said everything is in order and the farm can continue operations uninterrupted. You should have the report by tomorrow."

"Well, that's good news."

"When are you guys coming home?" Jamie missed her parents and wanted to share Sunday brunch with them again, and soon.

"Well, to be honest, I'm not sure. Mom and I want to enjoy spring in Scotland, and you know summer is the best weather here. So maybe for Christmas?"

Jamie wailed, "That's nine months from now! Is this your way of telling me it might be a permanent move?"

Dad's rich baritone laughter filled the car. "I'm not sure. It's up to your mom. I love Vermont, but you know my heart belongs to Scotland."

"I know." Her voice softened. "The girls and I miss you and Mom."

"Why don't you three put your heads together and pick a week or two you can come across the pond? We miss you something fierce."

"I'll talk to them at brunch this Sunday—we'll call in the afternoon."

"Looking forward to it, Jamie."

"Love you, Dad."

"And you more. Bye for now." With a soft click, the connection with her dad was gone.

After arriving at the office Jamie shot a text off to her sisters. *We're calling Mom and Dad after brunch.*

After setting her phone aside, she finished work for the day with thoughts of Steve Sullivan drifting in, distracting her. She remembered over dinner his cell buzzing at least once that she heard. Who knew a lawyer got business calls after office hours?

Jamie, focus. He's a good-looking guy. It's been ages since you've been anywhere with someone as smart, handsome and funny as Steve Sullivan. And all the man did was go horseback riding and have dinner with you. Who cares if he got a phone call? He didn't declare his undying love."

She jumped up and began to pace. "Where did that thought of love come from?"

She stopped at the desk, flipped open her appointment book and saw she had two more clients for the afternoon. Frustrated, she snapped it shut. *No escaping today.*

Her phone chimed, announcing a text message. Thinking it was one of her sisters, she slipped it into her bag. She needed to reconcile this checking account before her next client arrived. After a few minutes had passed her office phone rang, shattering her tentative concentration on the task at hand.

"Jamie MacLellan."

"Hello, Jamie."

Her pulse quickened at the sound of his voice. "Hello." She masked her delight at hearing his voice with a stiff and formal tone.

"It's Steve Sullivan."

"I recognized your voice." She smoothed down the front of her blouse, shaking her head at the absurdity of the gesture.

"I hope I'm not interrupting you"—his voice was smooth —"but I wanted to thank you for yesterday. I enjoyed the trail ride and dinner."

"I had a good time too. Thanks for buying dinner even though I lost the bet."

Steve's laughter filled her ears. "Let's be honest. You lost because of a bear. How could I, in good conscience, hold you to the deal?"

Jamie smiled into the phone. "Well, thank you very much. It was fun."

"Any chance you want to get together this weekend. Maybe catch a movie?"

She hesitated. "Um."

He rushed to reassure her, "It's not a date. I haven't made many friends yet. I've been too busy working and I hate eating a tub of popcorn by myself."

Jamie chewed on her bottom lip. "I guess we could. I love action movies, especially ones with high-speed car chases. So feel free to pick something you'd like."

"I'm surprised you didn't ask for a rom-com."

"I'd never make you sit through a chick flick," Jamie giggled. "Well, not until I know you better."

"Good to know. Do you want to head into Rutland or is there a movie theater in Easton?"

"A single screen, but I know there is a multiplex in Rutland, so I'll drive out. What time should I meet you?"

"Why don't you swing by my place around three?"

"Sure, I can do that, what's your address?" Jamie grabbed a pad with pen poised she waited for the details.

"I live at my office."

She chuckled. "Well, that's convenient."

"And cost effective. See you Saturday."

"You bet. Oh, Steve, just to clarify, let's go dutch for the movies, and I'm picking up dinner."

"Nice. Movie and dinner too." Just before the line disconnected, Jamie thought she heard him chuckle.

"Well, now what have I gone and done? It sounds like I asked *him* out for dinner."

The outer office door chimed and she peeked out through the doorway. Ralph gave her a wave and sauntered into her office. "Hey, Jamie. How's things?"

"This is a surprise. I don't think we have an appointment today." Jamie checked her book and flipped through the next few pages. "We're not scheduled to review your taxes until next week."

"I know. I wanted to see how everything went with Sully."

Jamie raised her eyebrows. "With…?"

"Steve Sullivan. The attorney I referred you to. You did meet with him, correct?"

"Oh, right. It went great. He's detailed-orientated, which I like, and said everything was in perfect order. In fact, I talked with Dad a little earlier and gave him the good news."

"Glad it worked out." He rocked back on his heels. "Sully's a smart guy."

She nodded. "I can tell."

"Well…" He glanced toward the door. "I was just in the

neighborhood and need to get back to the office. See you next week."

Jamie grabbed his sleeve. "Wait." Ralph stopped in his tracks. "Did you come for something more than to tell me Steve Sullivan is a smart attorney?"

"Eh, he's had a tough time before moving here and hasn't really gotten out much. I like you, Jamie, and Sully is one of my closest friends. I want the best for him."

"I understand. Given time, we might become friends. But don't hold your breath for anything more."

Color flushed to his cheeks. "Right, gotcha. See you next week." The door slammed behind him.

Jamie watched as he dashed down the driveway and hopped in his car. "I don't need a matchmaker."

❦

With the weekend on the horizon, Jamie tidied the office. Glancing at her watch for the third time in mere minutes, she moaned. She tapped the face and watched the second-hand move, *tick, tick, tick*. It wasn't even noon. How would she get to five?

Throwing up her hands, she packed her laptop bag, shut off the lights and locked the front door. Enough was enough.

Driving down South Street, she made a sharp right turn into an open parking spot. After grabbing her handbag and locking the car doors, she strolled down the sidewalk until she arrived at Hemz boutique. Why couldn't she buy something new to wear to the movies?

She hesitated and then pulled open the door. The bell tinkled.

Jamie loved to shop but didn't make the time very often. She wandered around the racks, soaking in the colors, and felt the fabric of several blouses. If there was one thing she couldn't stand, it was scratchy clothes.

"Good afternoon," the store clerk said. "If there's something I can help you find, please let me know."

"Thank you." Jamie held a long, jewel-tone sweater in front of her and peered in one of the cheval mirrors placed around the room.

"That shade of purple works well with your eyes and chestnut-colored hair," the clerk volunteered. "I have a print blouse that matches it perfectly. Would you like to see it?"

Jamie smiled at the girl. "Thank you. I'm a medium."

The clerk pulled a hanger off the rack and handed it to her. "As you can see, there is a tiny abstract print that has the same color as the sweater."

Jamie held the blouse under the sweater. "It does go together perfectly."

"Would you like to try them on?" The clerk pointed to the back of the store. "The dressing rooms are open, help yourself."

Jamie grabbed a pair of black leggings and took the blouse and sweater with her. She glanced at the price tags and cringed.

From the front of the store, the clerk called out, "We're having a thirty percent off sale today."

It's like she's reading my mind. Jamie changed, stepped out of the dressing room and peered into the triple mirror. She turned right and left, looking from all available angles, then walked toward the clerk. "What do you think?"

The clerk grabbed a long silver necklace. "Here, try this."

Jamie slipped it over her head. She could see the beads shimmered, reflecting colors from the blouse and making the entire ensemble pop.

"The necklace is seventy-five percent off."

"That's a bargain. How can I go wrong?" Jamie smiled. "I'll take the outfit."

"Is there anything else I can show you today? Maybe a skirt, in case you want to dress it up for a night out?"

Jamie started to say no, but changed her mind. "Do you have something casual, like a slim skirt?"

"I do. Let me get it for you. You can try it with the sweater so you can see how it looks together." The clerk selected a hanger with a black skirt and handed it to Jamie. "I think this will fit perfectly."

Jamie returned to the dressing room and changed from leggings to the simple skirt. She peered into the mirror. "I'm going to take the skirt too."

"Great, will there be anything else?"

Jamie laughed. "No, you've done enough damage to my checking account." She took one last look and murmured, "Perfect outfit for friends going to a movie and casual dinner."

The clerk leaned in. "When he sees you in the outfit, he won't have eyes for anyone else. The colors are stunning on you. And don't forget to wear tall black boots to set it all off."

Jamie handed the clerk her debit card and said, "Oh, it's not a date. I'm going with a friend."

"I've heard that one before. Have fun with your *friend*."

Jamie took the card and tucked it into her wallet. Taking the pink paper bag, she gave the girl a sunny smile. "Thank you and enjoy your day."

"Stop in again, we are getting new things all the time."

"I will." She grinned and bounced to the door. "I forgot how much fun shopping can be."

Swinging the bag, Jamie walked outside and detoured to her sister's gym. "Maybe Kenzie will have time for a coffee."

8

"Whoa, look who's been shopping." Kenzie grabbed the bags out of her sister's hands. She pulled the sweater out of the bag and groaned. "Oh my heavens, this is gorgeous. Just look at this blouse and the skirt." She crumpled the blouse to her chest, and her eyes narrowed. "Why did you shop?"

"I just felt like picking out a new outfit." Jamie grabbed the blouse. "It's not a crime to buy pretty clothes."

"No," Kenzie said slowly, "but you only buy new clothes when you have plans." She pointed an accusatory finger at Jamie in jest. "Do you have a date?"

"No, I don't." She stuffed her new clothes back into the shopping bags.

Kenzie studied her older sister. "Okay, since it's crunch time at the office, I know you haven't had time to meet anyone new. But I've got my eye on you, sis. You've been acting a little off since Chloe threw you."

Jamie stammered. "That's right, I did hit the ground pretty hard."

"Did you ask Grace to take a look at your head? I know

how you avoid everything medical and would have skipped a trip to the ER."

"No. But Steve—you know, the attorney I had look at the will—he was there and made sure I wasn't bleeding and I wasn't knocked out, so I'm fine."

"Hold on. The lawyer was with you?" Kenzie crossed her arms over her chest and tapped her foot. Frowning she said, "You neglected to tell me that little tidbit."

"It was no big deal." Jamie feigned boredom. "We had a meeting scheduled and I was tired of being stuck inside. When I called to postpone, I mentioned I was going riding, he asked if he could tag along. Turns out he's pretty good in the saddle."

Amused, Kenzie didn't attempt to hide her smirk. "What else is he good at?"

"I told him I'm not interested in anything more than friendship, and he agreed. I may have told you he moved to Rutland less than a year ago, so he doesn't know many people."

"Go on." Kenzie leaned against the counter. "Is he really good-looking?"

Jamie could feel the heat rush to her face. "I haven't noticed."

"You're not a good liar. So I'm going to guess he's hot."

Jamie held up a finger and exclaimed, "You know, you have seen him. He was the guy at the Pasta Bowl."

Kenzie almost purred. "He *was* cute." She winked. "And when are you going to see him again?"

Nonchalantly Jamie said, "Actually, we're going to a movie together."

"I knew it! You do have a date, and a new outfit to wear. You are interested in the hot lawyer."

"Kenzie, you don't just give up, do you? I'm going home to do some work, and we'll chat on Sunday." Jamie hugged her sister and kissed her cheek. "Don't forget to bring the salad."

Jamie dressed carefully in her new outfit, deciding to go with the leggings as the air had a sharp nip and the forecast was calling for snow later. She studied her reflection, and out of the corner of her eye saw Gran's wedding dress hanging on the door. Unable to stop herself, she crossed the short space. She reached out. Her fingers trailed down the skirt.

"Gran, I don't believe in enchantments. The dress is beautiful, but it was coincidence you found the love of your life after you put it on."

Jamie didn't know what she was expecting, maybe some sign from beyond to give her direction, hope for her future.

"Do you think Steve might be *the* guy?"

Silence filled the room.

"Before this dress arrived I never spent time talking to myself. That's for dreamers who believe in fairy tales. Not for a sensible, successful woman."

She walked away from the dress and ran a brush through her long hair. She plugged in the curling iron and looked at her reflection. *Why am I going to so much trouble for two friends going to a movie? Would I be so particular if I was going with one of my girlfriends?* She finished her hair and, with a final check of her makeup, she left the house for the drive to Rutland.

Honking the horn, Jamie waited in the car for Steve to come out. His driveway was a sloppy mess. She noticed a Jeep parked in the driveway, but Steve's opening of the passenger door diverted her attention.

"Thanks for picking me up." Steve grinned. "I thought we'd see the new pirate movie. It's gotten pretty good reviews for special effects."

"Sounds good." Jamie eased out of the driveway. "Whose Jeep?"

"Ah, my brother Caleb's still in town. I guess Europe lost its appeal and he wants to hang out in Vermont a while longer."

"We could have postponed the movie so you could spend time with him."

"Nah, it's not a big deal besides he's otherwise occupied. I left him a note and told him we'd be out for dinner too and I'd give him a call later, in case he wants takeout."

"He's welcome to join us if you want."

Steve shook his head. "He can eat takeout or cold cereal. Besides, he's here indefinitely, so there will be plenty of dinners together."

Jamie laughed. "You're a mean older brother."

Steve grinned. "Don't feel too sorry for him—Caleb has a way of everything going exactly the way he wants. Always has, always will."

"If you're sure…" Jamie hesitated.

"Enough about Caleb—any thoughts on where you're taking me for dinner?" he joked. "I've saved my appetite."

"I was thinking there's a good steak place downtown with live music on Saturday nights. We should be out of the movie in time to beat the dinner crowd."

"Sounds like a plan."

Jamie pulled into the Movie-plex parking lot. "Remember, the movie is dutch and dinner is on me."

"I know. You don't have to beat a dead horse." Steve smiled. "Jamie, relax. I'm not going to seduce you or something."

With a flick on the door handle, Jamie stepped into the biting cold. *What does he mean by that?* She hit the key fob, locking the car. She secured her scarf around her neck and dashed across the parking lot, the wind whipping in her face. The stinging freezing rain hitting the exposed skin on her face and hands.

Steve was casually walking behind her. "You know, you're still gonna get wet whether you run or walk," he called after her.

Jamie flipped a glance over her shoulder, losing her footing—she was going down. Before she could kiss the ground, his strong hands reached out to steady her. "Don't worry, I've got you."

Jamie looked up into his eyes.

There was no sense of a connection.

"Er, thanks."

"Are you okay?"

"Yeah. I guess you're getting into the habit of picking me up off the ground."

"Seems like." Steve opened the glass door. "After you."

Jamie's thoughts raced. *This guy is handsome and funny and despite a few flutters, which could be more from lack of male company, I'm not sure if I'm attracted to him.*

Wait! You've agreed, nothing romantic between you. Just stop dissecting each comment and enjoy the movie. Men and women can be just friends.

"Earth to Jamie?" Steve poked her arm. "Hey, go get the popcorn and I'll get in the ticket line. We can add up the cost and split the difference."

Jamie said, "Sounds good," and moved away.

Steve called after her, "Lots of butter and salt, please."

After a purchase of two waters, an extra-large tub of popcorn and a box of Junior Mints, Jamie looked around and found Steve sitting on a padded bench near the access door to the theatre. He was holding his phone—it looked like he was texting.

He slipped the phone in his pocket and rushed to help her.

Taking the tub, he looked down. "You remembered extra butter, right?"

Jamie pulled out a wad of napkins from her coat pocket, struggling to keep a straight face, she said, "Yes, and I got these too so you're not tempted to wipe your hands on my scarf."

"I'm not a child." Then he glanced at her eyes. "Oh, you're joking."

"Lighten up." She burst out laughing. "Well, I wouldn't let you use my scarf for anything other than a true emergency."

In his pocket, Steve's phone buzzed.

"Do you need to get that?"

"I'm sure it's Caleb. Do you mind if he meets us for dinner?" Jamie opened her mouth to say something, but Steve plowed ahead. "I wouldn't expect you to pay for his meal. But I'm feeling guilty, we're having fun and he's sitting home."

Jamie was confused. Before, Steve was saying Caleb could eat takeout and now he's joining them for dinner. "Yeah, sure. You can let him know when we're on our way to the steakhouse and he can meet us there."

"Thanks. It's really nice of you to extend the invite."

"I have two sisters, remember. There never seems to be any boundaries when it comes to them either."

"Let me get back to him and I'll meet you inside."

"Yeah, sure." Jamie walked into the semi-darkened movie and found two seats near the aisle. She sat down to wait for the trailers to begin, and for Steve to join her.

After a few minutes, he stepped over her outstretched feet. "Oh wow, these seats recline?"

"I guess so. It's been so long since I've been to a movie, I didn't know there was the option." Jamie pulled a bottle from her bag. "Water?"

"Thanks." Steve perched the tub on the joint armrests and

said, "Caleb wanted me to tell you thanks for taking pity on him."

"Really, it's no big deal." Jamie pointed to the screen. "It's starting."

The music swelled and Jamie was captivated by the characters on the screen. She sighed. The pirate captain was the perfect bad boy, good-looking, adventurous and slightly dangerous, with great comedic timing. Now there was a man she could fall for. But Gran would be very disappointed in her if she did give away her heart to a rogue like Captain Jack.

All too soon the end credits rolled and the house lights came up.

Steve said, "I'm going to let Caleb know we're leaving now. What's the address?"

Jamie rattled off directions and glanced at her watch. "We'll be there in about ten minutes. If he gets there first, have him ask for a table."

Steve's fingers flew as he wrote the text. He waited a moment and looked up. "He's on his way."

They picked their way through the puddles of icy rain in the parking lot.

Steve said, "He's a pretty interesting guy. You're gonna love him. Everyone does."

9

Steve held the door for Jamie as they entered the bustling restaurant. Her gaze roamed the dining room. A man looking vaguely familiar waved and Steve returned the gesture.

"Jamie." Steve touched her arm. "Caleb is over there."

Jamie allowed herself to be propelled forward. The closer she got, the heavier her boots felt. She was surprised to realize she really wanted to have dinner with Steve, alone. Despite what she thought, she wondered if maybe he was the guy, since she met him because of the wedding dress.

Caleb stood. Crossing the short distance between them, she couldn't help but notice his tall, muscular physique and captivating sea-green eyes, and how had she missed those dimples the first time they met? Her knees threatened to buckle beneath her, and Jamie could picture falling into his arms.

He extended his hand to her. "Hello. It's nice to see you again, Jamie." His eyes twinkled. His voice was low and smooth to her ears. "Thanks for taking pity on me and letting me tag along on your dinner date."

"Oh," she stammered, "it's not a date. Just dinner between friends."

Caleb didn't release her hand. "Good to know."

His eyes locked on hers. Her heart hammered in her chest. She could feel the heat rising in her cheeks. Struggling to keep her voice steady, Jamie said, "If you'll excuse me, I'm going to use the restroom."

She scurried away, blood racing in her veins. She shoved open the door. Grabbing the sides of the sink, she took a deep ragged breath and turned on the water faucet. Leaning over the sink she splashed her face. The cool water took the burn from her face and her heartbeat began to slow.

"What is wrong with you?" she chided herself. "Caleb is Steve's brother."

Two ladies came in and glanced at Jamie. "Are you okay, honey?"

Jamie nodded. "Low blood sugar."

"If you're sure." The ladies exchanged a look and went about their business.

Jamie took a moment to take some deep, heart-steadying breaths. With a fresh swish of lip-gloss, she was ready.

With slow and deliberate steps, she found her way back to the table. The brothers were deep in conversation and she thought she could just sit down with little fanfare.

Caleb hopped up and pulled out a chair for her. Sandwiched between the brothers, Jamie looked right and left. She could see the strong similarities in their looks. But there was something about Caleb, an intensity and kindness, that she was inexplicably drawn to. She said, "Steve tells me you've been traveling the world?"

"Steve?" Caleb chuckled. "You don't call him Sully?"

Even the way he chuckled caused an unfamiliar sensation in the pit of her stomach. "Well, no. Somehow it didn't seem appropriate to call my lawyer by his nickname."

Caleb smirked. "Are you still her lawyer?"

Steve shrugged. "I don't think so. Our relationship is evolving."

Caleb's head cocked to one side, a slow smile sliding across his face. "You've become friends."

Jamie's eyes met Caleb's. She thrust her chin up. "Is there a reason we shouldn't be?" she sniffed.

He held up his hands and leaned back in his chair. "Whoa. I was just teasing my brother. It's not often he has dinner with *just a friend*. And a pretty one at that."

She could feel the heat rush to her face, and she pushed back her chair. "Steve, I'm going to let you enjoy dinner with your brother." She stood up. "Caleb, it was interesting seeing you again. I hope you enjoy your visit to Vermont."

Steve followed Jamie through the dining room. "Don't leave. Caleb's just being his annoying self."

She stopped short as they entered the foyer. "It's fine. We can do dinner some other time."

Steve grinned. "I'm going to assume it will be after my brother leaves town."

"In my book, family always comes first." Jamie took her coat from the rack and slipped it on. "Have a good night."

Turning her back on Steve, she stepped out onto the walkway and looked up at the star-filled sky. "Well, at least it's not going to snow." Taking deep cleansing breaths of the cold crisp air, Jamie was determined to push all thoughts of Caleb Sullivan from her mind. After all she'd never see him again.

❦

Caleb watched Jamie hurry from the restaurant. He dropped into his chair and picked up his beer and took a long drink. This was the second time he'd met her and both times he never wanted her to walk away. What was wrong with him? She was a client and friend of his brother's.

He closed his eyes, remembering her crystal-blue eyes and ivory skin that looked as soft as silk. He longed to run a finger along her chin and tilt her lips up to meet his.

❦

Feeling out of sorts, Jamie picked up her coffee and wandered into the bedroom. Dropping to the edge of the bed, she studied the dress. "How can a dress find a husband I don't even think I want?"

She crossed the short distance and took the hanger down from the hook. Holding it in front of her, she gazed into the mirror. "Gran, I'm so confused. Why didn't you talk to me about all of this before you died?"

Letting her mind wander, Jamie could picture herself wearing the dress. Long white opera gloves covering her hands and arms as she carried a small bouquet of white tea roses and Picasso calla lilies. An amethyst teardrop pendant graced her neck, and earrings to match sparkled in her ears.

Jamie whispered. "Oh my." Her attention was pulled back to the present as the image faded from the mirror. "What am I doing?"

Rehanging the dress, she retrieved her coffee mug and closed the bedroom door. "You need to stop daydreaming about things that will never happen."

Laughter came from the back door and Jamie glanced at the clock—her sisters were early. She hastened to help carry in the bags of food she knew they'd brought.

"Hey." She took a bag from Grace and poked her playfully. "Did you bring the entire grocery store with you?"

Kenzie laughed. "You know with the MacLellan's there is never a small meal, and besides, I thought we could segue from brunch right into supper."

Grace chimed in, "You know how Mom and Dad proclaimed Sunday a family day, and I've been missing hanging out with my sisters, watching old movies and cooking together. So last night when I stopped at Kenzie's, we decided to make a day of it. Unless you have other plans?"

Jamie shook her head. "Nope, just hanging with my sisters." She shut the door behind them. "Time to stop heating the outdoors, girls."

"See, Kenz?" Grace beamed. "I told you Jamie would be fine with an impromptu family day."

Kenzie tugged Grace's curls. "Always the organizer, aren't you, Gracie? Herding us around, making sure that we can catch up on all the happenings of the week."

Grace's curls bounced and her head bobbed. "I'm not sure if that's a compliment or not, but I'm going to take it as one. I can't help it if I want to know what really happened on Jamie's date yesterday." She nudged Kenzie. "Admit it. You want all the gory details too."

"Yeah, I do." Kenzie glanced at Jamie's face. "Unless it's too personal. There are some details she can skip, if you catch my drift."

Snorting, Jamie gave them a shove toward the kitchen. "Mom and Dad first, and *then* I'll fill you in. Not that there is much to tell as it *wasn't* a date."

"If you say so." Kenzie winked at Grace. "Are you buying this line of bull?"

Grace giggled. "I might be the youngest, but I wasn't hatched yesterday."

Jamie sat down at her desk and fired up her computer. Within minutes, their parents' faces filled the large screen.

"Hi, girls!" Mom and Dad said in unison.

Jamie smiled at the screen. "Hey, Mom, Dad. It's good to see you guys."

"Let me take a good look at my beautiful daughters." Dad was beaming. "It's not easy being so far away from you."

"Oh, Dad. You and Mom are having a ball strolling hand

in hand over the moors, and I'm sure you're getting anxious to fish. Salmon season opens, what, in about a month?"

"Aye, it does. And your Mom's gear is ready. This year she's fishing right alongside me."

Mom giggled. "I'm not taking any wriggling fish from the hook, James, that will be your job."

"My dear Olivia, I'll even clean them for you."

"Darn tooting." Beaming, she planted a kiss on his cheek before turning her attention back to the screen. "What's going on with you girls? Is the weather starting to break?"

Kenzie gave Jamie a playful nudge. "Tell Mom about your date with the hot attorney."

"You're dating, honey?" Mom looked at Dad and winked.

"Hey, I saw that, and it's not what you think. It was just a movie and then dinner. Which was cut short due to his brother joining us."

"Sweetheart, in my day that was a date."

Jamie could hear the gentle prod in her mom's voice. "Trust me, it wasn't. I was paying back a bet. Steve joined me at Racing Brook Stables for a ride and I lost. Nothing more or less."

Dad chuckled. "Do you want to see him again?"

Ignoring the question, she said, "Enough about my dating life, or lack thereof—we're supposed to be talking about the farm, Kenzie's business or Grace's love of the medical biz."

"All right, Jamie," Mom said softly as she shot a warning look to Dad. "We won't ask any more questions."

Grace piped up. "Have you decided when you're coming home? It will be time to plant the vegetable garden soon. Well, at least the cool weather crops."

"We're not sure. Dad is really enjoying this time connecting with old friends. He hasn't had the luxury of an extended visit in many years. Retirement came at just the right time."

"I was afraid of that," Grace muttered, and then clearly

asked, "If you don't mind, I'm going to hire someone to rototill the garden as soon as it's not a mud pit."

"That sounds like a splendid idea. You always did enjoy puttering in the garden." Mom smiled. "Make sure you share the bounty with your sisters."

Grace leaned into the screen. "It sounds like you're not planning on coming home, at all."

"Don't go asking so many questions, lass. Your mom and I'll be home before you know it."

"Dad?" Kenzie interjected. "Do you hear yourself? Your accent has gotten thicker since you've been at the farm."

His eyes sparkled. "Ah, it has."

Mom tapped her watch and nudged Dad. "Girls, we're going to run. We're meeting some friends for dinner." Mom blew three kisses toward the screen and with a catch in her voice said, "We'll talk again soon. Love you."

Dad chimed in, "Love you." Before the girls could say anything more, they had disconnected.

Kenzie plopped onto the couch and groaned. "Sounds like they're having the time of their lives."

"And without us," Grace moped.

Jamie sank on the couch next to Grace and looked at her sisters. "Hey, Mom and Dad have doted on us since we were born. This is their time and I, for one, am glad they're having a great time. So what if Dad's accent is getting heavier? That happened every summer when we were at Gran's—even we'd come home with a Scottish burr."

Grace's lower lip trembled. "What if they never want to come home?"

Jamie put her arm around her baby sister. "They'll be back. It's got to be hard on Dad, losing Gran, inheriting the farm and retiring all within a few months. Let's give them some slack."

Grace glanced at Kenzie. Mischief gleamed in her eyes.

"Kenz, I think we should get back on the topic of Jamie's date."

Kenzie leaned forward with her elbows resting on her knees. "Time to fess up. What is going on with you and the good attorney?"

"Nothing. I keep telling you, we're just friends."

"He's good-looking. Like weak-in-the-knees hot, so what's the issue?" Grace asked.

Jamie laughed. "Gracie, when did you get so interested in weak-in-the-knees hot?"

"I'm not." She blushed. "Just an observation. You know."

Jamie walked into the kitchen. "Wine?"

"Add club soda to mine." Kenzie followed her and handed over a bottle. She winked at Grace. "I want to have a clear head as we drill you."

Jamie handed each sister a wine spritzer and poured one for herself. "You know, before last night I thought there might be something with Steve. He's handsome and very smart."

Grace said, "I hear a but coming."

"I want fireworks." Jamie stared out the window dreamily. "The kind from a movie where the guy causes the girl's heart to race deep inside, and that didn't happen with him."

"Really?" Kenzie said. "He seems to be perfect for you, right down to the horseback riding."

"That's just it, on paper he is. Besides, his phone goes off constantly and I have a hunch it's not business. He's distracted a lot."

"That is the stupidest thing I've ever heard," Grace said. "You have similar interests; he's good looking and available."

Jamie took a sip of her wine. "We think he's available. But what can I say?" She shrugged. "Maybe if we spend more time together, there would be sparks."

"Sorry, sis, if you're looking for movie or romance book sparks and they didn't happen yet, I doubt they will." Kenzie stated the obvious.

"Maybe it's for the best. I don't think I'd want to have a brother-in-law who drove me crazy every time we met," Jamie said.

Grace choked on her drink. Sputtering, she said, "Wait. Hold the phone, did you say what I think you said?"

With a twinkle in her blue eyes, Jamie said, "I'm considering the idea that maybe it might be nice to be married." She raised an eyebrow and took a sip. "But I need to find the right guy, of course."

Kenzie gasped. "Are you serious, and give up your independence *and* control of the remote?" She clutched her heart with mock horror. "I think you've been invaded by an alternate Jamie MacLellan."

"What do you mean? Maybe we've had this wrong all these years. Maybe we don't have to give up who we are as people to have a husband. After all, when we date a guy we don't have to morph into a single entity." Jamie looked between her sisters. "Mom has her own friends and hobbies, as does Dad. I mean, we know they love to spend time together, and with us, but Mom would be the first one to say in any relationship you need balance."

Grace bit her lower lip and slowly nodded. "I get what you mean—like we're best friends and sisters, but we have other friends. We don't spend all our free time together."

Jamie slapped her hand on the table and grinned with excitement. "Exactly my point. It's all about balance."

Kenzie took a plate from the cabinet and a few plastic containers from one of the bags. She arranged sliced cheese, crackers and some cut-up vegetables. After putting the plate on the breakfast bar, she pulled out a stool and sat down. Jamie leaned on the counter and Grace sat down too.

"If we're going to discuss the merits of getting married, we might be here a while." Kenzie took a piece of cheese and a cracker. Munching noisily, she said, "So if you don't think Steve is the guy, who is?"

"I don't know." Jamie remembered how she felt standing next to Caleb. Surprised that he would pop into her mind, she continued, "I…I haven't met him yet. But he'll make me smile, make my heart thump when he takes my hand in his and be excited to spend time together. He'll have to understand—family always comes first—and be willing to travel to Europe."

Grace fanned herself. "Don't forget hot." She tapped the counter top. "And has a decent job."

"Grace, I've dated good-looking men, and it never works out. Their vanity gets in the way."

Kenzie said, "A decent job goes without saying. We're not going to support some dead weight. If we're describing the perfect guy for any of us, I have to say he'll want to have kids. If I'm going to tie the knot I want to have the entire package, maybe even a dog or two." Teasing, she said, "Isn't that a pretty accurate description of the lawyer?"

Her eyes blazing Jamie snapped. "How should I know if he wants kids or a dog? It's not like we had a deep conversation. Besides, with his brother there all conversation went out the window."

Kenzie's eyes probed Jamie's. "Do you have plans to see him again?"

She snatched a piece of cheese from the plate and chomped down on it. "I guess. I still owe him dinner."

Grace sat up straight and grinned. "I have a great idea. Why don't you invite him to dinner here? Kenzie and I'll come too. It will give us a chance to check him out."

Kenzie pushed Jamie's cell phone across the counter. "Call him. We're free next Saturday night, right, Grace?" She grinned and leaned onto her elbows. "We'll even help with the cooking, so you don't poison the man."

"You're being ridiculous. I'm not going to invite Steve for dinner and have it be three against one."

Kenzie said, "So he can bring his brother if he's still in

town. If he's not, we'll drum up a few more people to come to dinner so it won't be the MacLellan girls against a poor, defenseless, handsome attorney." She drawled out the words *poor, defenseless* and *handsome.*

Grace perked up and said, "It'll be fun."

"Well..." Jamie picked up her cell. She moved the receiver away from her mouth. "It's ringing, so keep quiet." She mouthed, *Voicemail.*

"Hi, Steve. This is Jamie. Sorry about last night, but I was wondering...if you're free, would you like to come to dinner at my place next Saturday night with my sisters? And if your brother is still in town, he's welcome to join us. Give me a call. Bye."

She placed the phone on the counter. "Happy?"

Kenzie said, "Yup," with Grace quickly echoing her.

"Let's eat," Jamie said.

10

The sisters were lounging in front of the large-screen television watching a classic Bing Crosby movie when Jamie's cell phone buzzed. She got up and checked caller ID.

Flustered, she said, "It's Steve."

Kenzie said, "Don't keep the man waiting. Answer it!"

"Hey, Steve." Jamie turned her back on her sisters. "Thanks for calling me back."

"Hi, Jamie. It was nice to get your call. Dinner sounds like fun."

"Great, it won't be anything fancy, just my sisters and—"

Steve interrupted her. "I checked with Caleb and he'll still be around."

She nodded. "Oh good, you and Caleb. Why don't you come over around six?"

"We'll be there. See you Saturday."

Without another word the line went silent. She was perplexed as to why he was so short with her. She turned to face her sisters, who were grinning like a cat lapping up cream. "Satisfied?"

Grace and Kenzie looked at each other, and with a curt nod Grace said, "I am. You, Kenz?"

"Me too. So, what are you going to cook?"

She leaned on the sofa and mused, "He was pretty quick to get off the phone."

Kenzie suggested, "Maybe he was busy or he's not a phone kind of guy."

Jamie reminded them, "He called me, so he shouldn't have been rushed." She shrugged. "I have no idea, and since you got me into this, you're both bringing something."

Grace hopped off the couch and retrieved a pen and pad. "We should make a menu to divide and conquer." With pen poised on the paper, she said, "Jamie, you should make roasted chicken with sausage stuffing and smashed red potatoes." She scribbled something down. "Kenzie, can you bring a green veggie, maybe broccoli rabe? Oh, and wine. I'm thinking white. You are the best at picking out the perfect bottle or two."

Jamie laughed. "Okay, Miss Julia Child, and what will you make?"

Grace pushed the curls off her face. "Dessert, of course." She tapped the pen top on the paper. "How about…" Her nose crinkled up. "I've got it. Chocolate mousse and shortbread cookies."

Kenzie groaned in jest. "I'm going to have to hit the gym hard on Sunday just to burn it all off."

Jamie poked her sister and flashed a grin. "We'll be right there with you, the sweating sisters."

Grace finished her list and then handed Jamie and Kenzie each a slip of paper. "Don't lose this, it's your portion of the meal. Hey, we should include Jo and Robbie. We haven't gotten together with them in a while, and knowing us we'll certainly have enough food."

"Great idea. Kenzie can ask Robbie and I'll call Jo."

Grace tossed the notebook on the table. "Girls, Bing is

waiting for us." A dreamy look flitted over her face. She hit the volume button. "We've missed most of the movie but wow, Bing had the whole package. Looks and a voice that would melt chocolate."

The girls sighed in unison while Jamie thought of Caleb's voice. His would definitely melt ice in the Antarctic.

Jamie juggled three shopping bags, her laptop bag and purse while fumbling with her keys. She muttered, "Why doesn't this key work?" and jangled the keys. "Darn it. Office keys."

She dropped those in her open bag and balanced her purse on her knee. Pulling the keys out, she said, "Finally. With the right key, it's magic." Pushing the door open, she lost control of the bags. Onions rolled across the ceramic tiles, disappearing under the side table. Two whole chickens fell in the middle of the floor and red potatoes scattered. She carefully sidestepped the mess and dropped her handbag on the table before kicking the door shut.

Buzz, buzz.

"Now what?" Jamie pulled the phone from her coat pocket. "Hello?" She pulled the phone away from her ear to check caller ID. Annoyed, she said again, "Hello?"

"Hi, Jamie. This is Caleb Sullivan, Steve's brother."

"Hi, Caleb." Her pulse quickened and she pulled out a stool to sit on. Her knees wobbled.

"I hope I didn't catch you at a bad time." His voice slid over her like the sun, making her feel giddy and warm at the same time.

"Not at all, I just walked in the door." Shaking her head, she was helpless to say something clever.

"I wanted to thank you for the invitation to dinner, but if

it's just for three I'm happy to bow out since I put a damper on your dinner last week."

"No, it's not like that. My sisters and a couple of friends are coming. The more the merrier." Jamie brushed back a lock of hair. Kneeling down to scoop up the runaway produce, she sank to the floor instead, hanging on his every word. "Seriously, it'll be fun." She stopped breathing, hoping he'd agree.

"Well, then I'll be there. See you tomorrow night. Did you want us to bring something? I'm a pretty good cook."

"If you want to bring some cheese and crackers, that'll be plenty. My sisters and I have everything else under control."

He said, "All right then, see you tomorrow night. And Jamie…" The way he drawled her name out had her heart skip a beat. "Thanks again for taking pity on me."

She sat back on her heels. "I really want you to come." Her mouth dropped open. Why did she say that? "See you tomorrow."

She placed the phone on the table and grabbed the last onion. Dropping them into the bag, she crawled around making sure she got all the potatoes. Once she was positive she rounded up everything, she carried the bag into the kitchen. After putting the groceries away, she made herself a cup of tea and plopped into her favorite chair.

Her cell phone buzzed again. *For crying out loud, can't a woman have any peace after a long week?*

She grabbed her cell and put a smile on her face so it would be in her voice. "Hi, Gracie."

"I thought I'd swing by tonight and bring sushi if you're up for some company. Kenzie is going out with some people from the gym. She included me, but I'm too tired to be overly social. But I could use some company."

"Are you okay, squirt?"

"Just a little out of sorts."

"Sure, company would be nice. Pick up whatever you like, but skip the eel."

Grace's musical laughter was soothing to Jamie's jangled nerves. "See you shortly."

❧

Jamie flicked the button on the gas fireplace and it fired up with a whoosh. She sank back into her chair. What was bugging her, she wondered. She had hosted many dinner parties and this really wasn't that different. *With the exception that I'm trying to determine if Steve Sullivan is husband material, it'll be a perfectly normal night.*

She took a sip of her now cold tea. Frowning, she placed the mug on the table and wandered to her bedroom. Without turning on the light, Jamie shed her suit jacket and slacks, and left them in a heap for tomorrow's run to the dry cleaner. After slipping into cozy sweatpants and shirt, she then rooted around in her sock drawer until she found her favorite rag wool socks.

"Now I can really unwind and start the weekend."

A sharp knock came from the front door. Wondering who it could be, she went to investigate. Glancing out the sidelite window, she noticed a floral delivery truck in her driveway. She pulled open the door and was surprised to see Gus, a friend of her dad's and owner of the shop, holding a bouquet of tulips in a riot of colors and textures.

"Hey, Gus."

"Good evening, Jamie." He handed her the box, a vase secured inside.

Her eyes widened. She stammered, "Do you have the right house?"

"I most certainly do. Your name is on the card." He smiled. "Have a good night."

She closed the door and carefully carried the white cardboard box into the kitchen and set it on the counter. She drank in the subtle sent of the flowers and pulled the vase out of the box. A small white envelope was tucked into the center of the flowers. She tore open the card.

Looking forward to tomorrow.

Pounding on the back door caught her attention. Jamie dropped the card on the counter and went to open it. Grace stumbled over the threshold. Jamie took the bag filled with their dinner while Grace shut the door. "Why did you knock?"

"I couldn't reach my key." Grace looked around. "What were you doing?"

Jamie pointed to the flowers and wandered into the kitchen. "Look at what I just got."

Grace picked up the card. "Are they from Steve?"

"Who else would send me flowers?" Jamie looked at the card again. "I guess we'll have to see if there are any heart-skipping moments tomorrow."

Grace grabbed the card back. "Well, that's being a bit over-confident. Maybe you have a secret admirer." She snapped her fingers. "I know—they're from Robbie.

Jamie started laughing until tears ran down her cheeks. "I've known him since he was a baby. I highly doubt it's him. Besides, he's half in love with Kenzie."

"You're not going to ask Steve straight-out, are you?"

Jamie's eyes never left the flowers. She said, "Since whoever sent them wants to remain anonymous, we'll see how he reacts when they're the table centerpiece."

"Good idea, and I'll keep my eyes peeled and ears perked. Don't worry, sis, before dessert is finished we'll know if Steve is marriage material." Grace gave her sister a quick hug. "We've got your back." Laughing, she began to set out plates and chopsticks for dinner. "But at the moment I'm starving."

Jamie couldn't help but laugh. Whatever the sisters were dealing with, takeout always came first.

11

Jamie checked her makeup one last time as she heard the familiar chatter of her sisters' voices drifting toward her bedroom.

"JAMIE!" Kenzie's voice rattled the windows.

Grace admonished, "Kenzie MacLellan. Inside voice."

"Ah, jeez, you didn't need to jab me, and besides, you know she's primping in front of the mirror."

"Kenzie..." Jamie joined them. An impish smiled made the corners of her mouth twitch. "There's nothing wrong with putting a little effort into your makeup. You might want to take a peek at *your* mascara."

"What are you talking about?' Kenzie groaned. "I'm not wearing any."

"Exactly my point. You have those beautiful blue eyes, but you do nothing to accentuate them." Jamie turned Kenzie to face the mirror in the hallway. "We have basically the same eyes and see how different we look. My eyes pop and yours are just, well, there."

"If I started wearing mascara at the gym, I'd have to be constantly worried about black smudges under my eyes. That would scare off all my clients."

Grace grabbed the bags dangling from Kenzie's hands. Mildly annoyed, she said, "While you two debate the merits of mascara, I'm going to get busy in the kitchen." Jamie and Kenzie followed her down the short hall.

"There are many hours that you're not at the gym, and looking good doesn't have to be for anyone but yourself. Grace wears makeup every day, even when she's not going to work."

"If you haven't noticed, Grace is adorable. Always with perfect curly hair and just the right clothes. She's our girly-girl.

Jamie gave Kenzie a one-armed hug. "We each have our own style, which is a good thing. But you should accentuate your positives. You have great cheekbones, your skin is flawless and your eyes are one of your best features."

"Okay, I get it." She shrugged.

Jamie continued despite seeing her sister's cheeks flush with embarrassment. "When you're working you could skip the makeup, but they do have waterproof, also known as sweat-proof, mascara. A swish wouldn't hurt even at the gym."

"Jamie, let it go for tonight," Kenzie implored. "We should focus on your dinner party. Is everything ready?"

Jamie cocked an eyebrow and pointed down the hallway.

Kenzie held up her hands in surrender. "If you think I need a swish of mascara, I'll go put some on." She grinned. "After all, we want to make a good impression as potential future family."

"Now stop." Jamie gently shoved her toward the bedroom.

"What is the status of dinner?"

"The chicken is in the oven, the potatoes are simmering, I'm hoping Grace has dessert ready and I'm assuming we need to cook the vegetable?"

"Yeah, and I chilled the wine."

Grace interrupted her sisters. "Where's the wine?"

"It's in an insulated bag," Kenzie answered her.

"Got it." Grace pulled out four bottles. "Guess she's planning on us being thirsty."

Kenzie hurried off to Jamie's bedroom. Grace came out of the kitchen and handed Jamie a tray of appetizers.

"I hope we have fun tonight, and if by some slim chance there are sparks between me and a certain lawyer, well, that will make an interesting twist to the evening. If not, we'll have fun with friends." Jamie frowned. "Well, except for Steve's brother. Hopefully he won't be too annoying."

Grace said softly, "Cut the guy some slack. You met him for, what, a few minutes?"

Jamie nodded. "You're right. I'm sure it was a culmination of factors. I wasn't prepared for an extra dinner companion, even though I technically invited him, and he's new to town. Plus, Steve was really looking forward to spending time with his brother."

"It was nice of you to include him but now," with a wave of her hand Grace said, "put those on the coffee table and then you can set out some wine and beer glasses on the table." She glanced at her watch. "People will start arriving in less than five minutes."

"You're awfully bossy, squirt." Jamie grinned.

"It's self-preservation mode with two strong-willed older sisters."

Kenzie came into the living room. Turning her face from side to side, she said, "I'm ready for inspection. How's the paint job?"

Jamie leaned in. "For someone who doesn't use it every day, surprisingly well done."

Kenzie wiped fake sweat from her brow and smiled. "Whew. I was really shaking in my boots that I wouldn't pass."

"You're such a brat," Jamie teased.

Before Kenzie could continue the usual banter, Grace handed her a corkscrew. "You need to open the wine and set up the bar area." She winked at Jamie. "And if you don't stop harassing your sister, I'll call Dad."

"Well, Jamie..." Kenzie smirked. "I think Grace is using parent pressure to keep us in line tonight."

Jamie giggled. Before she could come back with a witty retort, the doorbell chimed. "I'm going to get the door, and you two? Behave."

Kenzie hurried to the fridge to open a bottle of white wine and set it in an ice bucket, then opened a bottle of shiraz. She then added a few bottles of beer to a tub full of ice. "I'm ready."

Grace nodded. "Me too."

Jamie pulled open the door. "Jo, I'm so glad you're here. Come in where it's warm." Jamie gave Jo a quick hug as she stepped inside.

Before Jamie could close the door, she heard, "Hold up, Jamie." Robbie ran up the walkway, slipping on a patch of black ice. Before he could hit the ground, he regained his footing. Grinning, he handed Jamie a bag. "I brought brownies. I baked Mom's recipe for you, double chocolate."

"Thanks, Robbie, but those are Kenzie's favorites."

"That's right...well, they're good at any rate." He stepped into the house and bumped into Jo. "Hey, Jo-jo."

"Hi, big brother. I didn't know you were coming too. We could have ridden together."

"Kenzie always includes me when she needs to have a little life injected into a party." Robbie's eyes sparkled and he stepped deeper into the house. "Hey, girls. Did you get beer?" His gaze met Kenzie's. Plastered across his face was a lopsided grin.

She pulled a bottle from the tub, popped the top and handed it to him. Robbie took the frosty bottle and glanced at the label. "Did you buy these just for me?"

Teasing, she said, "Don't let it go to your head. Mom drilled into us how to be a good hostess, and the top thing on the list was to always have the right selection of food and drink."

He gave a one-shoulder shrug. "Jeez, you know how to make a guy feel special."

Kenzie gave him a playful punch in his bicep. "Oh, Robbie, we've been hanging out forever—of course I know all your favorites."

Robbie bent low and pecked Grace's cheek. "Hey, squirt, how goes the medical biz?"

She smiled. "It was a busy flu season, but I think we're at the tail end. Next will be spring allergies."

"Being a junior doctor seems to agree with you."

Annoyance flashed over Grace's face and her voice grew frosty. "Robbie, I'm a physician's assistant, not a junior doctor."

"Isn't it the same thing?" His voice trailed off.

The murmur of voices from the front entrance caught Grace and Kenzie's attention. "Kenz." Grace nodded toward the door. "Are you thinking what I'm thinking?"

"Right behind you."

"Hey," Robbie said. "What's going on?"

Kenzie looked over her shoulder. "Help yourself to some munchies. We're going to greet Jamie's guests."

He mumbled, "I think there's more to it than that." He snagged a piece of cheese and plopped down on a stool.

Jamie felt her sisters hovering in the hallway as she hung Steve and Caleb's coats in the closet. "I'm glad you could make it tonight."

Steve said, "Thanks for extending the invite to include Caleb."

"It was my…" She glanced at her sisters. "Well, our pleasure. I'd like to introduce you to my sisters."

Kenzie stepped forward and smiled. "Hi, I'm Kenzie, the middle sister."

Grace piped up, "I'm Grace."

Caleb extended his hand, his smile warming his eyes. "It's nice to meet you. I'm Caleb, and this is my brother Steve. He's older than me by a few minutes."

"Oh." Color flushed Jamie's face. "I didn't know you were twins."

"Let me guess, Steve said he was the older brother but didn't bother to mention that it was by accident he popped out first?" Caleb chuckled. "It's a long running joke in our family."

"What can I say?" Steve winked at the girls. "I'm the oldest and better looking of the two."

Caleb held up a platter. "Where can I put this?" Jamie held out her hands to take it. "I hope you don't mind I whipped up a few appetizers. I had time on my hands since Steve was buried in contracts."

"You didn't need to bring anything so fancy, but thanks," Jamie said. "Come on into the living room and have a drink." She turned her back to the guys and mouthed *please* to Kenzie.

"Caleb, follow me and I'll introduce you to Jo and Robbie. Old family friends."

Grace went first, followed by Kenzie and Caleb. Steve and Jamie detoured to the kitchen. Casually she asked, "How were the roads on the way in from Rutland?"

Steve grabbed a spear of asparagus from the platter Jamie still held. "They were dry. It's gonna get cold tonight, but at least zero chance of snow or rain."

She set the platter down. "Can I get you something to drink—beer, wine or a mixed drink?"

"Beer's good." Steve looked around. "If you point me in the direction, I'll get my own."

"Sure, there's a tub at the end of the counter. Kenzie picked up a few of our favorites."

"Can I get you one too?" His hand hovered over a bottle.

"No, I'm going to have wine." She picked up a stemless glass and grabbed an open bottle by the neck. After sloshing the pinot into the glass, she set the bottle back on the counter.

The glass hovered at her lips. Steve put his hand on her arm and stopped the glass from connecting with her mouth. "Wait."

Her eyes widened. "What's the matter?"

He held up his beer bottle. "A toast. To our first party."

Jamie clinked her glass to his bottle. "Slàinte."

His brow wrinkled. "What does that mean?"

"It's a Scottish toast, it means 'health.'"

"Very nice." He sipped his beer.

"Our Scottish heritage sneaks into things we do and say," she murmured.

He leaned in as his voice dropped. "I like hearing you talk—you have a hint of Scots in your voice."

Jamie glanced at her sisters, who were keeping close tabs on her and Steve while staying engaged in light conversation with their guests. "We all do. Hazard of growing up with Dad."

"It's charming." Steve tucked a stray lock of hair behind her ear. "So, feel free to talk all you want."

She pulled back and stammered, "We should join the others." She picked up the tray and stepped in front of him. "I'm going to put this on the table."

He carried her glass for her.

Jamie said, "Jo, Robbie, can I persuade you to try one or two?" They selected a few appetizers before she could set it on the round wooden coffee table. Her gaze swept the room. "Does anyone need a refill?"

Robbie said, "I could," and Jo agreed.

Caleb said, "Jamie, let me help you." He stepped into the

small kitchen and set his glass on the counter, picking up the bottles of red and white wine. Holding them aloft, he said, "Jo, red or white?" He took a step forward.

"White, please." Jo held out her glass and murmured her thanks.

He refilled Grace and Kenzie's glasses and held the bottle of white to Jamie. "Would you like a bit more?"

"Thank you." She held out her glass and her eyes met his.

A shock rocked her system. She dropped her eyes, breaking their connection.

Caleb glanced in Steve's direction and replaced the bottle in the tub. Jamie looked at Steve but he was chatting with Jo. She took a drink, attempting to settle her pulse.

"Something smells good." Caleb pointed to the oven. "Do you mind?"

With a shake of her head, she said, "Not at all."

He quickly washed his hands and was drying them when Jamie opened the drawer next to the stove and handed him two mitts. He pulled out the rack and then the roasting pan. He pushed on the breast with his finger, took a large spoon from the utensil holder and basted the chicken before sliding it back in and turning the oven off. He glanced at Jamie. "The chicken's done."

Jamie peered into the oven. "How do you know? The little white button hasn't popped up yet."

His laugh was low and for her ears only. "Experience."

Jamie's brow creased. "Huh?" Her pulse started humming again.

"Steve didn't tell you?"

She shook her head. It was hard for her to concentrate on what he was saying instead of drowning in his eyes.

Amused, he said, "I'm a chef."

"I thought you were a vagabond, drifting around the world, cooking here and there."

Caleb smirked and shook his head. "Is that his story this

time? Actually, when asked, I travel with a few celebrities. It keeps me on the go and I make a pretty good living to boot."

"I had no idea." She frowned.

"What's the matter?" Concern filled his voice.

"I hope the meal lives up to your standards. I'm hardly a cook, let alone a chef." Jamie felt her hands get sweaty and she wiped them on the legs of her pants.

"Please don't worry. The aroma wafting throughout the house tells me it's going to be delicious."

She choked out a laugh. "You might want to reserve judgment until after you try it. The good news is there's always dessert and Grace makes sweets like no other."

He glanced at Grace. "Your sister has an eye like a hawk on us."

Jamie smiled over her shoulder. "She's just hungry."

He looked back at Jamie. "If you say so. What can I do to help serve? I'd hate to stand between her and dinner."

"That's really nice, but you're a guest. Relax and enjoy getting to know everyone."

Steve poked his head around the corner. "Yeah, little brother, I'll help Jamie."

Caleb snorted. "The king of takeout is going to plate dinner. Jamie, if you change your mind, the offer stands." He strolled into the living room but looked back over his shoulder, eyes smoldering with something Jamie couldn't read.

Steve put his empty bottle in the sink and rubbed his hands together. "What do you need me to do?"

Jamie pointed to a large platter and bowl. "If you can bring those over, I'll dish out the chicken and stuffing. My sisters will get the rest from the fridge."

"Sure." Steve stepped aside and watched as she placed the chicken on the platter and carved it. After scooping out the steaming stuffing, she handed the bowl to him. "This is ready for the table."

He hurried across the room and then touched Kenzie on

the shoulder. "Jamie said you'd help her finish getting dinner on the table."

Jamie couldn't help but notice Steve couldn't get out of the kitchen fast enough. Kenzie and Grace moved in with well-practiced motions. When Grace set the bread basket on the table, she said, "That's the last of it."

"Dinner's ready." Jamie ushered her guests into the dining area. "I hope you're still hungry after those amazing appetizers. And save some room—Grace made mousse and her world famous shortbread and Robbie brought brownies."

Steve held out a chair at the head of the table for Jamie and he sat on her right. Robbie sat next to Kenzie, and Caleb was between Jo and Grace.

Jamie took a sip of wine. She could feel Caleb looking at her. Averting her eyes, she stammered, "Please...help yourself before it gets cold."

12

As conversation flowed, Kenzie kept one eye on Jamie and the other on Steve. She was taking notes to compare with Grace later. A quick glance at Grace confirmed she wasn't missing a trick either. Steve was very handsome and smooth, but there was something that bugged Kenzie. She noticed he kept sneaking his phone in and out of his pocket.

Robbie nudged her foot, catching her off guard. "Earth to Kenz."

"What?" Kenzie's response was curt, and Robbie frowned.

He leaned over and hissed, "If you want to appear like you're *not* drooling over the attorney, you should talk to other people at the table."

Her eyes widened. She was taken aback at the annoyance she detected in his voice. "What are you talking about? I'm not drooling."

"If you say so." Robbie speared a piece of chicken and shrugged. "Could've fooled me."

"Keep your voice down." She lowered her voice. "I'm checking him out for Jamie. She thinks he might be the one."

"Huh?"

"Robbie, you're so dense." She dropped her voice to just above a hoarse whisper. "You know, the *one*."

Robbie started to choke. Sputtering and coughing, his eyes brimming with tears of laughter, he said, "MacLellan girls don't want to find the one."

Kenzie smacked his arm.

"Ouch." He rubbed it. "What did you do that for?"

Jamie's eyebrow arched. "Do I need to separate you two?"

Robbie shrugged and grinned. "Sorry, Mac."

Jamie looked at Steve. "They're best friends and Robbie works for Kenzie at her gym."

Steve set his fork down. "You own a gym?"

"I do. I've been open for a few years."

Steve anchored his attention on Kenzie. "Do you like being a small business owner?"

Propping her elbows on the table and clasping her hands, she said, "I love it. After college I thought about going on to be a physical therapist, but Grace's forte is medicine. I took my degree in sports management a different direction." Uneasy with the attention on her, Kenzie took a loud gulp of her water.

Robbie chuckled and took up the thread of conversation. "And then she took pity on her old friend and hired me."

Jamie redirected the conversation. Kenzie whispered behind the back of her hand, "Thanks."

He tapped the end of her nose. "Isn't it why you keep me around?"

Kenzie gave him a sharp look. "Huh?"

"Relax, Kenz, I'm the talker in this duo."

"Kenzie?" Grace said. "Will you help me clear the table?" She winked.

Jamie started to get up when Grace said, "We've got this."

Kenzie pushed back her chair. "Sure." She grabbed Robbie's plate despite his fork scooping up the last of the stuffing and veggies.

"Guess I'm done," Robbie muttered. He stood and picked up two serving bowls and placed them on the counter.

She smiled. "You can have an extra piece of shortbread."

He murmured, "I wanted to finish my dinner."

"Coffee, anyone?" Grace asked.

"Decaf?" Jo said.

"I'll brew a pot." Grace measured out the coffee, filled the carafe with water and hit the start button. The aroma of brewing coffee filled the cottage.

She placed shortbread cookies on a decorative plate and spooned chocolate mousse into stubby wine glasses, adding a dollop of whipped cream and a tiny piece of shortbread into the mound of cream. After setting them on a tray, Kenzie carried it into the living room, letting each person take a glass. Grace followed her with a handful of spoons and placed the platter of cookies and brownies in the center of the table.

"Does everyone want coffee?" Grace asked.

Five hands shot up. Grace dropped a hand on Jamie's shoulder. "You're on clean up duty."

Jamie smirked at her sisters and laughed. "I'm always on clean up duty around here." She relaxed into the cushions between Steve and Caleb, waiting for Grace and Kenzie to return with mugs, cream and sugar.

After delivering coffee, Kenzie perched on the arm of Robbie's chair and Grace sat on a hassock. "Dig in." Grace nibbled on a brownie. "Robbie, these are really fudgey."

Jamie moved the tiny cookie from the mousse and dipped her spoon into the whipped cream, then stirred it into her coffee.

"Jamie, sugar?" Steve held the bowl up.

"No, the whipped cream is sweet, and wait until you taste Grace's mousse—it's sinful."

Steve took a spoonful of mousse. Licking the spoon clean,

he exclaimed, "Wow, this is good! Are the three of you all good cooks?"

"We each have our specialty, and together we can turn out a decent meal."

Kenzie snorted. "Jamie's specialty is calling for takeout." Jamie shot her a withering look.

Steve's gaze roamed around the room. "Your home is charming, it suits you."

"Thank you." Jamie beamed. "I purchased it a couple of years ago and with a little sweat equity it's turned out quite comfortable."

"I see you have an unusual variety of tulips. Are they your favorite?" he asked.

She smiled. "I do. They were delivered last night. Aren't they lovely?" She paused. "Some of the colors I didn't know existed in tulips."

Steve said with a smile, "Our mother is passionate about tulips. As young boys Caleb and I'd help her every fall. If there was a new variety, she'd buy it and we'd plant it."

Caleb piped up. "Steve hated digging in the dirt—he'd rather be shooting hoops at the park."

"Cal would help Mom in the garden and kitchen. We didn't have any sisters, so I guess you could say he filled in a little of that void for her."

Caleb twirled his spoon in the mousse. "It was time well spent. She taught me that cooking was easy and hard at the same time. I chose culinary school because of her." He took a bite of a cookie. "Grace, these are really good. Maybe sometime you could show me how you make them?"

Grace smiled and with a shake of her head said, "Sorry, the recipe is top secret and it's only passed down within the family. But you can take a few home, if there's any left."

"Understood. Sometimes family recipes should be secret. It's like keeping your ancestors alive."

"Grace, Kenzie and I learned how to make a few traditional Scottish dishes from our gran. Unfortunately, she recently passed away." Jamie looked down and brushed a tear from her cheek. Steve took her hand, and she squeezed it. "We'll always have the memories of our summers in Scotland on the farm. She took us fishing and hiking. Every day was magical."

Steve gave her hand a tug and said, "I guess you could say your gran brought us together."

Jamie's head snapped up and she looked at her sisters. Softly she said, "I guess she did."

Without words, the girls shared the same thought: *the magic of the dress.*

Robbie's spoon scraped the edges of the glass and he broke the tension that seemed to be settling over the group. He looked up and grinned. "Is there any more mousse?"

Jo looked around sheepishly and held up her glass. "I could use a little more too."

Grace giggled. "Somehow, I knew you two would look for seconds, and yes, there's a bowl in the refrigerator. Help yourself."

Robbie pulled Jo up from the couch. "Come on, sis, I'm not waiting on you."

Steve leaned back and patted his midsection. "I don't think I could eat another bite without having to run a couple extra miles tomorrow."

"We'll be hitting the gym bright and early." Jamie flicked her thumb toward Kenzie and gave a lopsided smile. "She's a tough drill sergeant."

Kenzie held up her hands. "If I didn't push, you'd skate through and complain you didn't reap any benefits." She hopped up. "I'm going to see if Robbie left any mousse, but Steve, why don't you and Caleb come to the gym tomorrow? It might be fun to all workout together."

Jo peeked her head out from the kitchen and interjected, "Just for the record, she's gonna kick your butt."

Steve leaned forward, resting his elbows on his knees, and said, "I'd like to take a class with the MacLellan sisters. But I'm pretty sure we can handle it. What do you think, Caleb? Are you in?"

"Yeah, sure, sounds like fun." His expression was unreadable to Jamie.

Kenzie's eyes gleamed. She rubbed her hands together. "Care to make a friendly bet, Steve?"

Jamie waggled her finger at Kenzie. "No betting on a Sunday."

"It's Saturday. Besides, I don't think there's anything wrong with a little wager."

Steve looked at Jamie. "The last time I did, I got dinner. What are the stakes?"

"If I don't leave you dripping in sweat, you both can have a six-month membership on me."

Steve wore a cocky grin. "That sounds fair. And if by some chance we walk away smelling like a rose?"

Robbie chuckled. "Be careful."

Caleb chimed in, "If Kenzie successfully kicks our butts, tomorrow night I'll cook everyone a meal they'll never forget."

"There you have it, the Sullivan brothers against the MacLellan sisters. A battle of the sexes."

Robbie snorted. "Caleb, you might want to start planning the menu and shopping list tonight. And these ladies love wine, so be prepared to pick up a few bottles."

Steve grunted. "We're in great shape. I'm confident we'll be winning this bet."

"And Caleb, since your brother is totally underestimating these women, you should have him pay for the meal. These girls can eat." Robbie ran his finger around the inside of the glass, getting every last drop of mousse. "Kenz, I'll be in the gym at the usual time, so I can judge." He looked at Jo. "Are you in as a second?"

"Heck yeah. But I have just one question—since we're judging, can we be a part of the reward when Kenzie wins?"

Steve rolled his eyes and chuckled. "You're pretty sure of Kenzie?"

Jo's head bobbed as she laughed. "I've seen her reduce tougher guys than you to a puddle."

Steve glanced at Jamie. "You've been pretty quiet."

"Remember, I still have to pay off a bet with you, so I'm staying out of this one."

"Wise woman. What time should we meet?"

"Given that you have to drive over, let's say ten?" Kenzie looked at Grace and Jamie. "Or do you want to work out early?"

Jamie agreed. "Ten's fine with me. Steve?"

"Ten it is." He looked at Caleb. "Does that work for you?"

"Yeah. If we're going to be back tomorrow, we should be going." Caleb loaded all the dirty dishes on the tray and asked Grace, "Are you sure I can take a few cookies for the road?"

"Come on, I'll hook you up." Caleb followed Grace into the kitchen.

Robbie and Jo hung with Kenzie while Jamie went to get Steve and Caleb's coats.

"I'm really glad you and Caleb could come for dinner," Jamie said.

"Thanks for asking us. Sorry about dinner the other night." Steve's voice dropped low. "There'll be other dinners. He's not in town that often."

Jamie stepped back and handed Steve his coat. Caleb joined them and took his coat, slipping a small bag of cookies into the pocket. "Jamie, this was a lot of fun. Thanks again, and the chicken was fantastic. Oh, and I'll grab my platter tomorrow."

"You're welcome, Caleb. See you tomorrow." Jamie watched him walk out the door and down the driveway.

Steve said, "I'm looking forward to tomorrow." He took her hand. "Do you want to have dinner, alone, tomorrow night?"

Refocusing her attention on Steve, she laughed, "Did you forget Caleb is cooking dinner for us?"

He took a step back. "That's if we lose, but if not…" His voice trailed off. Steve turned and walked down the step. "Have a good night."

Jamie waited until the car had pulled out of the driveway before closing the door. She walked into the living room where four sets of eyes watched her.

Kenzie and Grace pounced. Grace demanded, "Well, is he the one?"

"Who?"

"Steve?"

A tiny smile hovered on her lips, and Jamie said, "Honestly, I have no idea. How can anyone tell after a few dates?"

Grace folded her arms across her chest. "You just spent an entire evening with Steve glued to your side. You must have felt something."

"I didn't feel any sparks or butterflies. I mean, even when he took my hand, nada."

Kenzie said, "When you're having dinner with a gorgeous guy and he flirts with you, shouldn't you feel something?"

"Ladies," Robbie said, "cut her some slack. It wasn't like they had a romantic dinner for two where sweet nothings could flow like wine. Her two sisters, a couple of friends and his brother were chaperones."

"Maybe. But I would have thought she would have felt a stirring of—oh heck, what do I know about love…" Kenzie said.

"Did I hear Steve ask you to dinner tomorrow night?" Grace asked.

"He did, but I reminded him they were going down after the gym. He didn't seem to be amused."

"Why?" Kenzie asked.

Jamie flopped into the chair and closed her eyes. "From what I gather so far, he's very competitive. Besides I just want to go to bed and sleep on everything."

Jo stood. "Robbie, that's our cue. We should get going."

Robbie tweaked Kenzie's nose. "I'll open the gym in the morning if you want to come in a little late. I want you well rested to kick a little lawyer butt."

She laughed. "So, you're betting on me? No worries. It's what I do best."

Grace said, "I'll get your jackets."

Jo gave Jamie a quick hug. "Thanks for dinner. I'll see you in the morning."

Robbie did the same, and they followed Grace down the hall.

Jamie heard the muffled sound of the door closing and Grace padded into the living room. She perched on the edge of the chair. "I loaded the dishwasher for you and Kenzie stored the leftovers in the fridge."

Jamie's eyes fluttered open. "Thanks, Gracie. Tonight was fun."

"It was. You're sure you don't know about Steve?"

Jamie shook her head. "I'm more confused now than before the Sullivan boys arrived."

Kenzie perked up. "The Sullivan boys?"

Jamie brushed back her hair. "Yeah, I didn't realize that Caleb is so easygoing."

"They're twins," Grace reminded her.

"Yes, but they're not clones. I thought he was annoying when I first met him, but he's really a sweet guy." Jamie kicked off her shoes and wiggled her toes. "What a day."

She failed to confess how Caleb made her blood pound through her veins or left her breathless with just a look. But the idea of dating a traveling chef was not her idea of a romance.

Kenzie said, "I think I'm going to head home. Grace, are you coming?"

"Yeah, since I can't lounge around tomorrow morning. I hear my bed calling me now."

Jamie pulled herself upright. "I'll be at the gym around nine-thirty tomorrow."

Kenzie hugged Jamie tight. "Sweet dreams, sis. And don't worry, you'll find the right guy when you're ready."

More to herself than the girls, Jamie softly said, "I wish Gran were here to ask her how she knew Granddad was the one for her."

Grace said, "I'd like to know more about the dress and its history. I have so many questions and no answers. Dad won't know since he's a guy."

Jamie kissed Grace's cheek. "And with Mom marrying into the family, I'm sure she doesn't have all the facts either."

Grace's face lit up. "We could Skype with them tomorrow. Maybe they could look around in the attic or someplace for a journal, something that would give us a clue."

As Jamie walked her sisters to the door, she agreed. "That's a great idea. We'll come here after we workout with the guys, have lunch and then Skype."

Jamie stepped into the crisp night air and shivered, wrapping her arms around her body until the glow of red taillights disappeared. She went inside and closed the door. It was too cold to wait for any kind of a sign from Gran.

13

Jamie woke with a start. She thought something banged against the back of the house. The house was dark and silence filled every shadow. She flipped back the covers and grabbed her robe. She shuffled to the kitchen to investigate and peeked out the window—then did a double take. "What the heck? Gran?"

Standing in the backyard stood Gran dressed in her favorite church dress. Jamie was hurrying to get out the patio door when the filmy vision disappeared. The lawn was empty except for a heavy coating of frost.

She rubbed her eyes. "I must be dreaming." She went back to bed and lay there for a long time, whimpering. "I miss you so much, Gran."

Despite tears dampening her pillow, she fell into a dreamless slumber.

Exhausted, and with a splitting headache, Jamie fumbled out of bed and into the bathroom. She filled a glass with water and tossed back three aspirins. She peered into the mirror, studying her face. Her eyes were blood shot and her skin, blotchy. "You look like you pulled an all-nighter."

Her phone chirped inside her robe pocket. There was an incoming message.

Are you up?

Morning, K. Yes, I'm up and I'll be on time.

K—ttyl.

Jamie mumbled, "Why does she always have to abbreviate in texts. Would it be too hard to type out *talk to you later*?"

Pulling on her workout clothes, she stopped midway through. *I can't wear this, it's got old sweat spots and is all stretched out.* She frantically pawed through her drawers. "I need something cute and not overly revealing."

Satisfied with black yoga pants and a long butt-skimming tee, Jamie pulled on a hooded sweatshirt and thick socks. Putting her sneakers and lightweight socks in her bag, she glanced at the clock. She had time for one cup of coffee.

Jamie pulled into the parking lot and noticed Steve's car was there, along with Grace and Jo's. A cold drizzle was just starting when she stepped from the car. She ran toward the front door. Looking through the drops, she saw Caleb was holding the door for her.

He grinned, "Morning, Jamie."

She noticed his workout clothes clung to his muscles, and smiled at him. "You're early."

"We didn't want to be late and lose the bet by default."

Her eyes lit up and she teased, "I wouldn't have pegged you for a competitive guy."

Steve wandered out of the locker room and chimed in, "You have no idea," as he walked past Caleb toward her. Giving her a friendly hug, he said, "Ready?"

"Are my sisters in the spin room?"

"Yup, you're the last to arrive."

The trio crossed the lobby. They could see into the spin room. Kenzie was sitting on a bike at the front of the room and Grace was putting her water bottle on a bike in the second row. They greeted them with welcoming smiles.

Jamie grinned. "I just need to put my sneakers on, and then we'll get down to some serious sweating."

Steve stepped to one side, letting her go in first. "After you."

Jamie walked into the familiar room and chose a bike to the far right in the first row. Steve claimed the bike next to her and Caleb took one beside Grace. Robbie and Jo were in the last row. It wasn't a huge spin room, three rows of bikes dominating the space, and of course Kenzie was front and center.

Kenzie looked at Caleb and Steve. With a goofy smile she said, "Have you done spin before?"

Jamie caught Grace's eyes in the mirror and winked. The boys were in for a brutal forty-five minutes, if they lasted that long.

Steve shook his head no and Caleb sat up a little straighter and said yes.

Jamie looked at Steve. "Here's the scoop. Class is forty-five minutes, but you can quit at any point. Once we get started, the music should give you a beat to focus on."

In a firm, authoritative voice, Kenzie said, "Steve, I see Caleb helped you set up your bike with resistance, seat height and handle bars." Handing him a bottle of water, she paused to check Caleb's settings. With a slight incline of her head, she smiled when she saw the large bottle of water in the holder. "In addition to a great leg workout, I'll combine other weighted moves to work the entire body. If at any time you start to feel breathless, slow your pace. Despite that we have a friendly wager going on, I don't want anyone getting hurt."

She strode back to the front of the room, cranked the music and hopped on the bike with ease.

In a loud, clear voice, she commanded, "Hop on and let's go—we're going to start with a slow warm up for two minutes, then we're popping it up."

Everyone eased into the rhythm of pedaling for a few minutes when suddenly Kenzie shouted, "UP!"

Everyone pedaled with butts in the air.

"And now drop to the saddle. Drop your speed to a working warm up. Then up again and pump it up. Your heart rate should be climbing and you should be working at about a seven. Hit the saddle again." Kenzie cajoled the riders, encouraging them with each passing minute. The music matched her cadence.

"Slow it down to the beat. Take a drink when you need it." Kenzie counted them down and back up double time, then back down, going from the base to double time repeatedly.

Jamie's heart was hammering inside her chest. She couldn't look at Steve sideways but could see his reflection in the mirror—sweat was dripping off his chin, his face grim as he followed Kenzie's lead. She gave him props for not quitting.

"Keep pushing," Kenzie urged. "Follow the beat of the music." She raised her finger and shouted, "Speed it up!"

She rose up, sweat pouring off her as she pedaled. "Up—three, two, one. Back in the saddle."

At seventeen minutes in, a sheen of sweat glistened on the group, Kenzie's voice driving them harder. "Don't give up. You've got this."

Her breath was steady as she encouraged the group to maintain their form. "Keep it going!"

Jamie gulped water and oxygen, oblivious to the water dripping from her skin, pedaling as if her life depended on maintaining her speed. She glanced at the clock—it was almost over. She might—no, scratch that, she *would* finish.

Finally, Kenzie shouted. "Five minutes!" The music slowed. "Time to start cooling things down."

Steve started to dismount when Kenzie barked, "Stay on your bike, you need to cool down properly, bring your heart rate down."

He grabbed his water bottle and drained it, while continuing to slow his legs.

"All right." Kenzie stopped peddling. "Let's hit the mats. There is a water cooler on the way in."

"Now what?" Steve groaned.

Jamie tossed him a towel. "We need to stretch our hamstrings, quad, calves, hips and back. Trust me, Kenz knows exactly what she's doing."

Steve filled his water bottle and drained it, refilling it one last time before collapsing on a mat. "For the record?" he gasped for breath. "Caleb's cooking tonight."

Kenzie let out a warrior whoop, high-fived her sisters and began talking the group through a thorough stretch routine.

Robbie nudged Jo. "See, I told you she'd kick butt."

"Doesn't she always?" Jo leaned over until her nose touched her knee. "Kenzie always gets what she wants."

Robbie looked at Kenzie and dropped his voice so only Jo could hear him. "More importantly, she will make sure Jamie finds someone who's worthy to be a part of her life."

"Steve!" Jamie called as he came out of the locker room. Caleb was behind him. "I hope Kenzie's class wasn't too hard."

"No, it's fine. I guess I should have asked what kind of workout we were doing today and I would have scoped it out on the Internet. Here I thought I was in good shape."

Jamie's laughter filled the room. "I don't know if that would have prepared you for Kenzie's class. I've taken others when I've traveled, and I think she's unmerciful."

He smirked. "Well, I guess I've been indoctrinated. Caleb says he loves to take these kinds of classes. Mixes things up from a basic run and lifting weights."

Caleb filled his water bottle, his eyes finding Jamie's. "I think being well rounded is the best way to stay in shape. Your muscles get conditioned to the same movements over and over."

"Yeah, yeah, I hear you, bro. Let it go." Steve glanced at his phone, missing the connection between his brother and Jamie.

Jamie's legs felt like jelly, as her eyes were locked with Caleb. "Am I sensing some tension?"

Caleb answered her with a smile, causing the blood to stop flowing to her brain.

Blind to what was going on between Caleb and Jamie, Steve said, "Nah. We're fine." He took her arm and steered her toward the door. "So, about dinner?"

Jamie felt the breath catch in her throat. "Right, dinner. Um..." Her eyes sought Caleb's. "Surprise us with whatever you feel like cooking. The market is just down the street."

Steve said, "Bro, let's hit the store and give everyone time to do their thing." He checked his phone again. "How about we come over around four?"

"Perfect. I'll tell my sisters and Robbie and Jo."

Caleb said, "Are you sure you don't have a request? I'll cook whatever is your favorite."

"We'll eat anything and after our workout, we've earned it." She gave Caleb a shy smile. Unsure what the heck was going on between them, she pointed to the other room. "I'll see you later."

The brothers each raised a hand and Steve called out, "See you later."

She brushed the hair off her face, taking a moment to settle her jangling nerves before walking into the other room.

"The guys are coming over later, but Kenz and Grace, are you still coming over so we can Skype with Mom and Dad?"

"Yeah." Grace picked up her bag. "I'll follow you."

"I'll be along shortly. Robbie's going to close up, and what time should they come over?"

Jamie said, "Four."

Robbie and Jo wandered in their direction. "What are you three up to?"

"Just making plans for tonight. Why don't you plan on coming around four?"

Robbie gave a salute, "We'll be there. I can't wait to eat something from a professional chef." He patted his stomach. "I hope he makes enough."

Kenzie chuckled. "If you don't get enough to eat, Jamie has enough leftovers from last night."

Grace handed Jamie her bag. "Ready to hit the road? I need coffee."

Kenzie chimed in, "Me too."

"It'll be ready and waiting." Jamie laughed.

"Thank heavens. I am about two cups short for the day," Kenzie said.

"Me too," Grace chirped. "And can I vote for no more spin classes on Sunday? It's just downright mean."

Kenzie chuckled. "People actually pay for me to be tough on them and you're complaining when you get it for free."

"I'll remember that when you grumble the next time I give you a flu shot and you don't have to pay me."

"Touché, little sister."

Jamie slung her bag over her shoulder. "Come on, Grace. If you want to take a shower at my place before Kenzie gets there, we need to put a wiggle on it."

"Now that does sound nice. You've got the best towels and I just love your shower—two heads and unlimited hot water." She sighed. "Someday I'm going to have a fabulous house and not just an apartment."

"Stop," Jamie scolded her. "You're doing great, better than some people you graduated with. You have an apartment, a nice vehicle and a job you love in your hometown, near family. Really, what more do you want?"

Grace thought for a moment. "You're right, let's get going."

Kenzie called after them, "Don't drink all the coffee."

Jamie followed Grace to her place and pulled her car into the small garage. Grace let herself in the side door as the garage door closed behind Jamie.

"I'm so glad you gave Kenz and me keys to your house." Grace dropped her bag on table.

"It just makes it easier if we all have access to each other's places. In case of an emergency or something." Jamie kicked off her boots inside her bedroom door.

"Oh, Jamie." Grace leaned against the doorjamb, her voice was soft. "You hung up the dress?"

"I couldn't leave it all folded up." Her eyes shone. "It's stunning, isn't it?"

Grace's eyes grew wide. She crossed the short space, her eyes glued to the dress. "Was it weird, wearing Gran's dress?"

Jamie wrapped her arms around Grace. "It felt wonderful. Like I was a girl getting ready to marry the man I love."

"And you said it fit perfectly."

"Like it was made for me. And if you remember, Gran was shorter than me, but it was the perfect length and fell in all the right places. When I saw myself wearing the dress, it was at that moment I knew I wanted to have someone special in my life. I can't really explain it any better than it was like a calmness fell over me. I could see my life laid out before—if I never opened my eyes to the possibility to love, it would be empty."

Grace's voice softened. "I understand."

"I wish you and Kenzie would rethink your life plans."

"Maybe we will. There's a part of me that's always wanted the fairytale life, my handsome prince rescuing me and all." Grace took it down from the back of the door. "Hold it up to you so I can see."

Jamie took the hanger and held it up in front of her.

"Oh, Jamie," Grace whispered. "It's beautiful. Can you believe Great-gran sewed this with her own fingers?"

"Remember Gran showed us her mother's sewing machine? I'll bet that's what she used." She held up the side of the dress. "Look at these seams. That wasn't hand-stitched."

Grace bent low and turned the seam inside out. "You're right."

The front door banged, and Kenzie shouted, "Hey! Where are you guys hiding?"

"Be right out." Jamie hung the dress up and pushed Grace toward the bathroom.

Kenzie was sitting at the breakfast bar. "Why haven't you started the coffee?"

"You know Grace, always going on about my bathroom." Jamie moved about the kitchen.

Kenzie popped a grape from the bowl into her mouth. "I'm starving."

"Feel free to grab the leftovers, and let's see what we can come up with for lunch."

Kenzie slid off the stool and dug around in the fridge. "Hey, Jamie, is there any leftover whipped cream for our coffee?"

"Um, Kenz, can I talk to you a minute?"

Kenzie shut the door. "What's the matter? Your face is all scrunched up like when you're upset."

"There's something I want to say."

"Go on." She sat down on a stool.

"When I tried on Gran's wedding dress, I got the distinct impression my life would be empty if I didn't open myself up to a future."

"I know." She reached for a mug and stuck it under the stream of hot rich coffee dripping from the machine.

"How do you know? No one knows other than me. Well, and now Grace."

She handed Jamie a mug of coffee and took another empty cup. "Just because you're the older sister doesn't necessarily mean you're the smartest. I knew you couldn't keep this dress in your house and not let your insatiable curiosity get the best of you. And if Great-gran says there is something to it, there is."

Jamie grinned and held up the mug before taking a sip. "How can you be so matter of fact? Am I that transparent?"

"Not to anyone other than me and Grace." Her voice held a note of certainty. "Gran could always read you like an open book." Kenzie held up a finger. "Maybe we're all a little psychic."

Jamie nodded thoughtfully. "You might be right and Gran always said there wasn't anything the three of us could hide from her."

Kenzie's face got a faraway look. "That would explain how we're always in tune to each other. Do you remember the first time we made shortbread with Gran? Grace had to have been about five. Mom and Dad hadn't come over yet—it was just us kids and Gran. I'm sure Grandad Rory was off fishing with his buddies or something."

"That summer was great. Grandad took us fishing almost every morning and Gran taught us how to bake the one thing she said every wee lass should know, in the proper Scottish tradition."

"Right. Gran went to bed and Grace snuck downstairs eating more than half of what was left. When she snuck back upstairs, she climbed in your bed and told you her tummy hurt."

Jamie clapped her hands together and giggled. "I figured I'd save her from getting into trouble and take the blame. So the next morning when Gran asked what happened to her cookies I 'confessed' to a nighttime snack attack."

"But Gran knew it was Grace. I never knew how, but she just nodded and never said another word until Mom and Dad arrived."

"I'm sure it was because Grace didn't want to eat breakfast. I can still see her now, the three of us sitting down at the table, and she pushed her food around."

"How can you remember that detail? You were only seven."

"Grace never misses a meal unless there's a darn good reason, and the way Gran cooked, no one ever left her table without eating something."

"That's a true statement," Kenzie said. "Even back then you took care of us, leading the way."

Jamie said, "When Mom and Dad arrived, she told them Grace had the most Scottish blood running through her veins."

Grace walked into the room with a towel wrapped around her hair, dressed in sweats and thick socks. "What are you talking about?"

"The time you ate half a batch of shortbread when we were at Gran's."

Grace smiled. "You know, I always thought I fooled her."

Jamie wrapped an arm around Grace. "Sadly, we didn't make shortbread for the rest of the summer."

Kenzie handed Grace a mug and dropped a dollop of whipped cream on the top. "Thankfully you learned how to make the best shortbread, just like she did."

Grace took a sip of the coffee, the whipped cream leaving a speck on her nose. "You know I've been wondering, do you think Gran left a diary or journal that talks about the dress? I remember she always had a book and a pen next to her bed. We could ask Mom to look."

Jamie handed her a napkin. "Your nose."

Grace giggled and wiped it off. "Don't you agree?"

"Yeah, Jamie, fire up the computer and we'll have lunch after. Curiosity is getting the best of me."

The girls huddled around Jamie waiting for Skype to connect.

"Well, hello, girls." Mom's face filled the screen. "This is a surprise."

Their dad came up from behind their mom. "Hello, girls."

"Hi, Dad," they said together.

"Mom," Kenzie began. "We were wondering if you know —did Gran leave a journal or diary?"

"Well, as a matter of fact, we found a box squirreled away in the attic. What makes you ask?"

Grace jumped in. "You know she sent us the wedding dress and a letter, but we have a lot of questions about how Gran met Grandad Rory and about Great-gran Ann and Granddad James. Would you mind shipping them to us?"

Mom looked at Dad. He said, "Gran left a letter saying to send them to you when you asked."

Jamie looked at her sisters. With a shake of her head, she said, "Gran strikes again."

They nodded.

"We've boxed them up for you. We'll ship them tomorrow. I'll send you the tracking information."

"Thanks, Mom," Jamie said.

"What are you hoping to find?" Dad asked.

"We're not sure. But when we do we'll fill you in," Kenzie said. "All right, we're going to run for now, but we'll call again soon."

Jamie, Kenzie and Grace waved to the computer screen

and blew a kiss to their parents. In unison the girls said, "Love you guys."

"Love you girls," Dad said, and Mom waved goodbye.

The screen went blank, and Jamie leaned back in the chair. "So once again Gran is at least one step ahead of us."

Kenzie breezed into the kitchen. "Who knows, maybe after we read her journals we'll understand how she did it."

Grace snorted. "Yeah, right. I think she took that secret with her when she went to live amongst the angels."

"One thing I know for sure, we'll have to wait until the books arrive, and until then we're still working on what I'm going to wear tonight."

Grace squealed and Kenzie rolled her eyes. "Are you excited Steve is coming over for dinner?"

Jamie stood up. Very nonchalantly she said, "I'm not sure either of you noticed, but at the gym he kissed me on the cheek."

"And…" Kenzie jabbed her side. "What was that like?"

"Truthfully? It was like being kissed by Dad. Nothing, zero, nada."

"Still? Not even one little twinge?" Kenzie prodded.

Jamie piled leftovers on her plate and slid it into the microwave. "No."

"What do you think that means?" Grace mused. "Shouldn't you be feeling some sort of excitement or tingles and blood racing?"

Jamie sat on a stool and watched the timer on the microwave, taking her time to answer. "It's either I was exhausted from our sister's punishing workout or he's not the guy."

"Don't blame me. You've done that same workout lots of times." The microwave beeped and Kenzie withdrew the plate, handing it to Jamie, and slid hers in.

"Then why go out to dinner with him?" Grace asked.

"One, I never renege on a bet, and two, I think if he tries to kiss me—you know, really kiss me—I'll know for sure."

Kenzie tapped her fork on the edge of her plate. "Logical. I like it." She grabbed her plate and slid in Grace's. "After we eat, let's pick out a killer outfit and do your hair. Getting dressed up always seems to help a girl's outlook."

14

A sharp rap on the front door at exactly four had Jamie hurrying through the living room. Flinging the door wide, she stepped back to let Steve and Caleb come inside. They were loaded down with shopping bags. Laughing, she took two bags from Caleb and closed the door with her foot.

"Come on in. Everyone is here and anxious to help cook." Her eyes twinkled. "Or eat."

Caleb stepped aside so Jamie could lead the way. She called out, "Hey, everyone, the guys are here." Steve passed off the beer and wine to Robbie, and Kenzie and Jo took a bag of groceries and set it on the other side of the kitchen counter. Grace greeted them warmly and offered to take their jackets.

Caleb shrugged out of his jacket and handed it to Grace, saying thank you before stopping Jamie from unpacking bags. "You can take a seat over there." He pointed to a stool. "And I'm going to do my best to not make a mess of your kitchen."

Jamie happily sat down and watched as Caleb placed salad fixings, thick pork chops and sweet potatoes on the counter, and stored pints of ice cream in the freezer. "I'm hungry already and you haven't even started cooking yet."

Caleb laughed and glanced around the group. "Any food allergies before I start?"

Robbie unscrewed a bottle of beer. "Just to hunger." Everyone laughed and heads bobbed up and down in agreement.

Caleb rubbed his hands together and said, "How about a little something to tease your appetites?" From another bag he pulled out a few covered containers. "Mushroom pate, of course brie, baguettes and marinated olives to whet your appetite."

Steve was uncorking wine and pouring white when Caleb said, "I think Jamie prefers pinot noir."

Jamie saw Kenzie's eyes grow wide. She too was surprised Caleb knew what wine was her first choice. Steve opened the red and poured Jamie a glass. "Anyone else?" He held up the bottle.

Grace took a glass of white and Kenzie held up a beer. Jo shook her head. "I'm good for right now."

Caleb smiled at Jamie. "I know it can be hard when someone starts to go through your drawers."

She found herself watching him instead of engaging in conversation around her. "What?"

He pivoted in the kitchen. "Where are your knives, pots and miscellaneous cooking utensils? Or would you care to be my sous chef?"

Reluctant to break away from Caleb, she glanced at Steve, who was having a spirited conversation with the rest of the group about the upcoming baseball season. "Sounds like a great opportunity to learn from a master." She hopped up and grabbed an apron.

"By the way, you look really pretty. That purple sweater suits you."

The timber of his voice rumbled down to her toes. Jamie could feel the heat creep into her cheeks. Fanning her face, her voice low, she said, "Wine makes my cheeks pink."

He angled a glance downwards. "Do you like the wine?"

She swallowed hard and nodded. "It's one of my favorites."

Caleb reached across her body, his hand grazed hers. "Here, let me show you the way to slice the onions for the brine."

She allowed him to put his hand over hers. With smooth movements, together they sliced the onion into fine slivers. He scooped them up and dropped them into a glass bowl. Stuttering, she said, "What's next?"

"We need to boil water, mix that with some spices, salt and some apple cider…"

"Maple syrup?" Looking up through her lashes, she paused. "I have some in the fridge." She stepped from his side and let go of the breath she wasn't aware she was holding. She found the jug and handed it to him.

"Do you need more help?" Jamie noticed Kenzie watching them. "I should go check on the others." Before he could respond, she moved out of the kitchen, taking bottles of wine with her.

Kenzie slid up next to her. "What's cooking out there?"

"Caleb was showing me how to make a brine for the chops. I learned a new way to slice onions too."

Teasing, Kenzie said, "I saw that." She peered around her sister. "Don't look now, but he's keeping an eye on you."

Jamie peeked over her shoulder and sighed. *What are you doing?* she chided herself. *Steve is supposed to be your date, not his brother.*

Grace broke away from the group and joined her sisters. "Everything okay in the kitchen?"

Jamie shot Grace a sharp look. "What's that supposed to mean?"

"Nothing, why are you so touchy? You looked like you were having fun with Caleb, that's all." Grace stepped back. "I'm sorry I asked."

Instantly Jamie was sorry she snapped. "Grace, wait." She held up a bottle. "More wine?" Grace gave her a smile that Jamie knew meant all was forgiven.

After refilling glasses, she went back to the kitchen. "So where were we?"

"While you were playing hostess, I got the potatoes in the oven, chops are brining, salad is chilling in the fridge and the fudge sauce is simmering."

Jamie stood in front of the stove, took the spoon and stirred the sauce. "Can I try it?"

Caleb pulled a teaspoon from the silverware drawer and handed it to her. "Careful, it will be hot."

She looked into the living room; Steve was laughing and having fun. She took the spoon and dipped the tip into the heavenly smelling sauce. She blew on it before sticking her tongue out.

Inwardly Caleb groaned. This woman was going to be the death of him if his brother didn't kill him first. All this flirting with the first girl his brother had shown interest in since breaking up with Yvette. What was he doing?

He turned away as she tasted the chocolate sauce. He could hear her say, "Caleb, this is the most amazing thing I've ever tasted."

If she could be so appreciative of a simple confection, how would she react if he really pulled out all his culinary talents to woo her?

"I'm glad you like it." Using his thumb, he reached out and wiped off a drip off her chin. Surprise filled her clear blue eyes. He held up the evidence. "Chocolate."

"I can't wait for dessert." She dropped the spoon in the sink. "We should go in the living room."

He took a step back and let her go before him, reminding himself one more time she was off limits.

The way her body reacted to Caleb's simple gesture had Jamie hurrying to her room.

With a soft knock Grace poked her head in. "Sis?" She closed the door behind her. "What's going on you've been off ever since the guys got here. Did something just happen?"

With a shake of her head, she pulled Grace into a one-armed hug. "Squirt, I'm tired and just needed a minute."

Worry lines appeared on Grace's forehead. "I'm not sure I believe you, but we should get back out there before Caleb serves dinner and we're left with pan drippings." Grace plopped a kiss on her cheek. "I'm here if you want to talk."

"Thanks, Gracie."

Jamie and Grace slipped into the kitchen, and Kenzie said, "There you are."

Jamie's smile was tight. "I didn't know we were missing." She looked at Grace and winked. "Did you?"

"We've been right here the whole time." The sisters exchanged a look and Kenzie dropped the subject.

Slowly, one by one, everyone gathered in the kitchen to help with dinner. Although Caleb insisted there wasn't much to do, he gave everyone a job. Jo tossed the salad. Robbie checked the potatoes, found a bowl for them and scurried out of the way. Caleb was patting the chops dry with paper towels and said to Steve, "Can you run out to the Jeep and get the cast-iron skillet?"

Steve did as was asked, and when he handed it to Caleb it went directly into the oven. Jamie's questioning look caught his eye.

"Trust me, you're about to eat the best pork chops in your life."

"I see you're humble, Mr. Sullivan."

His eyes gleamed. "That's Chef to you, Ms. MacLellan." His voice was laced with laughter.

With a mock salute, she said, "Duly noted, Chef."

Steve grinned. "I'm glad you two are getting along so well."

A stab of guilt reminded her she was supposed to be getting to know Steve, but in the span of the last hour she'd found herself drawn to Caleb.

Thankfully Caleb didn't respond, and pointed to the dining table. "Go sit down. Dinner's served in about ten minutes."

The group had taken the same spots as the previous night, putting Jamie next to Steve. True to his word, Caleb carried in a platter of chops; the aroma made Jamie's mouth water in anticipation. She loved pork chops almost as much as she loved pasta.

With a flourish of showmanship, Caleb served the chops, starting with Kenzie. "You're first since you brought my brother to his knees. A feat which is not easy to accomplish.

"My pleasure, any time." Kenzie took the bowl of potatoes Robbie passed, followed by the salad.

Silence fell over the room as the dinner was savored, save the occasional murmur of delight. Jamie said, "Caleb, give me your mom's address. I need to send her a thank you for encouraging your obvious passion for good food."

Steve chuckled. "She'd love that."

When all the plates were empty, Jamie pushed back from the table. Grace jumped up. "Stay put—since you hosted, we'll all clean up."

Steve started to stand when Kenzie interjected, "Keep Jamie company. We've got this."

Caleb avoided Jamie as she watched him go into the kitchen. She glanced at the small group laughing and chatting in her tiny kitchen trying to pick Caleb's brain for cooking tips. "Let's go into the other room."

Steve handed her a glass of wine and grabbed a beer as they moved to the sofa. "Did I pass muster with your sisters and friends?" His eyes twinkled and an amused smile graced his mouth.

"Were we that obvious?" Jamie sipped her wine.

"When you had your best friends and sisters at dinner last night, Caleb and I thought we were being vetted for potential."

"Sorry about that. So much for subtlety."

Steve laughed. "We had a good time." He leaned in and took Jamie's hand. "You're a good cook."

Jamie's heart maintained a steady beat. She paused, waiting to see if anything might flutter.

He let go of her hand. "What about you, did you enjoy dinner?"

"It's always fun having people over." She could feel she was wearing her polite smile. "Has business been picking up?"

"I can't complain. I thought I'd miss the hustle of Boston, but I really like the slower pace."

"That's good. I'm surprised you'd move up here by yourself."

Steve's eyes narrowed slightly. "That wasn't the original plan, but sometimes things just work out differently."

"If you don't mind my asking, what happened?"

He leaned back and his fingertips formed a triangle. "I'll give you the condensed version. I was engaged to a woman I had been dating for a couple of years, and we were supposed to get married next summer. When I got tired of city life, she said it was either the country or her. She didn't want to be like that old television show *Green Acres*. Remember, where the city folk move into the country?"

"Let me guess, she's a little more like Eva Gabor?"

"You could say that. I tried to make a joke that it was beautiful up here and a great place to raise our family. Rutland is a smaller city but still pretty close to Boston, so we could go back for the theater and shopping anytime she wanted."

"Was it about her job?" Jamie inquired.

"No, she's a copywriter and artist. I would have created a beautiful office space for her at the new house."

"What's her name?"

"Yvette."

"You really love her." Jamie stated the obvious.

He shifted on the cushions, visibly uncomfortable. "Let's change the subject. This is supposed to be our time to get to know each other, not me rehashing my previous entanglements."

"The past is what makes us who we are today and what we bring to the table for future relationships."

He looked at Jamie. "And who are you? What do you bring from your past?"

With a nervous giggle, she said, "I've had relationships, but I'm not willing to settle for anything less than someone giving me their whole heart."

He nodded. "I know exactly what you mean. After Yvette and I broke up, I realized so much of our lives were tangled up with the other. I had an enormous sense of loss."

"That's to be expected when you spend so much of your time with one person."

Steve turned to face her, seeming to hang on her every word. "You couldn't be yourself in other relationships?"

"I found that I lost part of myself." Jamie toyed with the wineglass. "I'd rather be content living my life as a single person than to have some guy expect me to give up parts of myself just so he can feel like the center of my life."

Steve let out a hearty chuckle. "I can't see any man not recognizing your strength and fortitude."

"Well, I've worked hard to be taken seriously." Jamie nodded.

He leaned closer. "I was thinking maybe this weekend you'd like to go into Boston, we can go to the aquarium or something."

Jamie hesitated.

"Then afterwards there is a great sushi place that pairs every dish with tequila."

Jamie wrinkled her nose. "That doesn't sound very appetizing. Tequila and raw fish, yuck."

He chuckled. "Is sushi unappealing or the combo?"

"Call me old-fashioned, but sushi goes with wine or sake and tequila goes with good Mexican food. The two should never meet."

Steve nodded. "Good to know."

She quickly rethought her hesitation. "The day trip sounds like fun if you can recommend another restaurant."

He grinned. "I can definitely find someplace else for dinner. We have a few favorites."

She cocked her head. *Did he just say* we? "What time do you want to leave?"

His cell rang. Steve held up a finger. "Hold that thought." He stepped away from her. Jamie heard him say, "I'm surprised to hear from you."

He walked out the front door and closed it behind him. She followed him to the door and sat down on the bench in the hallway. When he was outside, she sipped on her wine, taking her time to enjoy it, all the while keeping track of the hands spinning around the clock face.

The front door opened and Steve plunked down beside her. His gaze met hers before looking away. "Sorry for the interruption."

Jamie's voice was soft. "Is everything okay?"

"Just a legal issue that didn't seem like it could wait." He glanced around the room. "If you don't mind, I need to go."

"Of course."

Steve seemed torn. Jamie patted his arm. "I'll tell the others, go ahead. I'm sure you're anxious to take care of your client, and you have a long drive ahead of you."

He pecked her cheek. "Thanks for understanding. I'll call you tomorrow."

Before she could utter a single syllable, he was nearly sprinting out the door.

Jamie's mouth fell open. *What the heck just happened? What could be so critical that he has to get home?* Jamie ran her fingertip around the edge of the wineglass, replaying the last few minutes.

"Jamie?" A deep male voice caught her attention.

"Caleb." She whipped her head around.

Unable to peel his gaze from her face, he said, "Did Steve leave?"

"He got a phone call and had to rush back to the office."

"Who has a legal emergency on a Sunday evening?" Irritation laced his voice.

"How should I know?" Jamie's response was sharp. "I'm not a lawyer."

"Hey, I'm sorry." His tone softened. "I didn't mean anything. I'm just concerned that you're..."

Jamie pushed past Caleb to walk into the living room, and saw Robbie in the kitchen. She caught his attention. "I'm sure Robbie can drive you home."

"Jamie..."

For a brief second, she wondered what it would feel like to be pulled into his arms. "I'm fine," she snapped, annoyed at her thoughts, not his brother's actions. "I'll see you later."

15

If a girl could feel underwhelmed after a dinner with a gorgeous guy, Jamie did. She punched the pillow trying to get comfortable but flopped on her back, eyes wide. She turned on the bedside table and flipped open a book. The words blurred together. Unable to concentrate, she snapped it shut, climbed out of bed, and wandered into the living room to fire up her computer.

She checked the time. "It's nine AM in Scotland."

After striking a few keys, a synthesized ringtone emanated from her computer, breaking the silence in the shadow-filled room.

Mom's face appeared on the screen, concern flitted across her face. "Jamie? Are you okay, sweetie?"

"Hi, Mom. I couldn't sleep, so I thought of calling you. I hope it's okay?" She rubbed a hand over her eyes.

"Of course it is. Dad's out with Patrick. He's managing the farm now that his dad retired. I'm not sure what they're doing, but it's become a daily habit, the two of them traipsing around each morning, looking over the land and making a plan for the day."

It was nice to hear about daily life on the farm. "I didn't

know Paddy was retiring. It's nice that Patrick is stepping into the role." Jamie's smile waned. "Mom?"

"Talk to me. I know when something is troubling you."

Jamie wished she was sitting with her mom, but this was the next best thing. Taking a deep breath, she said, "Last night I had dinner with a handsome lawyer, and before dessert he got a phone call and couldn't get out of here fast enough. We've hung out a couple of times and he's always getting phone calls or texts."

"Did he say why he had to leave?"

"Not really. He said it was a legal problem. But I get the feeling it's more than that."

"Could this man be special to you?"

"I thought he might be, but now I don't know. I'm confused."

"Why don't you start at the beginning and tell me everything, and maybe I can help?"

Jamie mumbled, "I'm going to make a cup of tea."

"While you do, I'll make one too and we can have it together."

Jamie's heart lightened just a bit. "Just like when I was little."

She fired up the kettle and dropped a teabag in the cup. She scooped out a teaspoon of honey from the jar. The kettle was whistling, and as she poured, the honey melted from the spoon. Jamie carried the steaming mug back to her desk. Mom sat down at the same time.

"Cheers." Jamie held the mug up to the screen before taking a sip of tea.

"Kiddo..." Mom's voice was soft. "Start at the beginning." Her tender smile bolstered Jamie's spirit.

"We got the package that Gran left for us, and it contained the wedding dress both she and Great-gran wore when they got married. And you know how Grace, Kenzie and I have always said we didn't want to get married."

Mom interjected, "Which, by the way, I've never understood."

"We didn't want to lose our independence, but the real reason is we never thought we'd find anyone like Dad. He's perfect."

"Honey, there are many wonderful men out there, and you and your sisters shouldn't give up on a future with one just because you have put your dad on a pedestal. And I hate to break it to you, he's not perfect, but he is a very good husband and father."

"You have the best marriage."

Mom laughed out loud. "I'm so glad you think. We love and respect each other, which was our foundation. We've grown together from there."

"I guess." She swirled her mug in a circle on the desk top.

"Honey, go back to when you received the dress."

"The girls voted to keep it at my place. I hung it up in my bedroom, and late one night, I don't know what compelled me to do it, but I tried it on. It fit like it was made for me. Looking at the woman in the mirror, I realized getting married didn't mean I had to give up who I was, or am, as a person. But finding the right man to share my life with would only enrich it."

"I'm so glad to hear you say that." Mom grinned from ear to ear.

"Anyway," Jamie continued, "there was a letter from Great-gran in the box, along with a brooch and tartan. She writes that the dress is enchanted. It had been made with special thread, and if an unmarried woman from our family tried it on, she'd see her future."

"Well that's an interesting twist and it does explain a few lingering questions I had about Gran, but that's a conversation for a different day." Mom smiled. "I think I'm starting to see the problem. You tried on the dress but you haven't met someone who you feel is like your father, so you're worried?"

"Well, sort of. Steve, the guy I've dated a few times, is a nice guy, and well, I don't feel any sparks when I'm with him. There's that whole distraction thing. He's smart and good-looking, but should I feel something when he holds my hand or kisses me?"

"Jamie, just because the family lore says you'll meet your husband after you try the dress on doesn't mean it'll be the first man you meet. Maybe the real magic is for you to open your eyes to see the possibility of love. It sounds like that is exactly what it did. Looking into your heart, you could see a different path in life."

"I guess." Jamie chewed her bottom lip. "Do you think if the chemistry isn't there from the beginning it won't ever cause a spark and ignite?"

"That is something only you can answer. Do you like this man you've been dating?"

"He's nice, but it feels more like friendship than a romance. You know, like the kind of guys I hung out with in high school."

Mom smiled. "So, what's wrong with enjoying his friendship and taking the pressure off yourself? In time you'll find what your grandmother wanted for you."

"You might be right. Maybe I should give the dress to Kenzie or Grace."

Mom laughed. Her soft, musical voice soothed Jamie's tender heart. "If I read between the lines, everything has to start with you."

"Do you believe in magical dresses and all that stuff that Gran did?"

Mom looked away from the screen, and then her eyes met Jamie's. "It doesn't matter what I believe, it's what you believe."

"Do you? I really need to know if I'm crazy."

"Love is magical. When I saw your father from across the park, I knew. At that moment, for the first time, I believed in love at first sight. It knocked me off my feet. Call it magic, fate, kismet, I just knew I would spend the rest of my life with him. It took a few months for your father to fall in love with me, but we've been together ever since. We complement each other. Like two peas in a pod."

Jamie's chin rested in the palm of her hand. "You are both so good together. He supports whatever you've wanted to try, from painting, gardening or gourmet cooking classes."

Mom's voice was full of love and pride. "He has, and in turn, I was honored to be welcomed into his clan. His commitment to those he loves is an eternal flame that burns bright, and that includes me, his daughters and the people of Scotland. Spending time at the farm has made me see how much a part of this country is embodied in him. Including the legends and lore that linger in the Highlands."

"Does that mean you guys will live in Scotland full-time?" Jamie's words stuck in her throat.

"We'll live between Scotland and Vermont. We have our lovely family waiting for us there and you'll come here. We'll be bi-country."

"And *you're* okay with spending part of the year in Scotland?" Tears threatened to spill down her cheeks. Wait until her sisters heard this news.

"Home isn't an address, Jamie. It's where your heart resides. My home is with your dad and you girls."

Jamie wiped her cheeks on the sleeve of her bathrobe. "I miss you so much, Mom. It feels like you've been gone forever."

"We'll be home soon. It's a lifestyle change, but nothing says we can't be in Vermont any time we want."

Jamie didn't want to talk about her parents living in Scotland on a more permanent basis. "Getting back to the matter of my heart…any final advice?"

"Go out with Steve again and see if your feelings change. You'll know what to do after the next date or two."

Jamie brightened. "This weekend we're supposed to go to the Boston Aquarium. Maybe getting away for the day will help. Neutral territory."

"That sounds like a perfect idea. Let's talk on Sunday and you can tell me all about it."

"Thanks, Mom, for sharing a cup of tea with me."

"I'm never further away than a few clicks. Oh, and before I forget, that box should arrive tomorrow, with all of the journals we found. From the looks of them, some are pretty old."

With a slight laugh Jamie said, "What did you do, send it express?"

With a splitting-cheek grin, Mom said, "Dad wanted you to have them right away, so of course he chose the fastest method possible."

Jamie's smile reached her eyes. "I can't wait to read them. Did you take a look before you packed them up?'

Shaking her head, Mom said, "No. Dad thought it was best if you read them first and then pass them on to your sisters, one at a time."

With her curiosity piqued, Jamie asked, "Does Dad know what's in them?"

"I think he has a strong suspicion that his mother is trying to help you and your sisters make the right decisions for your future."

"Just what we need, Gran still trying to shape us into her version of the ideal lass." She chuckled. "If she said it once, she said it a million times. 'Now, girls. You need to grow into a strong Scots lassie.'" Jamie's words were punctuated with a thick brogue.

Mom smiled. "I can hear her now." She placed her hand over her heart. "You know, you're very much like her. When I first met Arabel MacLellan, I hoped her intelligence, strength and loyalty to family would be passed on to my future children."

Jamie laid a hand over her heart and smiled at her mom.

"With that compliment, I'm going to say goodnight and go back to bed for a couple of hours of much-needed sleep."

"Sleep well, honey." With a little wave, Mom blew her a kiss. "Good night."

Jamie sat in front of the blank computer screen and thought about what Mom had said about her being like her gran. "There's no one I'd rather be compared to than her. She was a very special lady."

Leaving her mug on the desk, she wandered back into her bedroom, yawning as she crawled into bed. She fell into a deep dreamless sleep as soon as her head touched the pillow.

❦

The doorbell rang. Jamie ran her fingers through the waves in her hair and hurried to the front door. Breathless, she pulled it open.

"Caleb." Jamie licked her lips. "This is a surprise." She leaned out the door and looked around the yard. "Where's Steve?"

Caleb shoved his hands into his coat pocket. "Well, that's why I'm here. Steve asked me to pick you up and he'll meet us in Boston."

Jamie brushed a stray lock of hair from her face. "I'm afraid I don't understand. We had a date." She held the door open. "Why don't you come in and tell me what's going on?" Caleb stepped over the threshold and wiped his boots on the mat. "Come into the kitchen. I'm just finishing up."

Caleb followed her down the hallway into the sun-splashed room. He pulled out a stool. Sitting quietly, he watched as Jamie wiped the spotlessly clean counter, she said, "Is Steve okay?"

"Yeah, he's fine. He got called into the city last night and decided to stay and handle things. When he called to let me know, he asked me to swing by this morning, pick you up and drive down."

Jamie could detect something in his voice, but she wasn't quite sure what it was. Was he annoyed Steve had asked him to drive her? "He could have called to reschedule. I would have understood business sometimes has to come first."

"He really wanted you to see the penguin exhibit today and I wasn't doing anything, so I'm happy to pitch in as your chauffeur and temporary guide." Caleb's smile warmed his eyes and Jamie's anger evaporated. She couldn't be mad at him for being a good brother and all-around nice guy.

"Before we go, would you like coffee? I've got travel mugs."

Caleb's sea-green eyes twinkled. "Is this your way of saying you're not going to kill the messenger?"

"No, you're safe." She held up a travel mug. "Coffee?"

"Strong with a shot of cream?"

"No sugar?" she teased.

He cocked his head and proclaimed, "I'm sweet enough."

"And who told you that?"

His rich laughter filled the room. "My mom, of course."

Jamie was buckled up in the passenger seat of Caleb's Jeep. She pushed her sunglasses up her nose. After taking a sip of hot coffee, she secured the tumbler into the in the center console. "You're a good driver."

Giving her a quick sideways look, he said, "Thanks. I love getting behind the wheel wherever I am. It's the best way to get a feel for the community."

She smiled. "You know, you are starting to make me rethink my original impression of you."

"Really?" He glanced at her and smirked. "And why's that?"

"Well, the night you horned in on our dinner, I thought you were a little rude."

"Ouch." He pretended to shrink in his seat. "In my defense, Steve said he was going to the movies and dinner with a friend and he asked me to come—he said it was your idea. I had no idea it was a date." He placed his hand over hers. "If I had, I wouldn't have shown up. I'm really sorry."

Jamie's gazed dropped to his hand on hers. "Oh. I guess *I* should apologize. All this time I thought you were being a jerk. You know, the globetrotter brother arrives in town and expects the world to revolve around his schedule."

"You sure know how to put a guy in his place." He smiled.

"Undeservedly so. And then we had dinner two nights in a row. You were a good sport to cook for all of us."

"It was fun and I love cooking for people who really like to eat." He grinned. "Your sisters and friends qualify there."

They fell silent for a few miles until Caleb said, "Tell me a little more about yourself, Jamie Mac..."

She smiled. "When we were kids, my sisters used to call me Mac."

He kept one eye on the road and one eye on Jamie. "I think it suits you."

"My dad's name is James." Picking up her coffee mug, she laughed, "Can you guess who I was named after?"

"Um, let me think. Your mom?"

She lightly punched him in the arm. "You're funny, you know that?"

"Yeah, again, my mom told me I'm the funny one in the family." Caleb slowed and merged onto the highway. Heading south, he picked up speed and then clicked on cruise control.

Jamie paled and clutched her seatbelt.

"What's wrong?" Concern filled his eyes.

"It's. Nothing. Really," she stuttered.

"Do you need me to find a rest stop or pull over?"

She shook her head and wrung her hands in her lap, her knuckles going white. "No, I'm fine."

Caleb slowed the car and pulled over to the shoulder. Putting the car in park, he turned to her. "You're not fine. Tell me what's wrong. Am I driving too fast?"

"No."

"Jamie, talk to me." Concern filled his voice.

Shaking her head, she said, "It's silly."

"You're sweating."

She brushed a hand over her forehead. "Really, it's nothing."

"Jamie. For you to break out in a sweat and get deathly pale, it's something. We're not going to move until you tell me what's upset you."

"You're going to think I'm stupid." She swallowed hard. "But I'm afraid of cruise control. I think the cable or whatever controls the accelerator will break and we'll crash."

Caleb took her hand and gave it a squeeze. Smiling sympathetically, he reassured her, "That's an easy fix."

Quickly she volunteered. "I can drive if you'd like. I really don't mind and I don't get tired."

"No, it's fine. I'll drive." He glanced her way. "Without the benefit of cruise."

"Caleb, thank you." Her voice was soft. She took a deep ragged breath. "Thanks for not mocking me."

"Everyone has something they're afraid of." He laughed. "I happen to be petrified of balancing my checkbook. It never comes out right."

It was Jamie's turn to smile. "I can help with that. I happen to be a cracker jack CPA, if I do say so myself."

"And you're modest too." He grinned. "I usually just take the bank's balance and run with it."

Astonished, she said, "You do know the bank can make a mistake, right?"

"No, they have all the best computers, and how can a computer make a mistake?"

"Are you serious?" Jamie raised an eyebrow. "People enter the information into the computers, so there is always a chance for an error."

"Now you're teasing me."

"I'm being totally serious. If you ever want to do a review of your checking account, I'm happy to help. I can show you a few tricks I've come up with over the years to make it easier."

"Thanks, that's mighty kind of you, little lady." Caleb smirked and added a bit of a fake Southern drawl to his voice.

Jamie relaxed and laughed. "Consider it a standing offer. Although I'm not sure when you're planning on hitting the road again. It would be harder to show you if you're not in town."

"It depends. I'm kind of digging Vermont and looking forward to seeing the farmers' markets start up again. There something about cooking with local items that I can't seem to get enough of, and I've done enough bouncing around to justify hanging out for a while."

Jamie was really enjoying the drive as the mile markers slipped by the window. Her inquisitive nature propelled her to ask, "Does it get old, not having roots?"

Caleb drove for a few minutes without answering her. "Yes and no. But I've never found a place that felt like it might be home."

"What about Steve? Isn't there supposed to be something about being a twin that keeps you connected to each other?"

"Physical distance has never been a problem for us. We talk all the time."

She nodded, understanding the bond of siblings, but was sad they weren't closer physically. She couldn't imagine not living close to her sisters. They drove in silence for quite a while as the scenery became less mountainous and more urban. From time to time Jamie stole a look only to discover Caleb was doing the same to her.

After they crossed the state line Jamie asked, "What about your parents?"

He glanced at her. "They're still in the house we grew up in, just outside of Boston."

"Do you see them often?" Jamie's curiosity bubbled over.

"You sure do ask a lot of questions." His laugh was slow and lazy. "But it's been hard, with my traveling. Sometimes they've flown to where I've been staying if I can't get back home. Like, they've shown up a few times on my birthday, with Steve."

"That must have been fun." She looked out at the passing landscape change from countryside to more urban. "I can't imagine spending birthdays and holidays away from my sisters."

"You're all close. It's nice." He kept his eyes on the road as they cruised along.

"We're best friends, but sometimes we're in each other's personal lives a little too much." She toyed with the locket she was wearing. "But I wouldn't change a thing. I couldn't begin to imagine one of us living on the other side of the ocean."

"Aren't your parents in Scotland now?"

She nodded. "They are. With my gran passing away, my parents are staying at the family farm. They're probably going to live here a few months and then live in Scotland a few months and bounce back and forth."

"Will it bother you to have them live in both places?"

Jamie was impressed the way Caleb handled the increasing traffic. "I haven't given it a lot of thought, but now that we're talking about it, I guess it would be okay. As long as they were home for the important stuff, like holidays and our birthdays."

"And when is your birthday?"

With a cheeky grin, she said, "Only if you tell me yours."

"A funny story. Even though I'm a twin, Steve and I don't share a birthday. He was born just before midnight and I was just after."

"That's so cool." Jamie had a funny feeling in her stomach. What was happening to her?

Caleb beamed. "I love my brother, but it's nice to have our own special day."

"Did your mom make each of you a cake?"

He smiled. "She did. Double chocolate for Steve and for me, well, I liked something different every year. What about you? What's your favorite kind of cake?"

Jamie didn't hesitate. "German chocolate. All that chocolate, coconut and pecans." She smacked her lips. "Pure decadence on a plate."

"And when is your special day?" Caleb prodded as he exited the highway and drove down the city streets.

"My birthday is May 11th, Kenzie's is April 11th and Grace is on March 11th. We're born eleven months apart."

He nodded and looked totally engaged as they chatted. "That's an interesting factoid. So who bakes your cake?"

"Usually my mom does, but this year I don't know if they'll be back in the States. They missed Grace's and I don't think they're coming home for Kenzie's either." Jamie tried to keep her tone light, but the sadness was evident even to her ears. "I'll make Kenzie's just like I did for Grace, and I'm sure one of them will make mine."

Caleb studied his passenger. "If you need any help, just holler."

"I have Mom's recipes, it'll be fine." Jamie pointed. "Look, there's the aquarium!"

"You're pretty stoked to see some fish." He hoped it was the fish and not his brother that had her excited. Caleb pulled the car to a stop and took an entry ticket at the parking garage. He placed it over his visor and slipped off his sunglasses as he drove up the darkened tunnel.

"Where are we supposed to meet Steve?"

"I'll shoot him a text once we get parked and I'm sure he'll be along shortly."

Jamie pointed to an open space and Caleb expertly slipped the vehicle in the tight spot. "I'm sorry you had to spend your day driving me three hours to meet up with your brother. You must have had something better planned."

He shook his head. "I've had fun. The car ride flew by, and it was great that we cleared the air."

"It was." When Jamie grinned, his heart melted. He was in serious trouble.

Caleb's cell phone vibrated. He looked at the screen and frowned. "It's from Steve. He's still in a meeting and we should head into the aquarium without him."

Caleb saw the hurt flash in Jamie's eyes, but it disappeared as quickly as it came. "I happen to be a sucker for the aquarium. All the darkened water-filled tanks with sea life floating around. I find it soothing."

Jamie squared her shoulders. "I've been looking forward to the penguins and jellyfish, so let's go."

"That's the spirit." The pair got out of the car and Caleb hit the door locks. He pointed to the left. "The elevator is over there." He started to reach for her hand but instead slipped it into his pocket.

Jamie pulled out her cell and took a picture of the cement pillar next to Caleb's Jeep. "We won't forget where we parked."

He tapped his forehead. "Smart lady. I like it."

She dropped her cell phone back into her bag and zipped it up. "Onward."

Caleb linked arms with her and took a big step. "Does this remind you of anything?"

Jamie grinned and sang off-key, "We're off to see the wizard…"

Laughing, Caleb joined in. "The most wonderful wizard of all…"

Jamie looked up at him and, smirking, said, "You're a terrible singer."

"Everyone's allowed to stink at something." His heart soared. "And you're not such a great singer either."

She laughed. "No, but I'm a great CPA."

He winked. "So you keep telling me."

16

Jamie and Caleb meandered through the aquarium. After seeking out the shark exhibit, Caleb insisted they get up close and personal with a baby nurse shark and cownose ray in the touch tank. Jamie was hesitant but bravely stuck her hand into the warm water. Her fingers trailed over the scratchy skin of the shark, and she was surprised the ray's skin felt like soft velvet.

She dried her hand and, giggling, said, "Wow, I never expected something scary to be so soft. You touched the ray—didn't you think it was like velvet?"

Caleb said, "It was." He began to steer her to the next room. "Are you ready to see the penguins?"

Her eyes lit up. "I can't wait. I've never been this close." She glanced at the booklet in her hands. "It says here they have more than eight varieties living in the colony." She tugged him by the hand along the hallway. "Let's hurry. I don't want to miss them."

He chuckled and happily allowed himself to be pulled toward the exhibit. "Slow down. We still have two hours before they kick us out."

Jamie stopped short. "Do you think Steve will meet us for dinner?"

He avoided her eyes. "I'm not sure. I'll call when we're ready to leave. Worst case, we'll have dinner at a seafood place I know and we'll drive back to Vermont together."

She wrinkled her nose. "Do you think you should talk about eating"—her voice dropped to a hoarse whisper—"seafood?" She pointed to the tanks surrounding the room. "You know, they might hear you."

He laughed. "I don't think they can hear me through the tank walls, but just to be on the safe side…" He winked. "Let's go for steak."

Her head bobbed. "Steak it is. That is, if Steve is still tied up."

Caleb held his temper in check. He wished he could sneak a text to his brother and find out what was really going on. Jamie was an amazing girl and didn't need to get ditched. *Just like always, thinking of Yvette before everyone else.* At least he was pretty sure that's what was going on.

"Caleb!" Jamie was standing in front of an information monitor. "Listen, it says here the little ones are called blue penguins and they're the smallest species in the world, and all penguins live south of the equator."

"I like the punk-rock-looking ones." Caleb peeked over her shoulder. "What do they say about them?"

"They're rockhoppers." Jamie watched the penguins waddle toward the edge of the pool and dive in. "Look at how graceful they are, gliding through the water." She pointed to the wild yellow feather spurting up from the head of one penguin. "There's your buddy."

Caleb couldn't tear his eyes away from Jamie's face, it was filled with pure joy. "Watching you watch them is fun."

Jamie's cheeks grew pink. "You paid to see the penguins, not me."

"Can't I do both?" He leaned in. "I'm not sorry my brother got derailed."

She took a step back. "I think we should call Steve and find out if he's able to meet us."

Caleb pulled out his phone. "I'll text him."

Dinner?

He waited a minute for a response. He cringed when he read, *Not tonight. Can you cover for me?*

YEAH.

"Um. Jamie?" He was sorry for her but happy for himself. Now they could have dinner together.

She sighed. "Let me guess. We're on our own?"

"Yeah. He said he was sorry. He hadn't expected this emergency to take so long and he wanted you to know he'll call you tomorrow."

She frowned. "Okay."

"Do you want to leave?" *Please say no…*

Shaking her head, she said, "I'd like to spend a little more time watching the penguins play." She didn't look at him. "Do you mind?" she said in a hushed tone.

He rushed to say, "Of course not."

Jamie wandered closer to the glass, putting distance between them. He longed to ask her what she was thinking, but he could guess. Having a date planned with one man and his brother showing up instead must have felt pretty lousy. He'd do his best to make sure she had an amazing dinner and an uneventful drive home, and tomorrow he'd give his brother a piece of his mind. This was one girl who didn't deserve to be treated as an afterthought.

"Caleb, look." Her hand reached out to touch the glass. He was at her side in a flash. Her voice was filled with wonder. "It must be a baby. See how much smaller he is than some of the others?"

"He's pretty cute." Caleb's hand brushed hers. Electricity flashed through him. "Um. Are you hungry?"

"Famished. After all, breakfast was forever ago and we skipped lunch."

Caleb's voice was filled with regret. "Sorry about that. I can promise you dinner will be extra delicious."

She flashed him a megawatt grin. "Then let's get out of here and lead me to a glass of wine and a menu."

"I know just the place. It's right across the street, with excellent food and ambience." He placed his hand on the small of her back, steering her toward the exit.

She stopped mid-step. "Would you prefer to get outside of the city?"

"As you so eloquently pointed out, I've been starving you and you're going to love this place. It's rich with historical architecture and has a 110-foot bar crafted from walnut wood. They have a great wine list and the food is fantastic, lots of fresh seafood or steaks, and if you're really not interested in those options they have a risotto that will make you think you've been transported to Italy."

She looked into his eyes and smiled. "Sounds like you know it well."

"Once upon a time, I worked there. Mom encouraged me to become a chef, but working in that kitchen tipped the scales—it was the final decision maker."

The door to the aquarium closed behind them. Caleb and Jamie walked side by side down the pier. He breathed in the cold, salty air.

Jamie pulled up the collar of her coat and shivered. "That breeze is cool."

"It's like that right on the wharf." They turned the corner. "Here we are." He pulled the restaurant door open and Jamie stepped into the warmth. The smell of wonderful things cooking lingered in the air.

"Table for two, please?" Caleb ushered Jamie ahead of

him. This was his turf and he was going to make the most of the experience for her.

He held a chair for Jamie and asked for a wine list before sitting. "Not to come off sounding pretentious, but would you mind if I order for us?"

Jamie's eyes grew wide, unblinking. "I'm capable of ordering my dinner."

"That's not what I meant, but I'd love to have you taste some of the house specialties. They're created to dance on the taste buds, and most people tend to gravitate toward what they're comfortable ordering."

The waiter came over with the bread basket and filled their water glasses. Jamie waited until he moved away. Studying Caleb carefully, she said, "Okay, but if I don't like something after the first taste, you won't push me to try another bite?"

He stuck out his hand, longing to feel the smallness of hers in his. "Agreed. You're not allergic to shellfish, are you?"

"You're not instilling confidence in me, Chef." She laughed. "But no allergies."

"Last question, do you prefer white or red wine tonight?" He knew she drank red on the occasions he had been with her, but he didn't want to weird her out by assuming he knew her preference.

"Red, please." She looked around the room. "This place is amazing."

His eyes met hers over the menu. "It is, and just wait until you have dinner." Caleb studied the list, and when the waiter approached the table he ordered wine, polenta fries, roasted beet salad, risotto and the duck. "Do you mind if we share everything?"

Jamie's eyes sparkled in the candlelight. "Sure. It all sounds delicious."

They chatted through dinner and the conversation continued well into dessert and coffee. Jamie said, "Every dish is as you promised, tantalizing my taste buds. I'm surprised I like everything." She looked around and whispered, "The one and only time I ate duck, my mouth felt like I was eating flavored grease."

"That's because it wasn't cooked properly. But you liked the duck tonight?"

"Very much and the pinot noir was delicious too." She leaned on her elbows. Her eyes sparkled. "Tonight has been fun."

"I'm glad you're having a good time." Caleb watched a shadow flit over her face. He was sure Steve standing her up crossed her mind, but he wasn't going to ask.

Jamie finished the last drops of her wine. "It's going to be a long drive home—we should probably get going." She glanced at her watch. "Wow, it's already nine." She pushed back her chair. "We're not going to get home until the wee hours of the morning at this rate. Are you okay to drive?"

"I had one glass of wine, lots of water and coffee. But I would like to stop for another before we get on the highway."

Caleb took Jamie's coat from the back of her chair and held it for her. Slipping her arms in the sleeves, she said, "Absolutely, and I'm sure we'll talk all the way home. It doesn't seem we lack for conversation."

They stepped into the crisp night air. Stars dotted the skyline. Jamie's gaze lingered as she looked up at the sky. She took a deep, cleansing breath. "There's nothing like fresh ocean air." She tucked her hand into the crook of his arm and smiled. "Well, except for mountain air."

Caleb savored the moment. "It's nice to be able to have the best of both worlds just a short drive in either direction."

They got back to the Jeep and Caleb pulled into light city traffic, navigating like a pro. After pulling into the drive-thru, he ordered two extra-large coffees with cream and sugar on the side. He handed Jamie the two cups as she placed them in the console and juggled their stainless-steel travel mugs between her legs.

"Can you pull up over there? I'll dump out the old coffee."

Caleb took one cup and emptied it out the window and handed it back to her. Jamie filled it with hot coffee. The same procedure for the second cup.

She flicked the little white packets. "No sugar, right?" She set them on the dash.

"Good memory." He held the other cup while she added cream to top it off. She carefully replaced the lid on the mug.

"Here you go." She pushed a stray lock of hair off her face.

"You didn't need to fix mine, but thanks."

"Oh, shoot. I need to add sugar to mine."

"No need to rush." He watched as she concentrated on adding sugar and then secured the top to her cup. In his side-view mirror, Caleb caught sight of a familiar SUV. Inwardly, he cursed. "Don't forget to give it a good stir before the sugar settles to the bottom."

"Oh, right." She popped the top and took a few moments to give it a good stir getting the sugar up from the bottom. Replacing the lid, she said, "All set."

Caleb double-checked his mirrors; no sign of his brother. He backed up and pulled into traffic. "Next stop, Easton."

"Well, I might need a bio break at some point."

Caleb grinned. "Do me a favor—let me know a few minutes before you get to the desperate zone."

She gave him a thumbs-up sign. "Gotcha covered, Chef."

"Do you like calling me Chef?"

"It rolls off the tongue and I've never hung out with one before. You've got skills I only dream of having." Jamie turned on the radio to a classic country music station. "Do you mind?"

"No. Classics are good."

Jamie sang along, partially in tune, and Caleb admired her pluck. Soon they were both singing with the radio, laughing and telling more stories about their childhood highs and lows.

"Do you ride horses too?" she asked.

"I do. Why do you ask?" He merged into the passing lane as they left the city behind them.

"If you ever feel like getting out you should go to out to Racing Brook Stables. Jo owns and runs the family farm, and it has some great trails."

"Good to know. Do you ride often?"

"Not as much as I'd like. Actually, Steve went out there with me once. That's where I lost the dinner bet."

"Ah, that's right. Let me guess, he didn't tell you he's an accomplished equestrian."

She giggled. "Nope, that never came up. But in all fairness, my mount got skittish when a bear crossed the trail and threw me."

"Wait, you got thrown and *you* lost the bet?" As he looked at her, he knew why Steve made the bet. To spend time with Jamie was a win win, no matter what.

Jamie laughed again. "Well, it's not like that, exactly. I agreed I lost. He was very much the gentleman and said I hadn't. But I'm one to live up to my obligations no matter what the circumstances are."

"I'll remember that." He tapped his forehead. "It's filed away in my vault. You never know when these tidbits will come in handy."

"I've learned my lesson, betting with a Sullivan."

Caleb put his blinker on and turned into her driveway. "We're home."

Surprise crept into her voice, Jamie said, "That was a short drive. Why is it the trip home is always shorter than the drive there?"

Caleb chuckled. "It always seems that way. It's easy with zero traffic."

Looking at the clock on the dash, she said, "It's after one. You still have more driving ahead of you."

He reassured her, "I'll be fine."

She chewed on her bottom lip. "I don't want this to come out wrong, but if you want you could sleep in my guest room."

Caleb had a very quick internal debate. Shaking his head, he said, "No, I think I'll just head home, but thanks for the offer."

Jamie looked at him. "Are you sure?"

Caleb leaned toward her and, caressing her cheek with his hand, pulled her closer. Laying a feather-light kiss on her lips, he said, "I really can't."

"Oh. My." She leaned in and whispered, "Good night, Caleb. I had a wonderful time."

"Me too, Miss Jamie MacLellan." His lips teased hers. "Me too.

She got out of the Jeep and started to walk away. He was waiting until she closed the door before driving away, but she turned and hurried to the driver's side. He slid the window down.

She leaned in. Her lips brushed his, tentatively at first, and she took another step closer to the door. Slipping her hand around his neck, she pulled him closer, almost out the window. Her lips hovered over his for a moment. She kissed him again, deeper this time.

"Do you want to come in?" she whispered.

"Jamie?"

The moonlight reflected in her eyes, beckoning him to follow. He slid the window up and turned the key. Pushing the car door open, he held out his hand. She took it. He hesitated. "Are you sure?"

In a low, husky voice, she said, "Let's go inside."

Every cell tingled as he walked beside her. She unlocked the door and pushed it open. They stepped into the hallway, and she turned on a small lamp. Caleb shut the door and turned the lock. The small *click* filled the quiet space.

"Jamie, at any time you can tell me to go, and I will."

She laid a finger on his lips. "I'm asking you to stay."

He pulled her to his chest, his eyes locked on hers. He whispered, "There's nowhere I'd rather be."

17

Deep inside her heart, the vise broke loose. Somehow, in the span of a single day, he had found the key to the rusty lock on her heart, to her very soul.

Her coat slid from her shoulders and dropped to the floor. Caleb's coat followed. Reaching out, she grasped the front of his shirt and pulled him deeper into the house, leaving in her wake her handbag, keys and shoes. Her insides jangled, anticipation building.

At her bedroom door, she paused. In a low, sexy voice, she said, "I want you."

He watched her intently. A shiver slid over her. Her pulse pounded. She raised her face and wrapped an arm around his neck, pulling his mouth to hers. Grazing his lips, she murmured softly, "You smell so good."

He crushed her to his chest, his mouth claiming hers. "You have no idea what you're doing to me."

Her teeth teased his lower lip. She whispered, "Show me."

Walking backwards, Jamie drew him deeper into the room. She released him to pull back the covers on her bed. The room was washed in moonlight. Her blood hummed as it raced throughout her body.

She turned to him. His finger traced the line of her nose, sliding from the curve of her cheek to her jawline. He continued in triple-slow motion down her long, graceful neck with a featherlike touch. His hand floated over her collarbone, stopping at the hollow at the base of her throat.

She trembled and, with eyes closed, a soft moan escaped her.

"Open your eyes." His voice was deep and gentle.

Her crystal-blue eyes fluttered open and locked with his. She was caught under his spell.

His eyes widened slightly before his finger continued its downward trail, over her breast to the hem of her shirt. He hesitated and pulled it up over her head, then tossed it aside.

She took a step closer, moving slowly, and undid the buttons on his shirt. Her hands grazed his skin, smooth and warm under her touch, as she pushed the shirt off his shoulders. It fell to the carpet. Entirely caught up in the moment, she relished caressing his skin for the first time, fingertips tracing the outline and the contours of his muscles.

"You are so handsome." She nuzzled the base of his throat. "I want to see all of you."

She popped the button on the top of his jeans and pulled the zipper down, inch by inch. He mirrored her movements. Stepping from her jeans, clad in mere slips of lingerie, Jamie held her breath. Nerves flipped her stomach over and over.

Caleb's arms wrapped around her body and lifted her as if she were weightless, and placed her on the sheets. The bed dipped with her weight and he leaned in, claiming her mouth, passion raging.

"I'll stop if you say the word." His kiss stoked the already raging fire inside of her.

"More," was all she could manage.

His fingers found the clasp on her bra, and within moments another filmy barrier was gone. She wiggled underneath him, and with a flick of his hand the remaining fabric was history. He lay next to her, skin to skin. Her eyes widened, and she smiled. How or when did he…it didn't matter. All that was important was nothing was between them.

In the soft moonlight, the air around them sizzled. His mouth trailed over each inch of exposed flesh. Her breath caught; she wanted—no, needed—more.

Her fingertips trailed down his biceps and, making little swirling motions over his chest, she could hear him suck in a breath, his muscles tense under her touch. Her hand rested over his heart; it hammered beneath her fingertips. He bent to kiss her, but paused and slid from the bed.

Her eyes flicked open. "Where?" Her voice trailed off as he withdrew a small packet from his wallet and ripped it open. "Are you always prepared?" she teased.

In response he rolled on top of her and wrapped his arms around her, holding her close. His hands slid down the length of her spine, pressing her to him, her body molding to his in all the right places. She sighed, never expecting it, him, to feel this good, this right.

They came together as one, moving in unison with slow and steady rhythm. She urged him on, faster. He sped up, then slowed down, bringing her to the edge of release and holding her there.

A soft gasp escaped her. No one had ever discovered the tender spot of her heart, which she had protected at all costs. With a stroke and a caress, Caleb destroyed her final defense.

Her fingertips stopped their exploration and she looked into his half-closed eyes, dark with desire. The intensity of his gaze matched how she felt. Her mouth claimed his, tongues dancing to the beat of the pounding of their hearts. She couldn't get enough, she wanted so much more. As she indulged her curiosity, she allowed her hands to roam with abandon, and he groaned.

She threw her head back. Her breath came in deep, ragged

gasps, and wordlessly she encouraged him to drive her to new and higher peaks. Her breath hitched, her mind and body immersed in pleasure.

"Oh, Caleb…" With a shiver she burrowed her head into his chest, his arms tightened as powerful thrusts began again, deeper inside of her. With each stroke, he was driving them, higher and higher.

With a final thrust, they shuddered, bodies limp.

Jamie gasped for breath as Caleb rested beside her, his hard body molded to her soft curves. Her hand stroking his chest. His skin slick with a fine sheen of sweat. It seemed time stood still as her heart returned to normal. She could feel his quiet under her touch.

His hands smoothed back her hair and he gently tilted her chin upwards, kissing her tenderly. "That was. Wow." Lovingly he kissed the top of her head.

She nuzzled closer. "Ditto."

He gave a low chuckle. "I'll take it."

The delicious feeling of release made Jamie drowsy. Caleb pulled the blankets over them and held her close as they drifted to sleep.

Jamie paced in the driveway, oblivious to the warm sun on her face and the birds chirping. What was she supposed to think after last night and this morning? Yesterday she left this house thinking she was spending the day with Steve when instead she ended up locking lips with his brother, and so much more. What kind of girl did something like that?

Grace pulled into the driveway and parked. Kenzie was right behind her.

Grace rushed over. "I came as fast as I could. What's the matter, are Mom and Dad okay?"

Impatiently, Jamie waved her hand through the air. "They're fine, but I've gotten myself in a pickle."

Kenzie sprinted up the driveway. "What's happening?"

"I don't know where to start!" Jamie cried. She turned and hurried toward the backyard, stopped and turned. She shouted, "Are you coming?"

Kenzie and Grace fell in step behind her and walked through the garage out to the small fieldstone patio. Jamie flopped into a wooden chair at a small bistro table with two empty chairs. "Have a seat."

Grace looked at Kenzie and shrugged. "Jamie?"

"I'm sorry. I'm so mad at myself—I've really screwed up." Distracted, she ran her hand through her hair, stalling for time. "I might as well start at the beginning."

"I find that's the best place." Grace patted her hand. "And nothing is really that tragic, right?"

"Oh, wait until you hear what I've done."

Kenzie said, "Hold on. We're going to need coffee, and lots of it. I'll go brew a pot."

Grace hopped up. "I'll come with you, Kenz."

Grateful for another moment alone Jamie wondered how to tell her sisters she'd slept with the twin of the man she thought she was supposed to marry.

Kenzie came out of the house carrying a tray with mugs, a cream pitcher and a plate of cookies. Grace closed the door behind her.

Setting a mug of hot steaming coffee in front of Jamie, Grace said, "Spill your guts."

Jamie took a sip and added a touch more cream. "It started yesterday morning when Caleb came to pick me up."

"What do you mean? You had a date with Steve," Kenzie said.

Jamie nodded. "I did, but Steve was called into the city for some legal thing and Caleb showed up to drive me. Steve was going to meet me—well, us—at the aquarium, but he never came. So, Caleb and I ended up spending the day together."

Grace leaned forward. "How was that?"

A smile tugged at the corners of her mouth. "I had a really great time." Jamie looked off in the distance and continued, "Steve couldn't get away, so Caleb asked me to have dinner with him at some historic site in Boston. I haven't had that much fun in a long time." She let out a huge sigh. "In fact, the whole day was a blast. I can't remember the last time I've been that relaxed. He ordered dinner for us and it was amazing, and then we drove home and the time just evaporated."

Kenzie stared at Jamie. "So, what's the big deal? Steve got caught up with work and his brother stepped in so you could have a fun day."

"I kissed him." Jamie's simple statement caused Kenzie's mouth to drop open and Grace set down her mug, spilling coffee on the table.

Grace leaned in and asked, "Like a peck on the cheek, thanks for hanging with me today, or like a rock-my-world kind of kiss?"

Jamie's laugh was strained. "Well. If it was the first kind I wouldn't be confused, would I?"

Kenzie and Grace hung on every word. Jamie continued, "It was really late when he drove me home. I asked if he wanted to come in, which he declined, and then he leaned in close. When his lips brushed mine—you know, almost like grazed them—my heart pounded, blood rushed out of my head, and all I could focus on was his mouth and how it felt to have it on mine."

"Oh, Jamie." Grace placed her hand over her heart. "Isn't that how it's supposed to feel?"

Kenzie poked Grace. "I'm sensing there's a little more to this story."

"I thought Gran sent me Steve, and here I am having

roaring feelings for his brother. And I've been asking myself this all morning, what kind of girl am I to be sort of dating one man and find myself sleeping with the other, and liking it!"

"What?" Grace eyes went saucer-sized. "You slept with him?"

Kenzie said in no-nonsense voice, "Apparently you're attracted to Caleb, not Steve."

"But Steve is perfect for me. A professional man…we like similar movies and restaurants…"

"Just because Steve has all the check marks next to his name on some imaginary list you have doesn't mean he's the right guy for you."

"Kenzie's right, Jamie. You've gone out with Steve a few times and you haven't had the zing or spark or whatever you want to call it. You've never said you've laughed an entire evening away when you've been with him."

"I guess you're right, but now what do I do? Maybe Caleb and I were just caught up in the moment." Confusion clouded her eyes. "Do I tell Caleb it was a mistake?"

Always the logical sister, Kenzie said, "You need to take some time and see what comes next. Then you can make a decision."

"I can't go back to dating Steve. For that matter, I don't want to. But what if Caleb was just a one-night stand? Gracie, what do you think I should do?"

"Are you curious about what happened to Steve? Like, why didn't he call you to cancel? It seems odd to me that he'd just have his brother show up and basically do the date for him."

"You know, I never thought of it that way." Jamie picked up her cell. "I'm going to call him and let's see what he has to say for himself. Or do I ask to see him and tell him that we won't be seeing each other anymore?"

She hit a few buttons and covered the receiver. "It's ringing." She held up a finger to her sisters. "Hi, Steve, it's Jamie."

Kenzie was gesturing, but Jamie put a finger to her lips.

"Hi, Jamie." Steve's voice was strained.

"I wanted to make sure everything was okay. You know since you were tied up yesterday." Jamie stood up and began to pace.

"Everything is fine, but we need to talk. Today if possible."

"Sure, what time do you want to come by?"

"Mid-afternoon?"

She picked her mug up and set it back down. "Sounds good. Around three?"

She could hear Steve sigh, and wondered if it was from relief. He said, "Three's good."

"See you then." Jamie dropped the phone to the table and plopped down. She looked from Kenzie to Grace. "He didn't explain anything. Other than he wants to come over and talk."

Kenzie drained her mug and said, "I wonder what that's all about?"

Grace mused, "That's really odd, why couldn't he just tell you over the phone?"

Jamie shook her head. "I have no idea, but since I have a few hours to kill, who wants to go for a run?"

Grace groaned. "Not me—I need to clean my apartment and get to the grocery store."

Jamie's face fell.

"I'll run with you." Kenzie pushed back her chair. "Just let me pop home and get my gear. I'll be back in twenty minutes."

"Thanks, Kenz, I need a distraction."

Kenzie jogged out through the garage and disappeared from sight. Grace picked up the tray and carried it into the kitchen with Jamie trailing behind her. Grace rinsed them and placed them in the dishwasher. "Do you want me to hang around until Kenzie gets back?"

"No, I'm fine. I need to get changed too." Jamie gave her sister a warm hug. "Thanks for coming over this morning. I know you're busy with work and I'm pretty sure you were on call last night."

"It's nothing you wouldn't do for me if I called." Grace held her sister tight. "You'll figure out what's the right thing, don't worry about it."

"Thanks, Grace. Hey, I forgot to say anything, but we should have Gran's journals within a day or so. Want to come over for dinner and we can check them out some night this week?"

"That'll be fun. I wonder what family secrets we'll learn."

Joking, Jamie said, "Maybe we'll find out we're somehow connected to royalty."

Grace laughed. "Don't get your hopes up, sis." She pulled her keys out of her jeans pocket. "Have a good run and if you need to talk I'll be home later."

"Thanks, squirt. Talk to you later."

Fresh from a hot shower, Jamie dressed casually in her favorite yoga pants and a long tunic. She glanced at the clock just as the doorbell chimed. Three o'clock on the dot.

"Steve." She pulled open the door. "Come in."

He ducked his head as he stepped over the threshold. "Hi, Jamie."

She closed the door behind him. Her voice somber, she said, "Why don't we go in the living room?"

Steve walked down the short hallway and entered the cozy room.

"I made coffee—would you like a cup?"

"Yeah, sure, if you're having one." He shifted from one foot to the other.

"Have a seat." Jamie walked in the kitchen and poured coffee, adding cream and sugar to one mug. "Cream?"

"No, black. Please." He perched on the edge of a chair.

Jamie noticed he looked like a cat on a hot tin roof. She carried the mugs into the living room, and Steve stood and took one from her. He mumbled thanks and waited for her to sit down. Jamie placed her mug on the coffee table and sat in an overstuffed chair across from her guest.

"I wanted to explain about yesterday." Steve didn't seem to be able to look her in the eye.

She spoke in a calm soft voice. "I'll have to admit I was surprised to find Caleb standing on the doorstep, and even more surprised that you hadn't called."

Steve said, "I know. The last couple of days have been a little out of whack."

Jamie took a sip of coffee, giving him time to elaborate on his statement. Sensing he needed encouragement, she said, "Would you care to explain?"

"Well, I, um." He fidgeted in his seat.

"Steve, if you didn't want to go out with me, you certainly didn't need to send your brother as a stand-in. I'm a big girl—you could have just called to cancel."

"It's not like that, really." Steve took a gulp of hot coffee and grimaced. "Do you remember me telling you about my girlfriend, Yvette?"

A light bulb went off in Jamie's head. "I do."

"Well, she's been calling, and the other night when we were at dinner, that phone call I got was Yvette."

Jamie remained silent, waiting for Steve to continue.

"She asked me to come into Boston. Over drinks she said she was still in love with me and she wants us to work out our problems and get back together."

More annoyed than mad, Jamie asked, "Why couldn't you

have been honest with me? I thought we were friends, and in my book, friends don't skirt the truth no matter how uncomfortable it might be. If you had told me what was going on, I would have understood."

He let go of the breath he had been holding and smiled. "So, you understand that I need to give her another chance. That's great."

"What you decide to do about your relationship with Yvette is your business, not mine. I feel like you led me down a garden path when you had no intention of meeting us at the aquarium. That was rude and unfair to Caleb."

"Jamie, I'm sorry. That's not what I meant to do. It's just, well, she's always been able to tie me up in knots, and this time wasn't any different."

Jamie got up. "It's time for you to leave."

"Wait—I want us to be friends."

"Friends can still be mad at one another, and for right now I need you to leave so I can be mad at you."

Steve got up from the couch. "I'm really sorry I treated you unfairly. But Caleb said you guys had fun yesterday, and I understand you had great dinner too."

Jamie kept her expression neutral. "We did. But it doesn't give you a pass on being a jerk."

Contrite, he said, "I know, and I'm sorry." He opened his arms. "Can I hug you?"

Jamie hesitated for a fraction of a second. "Come here. But I'm still annoyed with you."

He gave her a quick hug and asked, "Can I call you later in the week? Just to say hi."

"I may or may not answer." She led him to the door. "Moving forward, if we're going to be friends, you have to be honest with me. That's the only kind of friendship I have."

Steve grinned. "Sounds good to me. Thanks, Jamie. You're a really good person."

She closed the door and sagged against it. "Well, that

solves part of my issue about Steve. But did Caleb really want to be with me or just get caught up in the moment?" She walked back into the living room and plunked down in her chair. "I've been such a jerk."

She shot a quick text to her sisters. *Steve's talking to his ex. We've decided to be friends. Now I wait to hear from Caleb.*

18

Caleb wiped the steam from the mirror. "How could you have slept with the woman your brother is dating?"

The man in the mirror shrugged.

"What was he thinking, ditching the bewitching Scottish girl with those incredible blue eyes a man could drown in?"

Lathering his face with cream, he ran a razor over the scruff. He towel-dried his hair and dressed in jeans and a long-sleeve tee. Jogging down the back staircase, he discovered Steve's vehicle was parked in front of the garage doors.

"Steve?" he shouted down the hall, and poked his head into Steve's office. He was sitting in a large leather side chair staring out the window. "Hey, when did you get back?"

Steve glanced at his brother. The weight of the world lay in his eyes. "About ten minutes ago."

"How was the trip from Boston?"

"Oh, Boston. That was fine. I drove out to Jamie's before coming home."

"You did?"

He nodded, and Caleb dropped into the chair opposite Steve. "How did that go?"

"Fine, we're good. But this thing with Yvette…"

The last person Caleb wanted to talk about was Yvette. He longed to hear what happened between Steve and Jamie.

Oblivious to the fact that Caleb wasn't paying attention, Steve continued, "I just don't know if I can trust her. What if she's calling me because she's lonely?" He looked at Caleb and snapped, "Are you going to help me or just sit there like a lump on a log?"

"Right—you'll only find out if she's sincere by giving her a shot." Caleb's heart thundered in his chest. "That's if you want to get back together with Yvette and stop dating Jamie."

"Jamie?" He shrugged. "Oh, we decided to be friends, nothing more, and I think she's good with me trying to reconnect with Yvette."

"Did she say those exact words?"

"I don't know what her words were specifically, but we both agreed we're better off as friends."

Caleb shook his hands, releasing the built-up tension. "Have you talked to Yvette since you got back?"

"I've been home all of ten minutes before talking to you—when would I have had the time to call her?"

"From the car?" Caleb stood. "Do us all a favor—unravel your shorts and figure out what you want to do about her. It's not fair to keep her dangling."

He turned to leave the room when Steve asked, "Are you going to ask Jamie out?"

He spun around. "What are you talking about?"

"I'm not blind, little bro. I know you sent the tulips."

Caleb shifted his weight from one foot to the other. "Did you tell her?"

"Nope, but you should." He smiled.

"I'll give it some thought." He studied a spot on the floor, unsure how Steve felt about what he had done.

"Caleb."

Caleb lifted his eyes to meet his brother's.

"Don't wait too long. If she had been right for me, I wouldn't have given you an inch to worm your way into her heart. There's a good chance, in some small way, you're already there."

In a flash of anger he demanded, "Do you think we're interchangeable?"

"Of course not—now you're being an idiot. We didn't have that kind of chemistry. However, I've been in the same room with you two, and if I noticed the sparks, chances are she has too."

"Would it bug you if I asked her out?"

Steve grinned. "Bro, like I said, don't wait too long. She's one in a million."

Caleb said, "Call Yvette." He closed the door on his way out of the office and wandered into the kitchen where he popped open a beer. Drinking a third of the bottle in one gulp, he wondered, *Should I call her or give it a day or so?*

He pulled out the makings for dinner and came to the decision—he'd give her a few days before calling. He wanted to make sure Jamie was ready and then he'd court the heck out of her.

He grinned and could hear his mother saying, "Courting equates to love. If she's worth it, put the time in."

Hump Day came and went, and Jamie's phone hadn't rung. She checked her messages more times per day than she could count, and still Caleb hadn't called.

"Maybe it was just sex." She replayed Saturday night in her head and examined it from every angle, and it was the only logical answer. Nothing more, nothing less.

To keep her mind off the silence from Caleb, at the end of the day she was meeting the girls and Jo at the gym for a workout, and they planned to grab burgers at the local pub. The day dragged and finally it was quitting time. As she was locking the door, her cell phone beeped. An incoming text from a number she didn't recognize. Her heart skipped a beat. Caleb?

Just checking in to see how your week is going. Caleb.

The urge to text right back was tempting, but instead she slipped the phone into her gym bag, locked up and headed over to Kenzie's. Let *him* wait.

Robbie was on his way out as Jamie was walking in. "Hey, Jamie, everyone's waiting on you."

She greeted him with a smile. "Hey yourself—not sticking around tonight? We're going for burgers after."

With a shake of his head, Robbie said, "Nah. Its girls' night and you don't need me tagging along. Another time."

"See ya."

The door clanged behind her. Kenzie came out from the weight room. "'Bout time you got here."

"Sorry. I got a text before I left the office. From Caleb."

"That's interesting. We'll talk later. Go change and we'll meet you inside for a warm up before we hit the weights."

Jamie hurried through the locker room door with Kenzie reminding her to grab a bottle of water. Ignoring her heavy heart, Jamie changed and headed out into the overly bright, mirrored room, filled with racks of free weights and some machines.

"Hey, ladies. Are we ready to get down to some serious work?" Kenzie wore a wicked grin.

Grace's voice held a humorous tone. "I know that look. You love this, don't ya? Bossing us around like a drill sergeant."

Beaming, Kenzie said, "I do."

Jo said, "We'll chat later, if I have the energy."

Jamie patted her arm. "I won't let her drain us completely.

After all, we have to have enough energy to stuff our faces and have a cocktail."

"Or two!" Grace shouted.

Kenzie frowned. "Is that all you girls can think about, eating and drinking alcohol? It's the same every time you come in to work out. You can't wait to put extra calories in that we just burned off."

Jamie did a biceps curl and laughed good-naturedly. "Then what's the point of working out?"

Happy chatter filled the room, and Jamie was glad she decided to surround herself with the women she was closest to. Men would have to wait.

Caleb looked at his phone for what seemed like the umpteenth time. It had been hours since he sent a text to Jamie and still no response. Was it a deliberate decision since he hadn't contacted her for three days?

A hand clapping on his back caught him off guard. "What the heck?"

Steve chuckled. "Lost in your own world again or plotting your next big adventure?"

Caleb mumbled, "Something like that."

Unscrewing the cap from a bottle of water, Steve studied his brother. "You look like crap. What's got you all worked up?"

"Ah, nothing worth talking about." Caleb opened the refrigerator door and peered inside. "What do you want for dinner?"

"If you plan on cooking, whatever you can find."

"It's pretty empty in here. When was the last time you stocked up?"

Steve shrugged. "A couple of weeks ago. You know I'd

rather eat out than cook." He took a long drink, draining the bottle.

Caleb snorted. "That's obvious." He shut the door. "I'm going to pick up something for dinner. That is, if you're gonna be around."

"Yeah." Steve glanced at his phone. "Yvette wants to see me this weekend. She's asking if she can come up."

"And you said what?"

"If she's serious about getting back together, then maybe spending time here would show me whether she's committed to the real me or the idea of me." He tossed the empty bottle into the recycle bin. "What do you think I should do?"

"We've been over this before and you still haven't said if you're in love with her."

Steve rubbed his eyes. "I've thought about everything so many times, my head aches."

"If you can't get her off your mind, that must tell you something."

"Huh?" Confusion filled his eyes.

Caleb playfully jabbed his brother in the chest. "You're still in love with her, dummy, but you're afraid of being hurt again."

A slow smile crept over his face. "I'm gonna ask Yvette to come up for the weekend. I'll get her some flowers and cook her a fabulous dinner, show her around town, and maybe we can go for a hike or something outdoorsy."

"Want some help with dinner?"

Steve grinned. "If you'd set up something simple, write down the directions, step-by-step, I can handle the actual cooking."

"That I can do." On his way out the back door, Caleb grabbed a cloth shopping bag from the hook.

"Hey, Cal, before you go, any luck with Jamie?"

"I sent her a text but haven't heard from her. I have no idea if she's interested or done with the Sullivan men."

"Don't give up on her. She's a really great gal. If it hadn't been for Yvette coming back around, I would have tried to see where we might have gone." To make his point crystal clear, Steve chided, "Don't forget we really only had one date, if you call the movies and almost dinner a date. The other was me showing up at the horse farm. Unless Jamie finds it's odd, go for it."

Caleb filed away Steve's comments to ponder later. "Yvette will be here tomorrow?"

"That's the plan, so let's hang out tonight, watch some sports, drink a few beers, and tomorrow you can make yourself scarce for the weekend."

"Maybe I'll drive down and see the folks."

"Even better, and it'll give time for Mom to try to convince you for the zillionth time to put down roots someplace."

"All right, you go do your legal beagle thing and I'll be back in a while."

Caleb slammed the door behind him and jogged down the back steps. Backing out of the driveway, he hit the hands-free button on the cell and called his mom but got her voicemail, so he left a message. "Hey, Mom. I'm coming down for the weekend. See you tomorrow."

After making the short drive to the market, he parked the Jeep and checked his phone to see if he got a return text from Jamie. He sighed and started to slip the phone into his jacket when it beeped. He grinned.

Busy week. All's good here. J.

"I'm taking that as a good sign for Team Caleb." Smiling, he strutted to the main door.

19

After arriving home, Jamie discovered a large cardboard box tucked under the eaves on her front porch. She hurried inside through the garage and opened the front door to get it inside. Groaning, she shoved it through the door and onto the wood floor. After sliding it over the polished surface, she did a little jig.

"Gran's journals." She hesitated. Should she call her sisters and they could read them together, or should she try to find the one that pertained to Gran falling in love with Rory MacLellan and the history of the dress?

Family loyalty won. She texted her sisters that the box had arrived, and did they want to come over? Moments later she got a response in the group text—*YES*.

Jamie carefully slit the tape on the box and gently lifted out one book at a time. She opened the front cover of each one and set them on the coffee table according to the dates written inside. The last book she pulled out was wrapped in plastic. Peeling back the bubble wrap, she looked inside. She sucked in a breath as she discovered dried bluebells and a faded photograph of her grandparents on their wedding day.

Jamie whispered, "Thanks, Gran—we'll start with this one."

The back door banged open. Grace and Kenzie burst into the living room.

"Are those Gran's?" Grace asked.

Wearing a grin, Jamie teased, "What did you do, drop everything and come running?"

Grace shrieked, "You bet we did! We're dying to read them."

Jamie pointed to the stack and said, "I put them in what I think is the right chronological order." She gestured to the book she was holding. "But this one has their wedding picture and dried bluebells, so this is where we start."

Kenzie ran her fingers lightly over the cover. Tears sprang to her eyes. "I can't believe Gran never told us she kept a journal, and by the looks of the stacks, for most of her life."

"Maybe she wanted it to be a surprise. You know she was always trying to get one over on us." Grace curled up in the corner of the couch. "Jamie, will you read the first one out loud?"

"Sure." Jamie moved to sit in her favorite chair and tucked her feet underneath her.

Kenzie stuck a finger up. "Wait. I'm gonna need coffee."

"That sounds good. Brew a pot and grab some snacks. We're going to be a while."

"Don't start until I'm sitting down. I don't want to miss a word."

"Well, then put a wiggle on it. I'm dying to see what Gran has to say about the dress."

"I want to know how she met Granddad." Grace pulled a blanket off the back of the sofa and tucked it around her feet and legs.

Jamie giggled. "Get cozy, Gracie, it's gonna be a long night."

Kenzie carried a tray in and set it on the side table. She

passed a mug to each sister and took one for herself, and opened a bag of cookies. "I'm ready."

Jamie opened the cover. In a clear, calm voice, she began. "'Arabel Mackenzie, age eighteen.'"

Kenzie blew on her coffee. "Wow, she was young."

"Back then people got married at a young age," Grace admonished her sister. "Now shush so Jamie can read."

"The handwriting is a little faded, so this is going to be slow going." Jamie adjusted the lamplight so it would illuminate the book. She cleared her throat. "Gran writes:

I'm worried. I've just celebrated my eighteenth year on this wonderful earth and still no beau comes calling. When I peer into the mirror, I see a fair lass looking back. My eyes may be a bit too blue and my hair too much copper, but still somewhat pleasing to the eye. Mother says not to worry. For some, it takes more time for a good man to call. I'm not so sure. There aren't many good men left in our town. Mother says if I'm still an unmarried woman by the new year, she has a surprise for me. I wonder what it could be?

Grace said, "It sounds like Gran didn't know about the dress. She doesn't mention it, anyway."

Jamie skimmed the next few pages. "There's stuff about the sheep and growing season and the occasional church social, but nothing about the dress yet." She turned a few more pages and said, "Oh, here we go."

The Christmas season has come and gone and the new year has rushed in with bitter cold air and snow. It's been many months since I celebrated my birthday, and I wonder if Mother has forgotten her promise to me. I may ask her.

Jamie turned the page. "Here she goes on about another snowstorm and the bitter cold."

Glancing at her sisters and then back to the book, she continued.

Mother has promised tomorrow evening we will talk. Dad will be reading his Bible and it will be the perfect time.

Jamie carefully turned the page. Her eyebrow arched. "Now it's getting good."

It's late and I must say Mother surprised me tonight. She had me come into her bedroom. Her hope chest was standing open and draped over the top was the most beautiful dress I've ever seen. It was her wedding dress. When I asked her why she was showing it to me, she smiled and told me to have a seat. She then told me the most wonderful story about how she met and married my dad.

She said when she was a little older than me, she too was unmarried and her family feared she would never find a husband. She had become resigned to caring for her aging parents as a dutiful daughter should.

Jamie took a sip of coffee and said, "She goes on to write about the old village woman."

Kenzie interrupted. "And?"

Jamie held up her finger. "Let me keep reading and we'll find out."

Mother did as she was told. And then, one Sunday, a stranger came to church. His name: James Mackenzie. When they were introduced, James boldly took her hand. He then asked her father if he could come 'round. That was the beginning of my parents' life together.

"Let me get this straight," Grace sat up straight and leaned forward. "Great-grandmother Ann met her husband at church and she had never met him until after she finished the dress and put it on? That's unbelievable especially since the old woman called him by name."

Jamie flipped back through a few pages and skimmed them again. "It would appear so."

"Holy cow," Grace murmured.

"I don't know," Kenzie said slowly. "It might have been just a coincidence."

"I'm going to keep reading and see what happened next." Jamie rubbed her eyes. "Grace, can you hand me my reading glasses?" She pointed to the side table. Slipping them on, she looked down at the book.

Of course, I was surprised. I never knew the story of how they met. Mother making a dress from thread given to her by an old woman—what did this have to do with me? It was then Mother told me if I wanted to marry I needed to put the dress on and then put it away for safekeeping until the day came where I would wear it. She placed the dress in my arms and I went back to my tiny bedroom under the eaves. I laid it on my bed and stared at it for what seemed like hours. After careful consideration, I folded it and tucked it away in my hope chest.

Jamie looked up. "I remember the chest. It sat under the window in her bedroom. Remember, she would never let us open it."

Grace nodded. Her eyes had a faraway look. "Maybe if she opened it, some of the magic would slip away."

"Grace." Kenzie's voice was sharp. You can't be seriously thinking that dress is the reason Great-gran met and married James Mackenzie."

"Uh, yeah. And just as a reminder, who are you and Jamie both named after? Great-grandfather. So, we all got something from that first marriage."

"If you two are done bickering, I'd like to keep reading." Jamie's voice was stern, causing Kenzie and Grace to fall silent.

"Thank you." Jamie cleared her throat. "Now, where was I?"

Several weeks passed and the days were growing warmer. But I wasn't any closer to meeting anyone new. The dress called to me. Several times I took it out and held it up, looking in the mirror and wondering if I should put it on. Late one night, when I should have been sleeping, I got out of bed, tiptoed across the room, took the dress out of the chest and unfolded it. I waited. I'm not sure what I thought might happen as I watched it. The first blush of the morn hovered outside my window when I made the decision.

I slipped off my nightdress and pulled the soft folds of white over my head. Only one moment of hesitation as I wondered how it would look. Mother and I are not the same shape; I'm curvy where she's more angular and tall. Words fail me as I will attempt to describe how I felt. It fit perfectly. It was as if the longing for a husband evaporated. I was beautiful. When I took the dress off and put it away again, I knew in my heart of hearts that I would wear this dress as a bride.

Kenzie whistled. "Wow. She got all that from putting the dress on?"

"I guess she did." Jamie noticed Grace wiping her eyes. "Grace, what's the matter?"

"Nothing, really. When Gran says she was curvy and Great-gran was angular, it made me think that you're a combo of both body types, but Kenz and I each take after them."

"You know, I never really thought about it, but you're right." Jamie cocked her head. "Out of the three of us, you do look the most like Gran."

She held up the wedding dress picture and passed it to Kenzie, who in turn gave it to Grace. "I do look like her." Grace studied the picture. In a hushed voice she said, "I never realized." She set the picture on the table. "What happens next?"

It's been several weeks since I wore the dress, and I've wanted to ask Mother what I should be doing or if I've done something wrong. We need to go into the village tomorrow and Easter festivities are soon. That will be enough to keep my mind off the dress.

"How long do you think this is supposed to take?" Grace asked Jamie.

"It's got to be the luck of the draw. Back then Scotland wasn't exactly teeming with people."

Ever the skeptic, Kenzie sighed. "If you ask me, I don't think it's so much luck as it is being in the right place at the right time."

Jamie nudged Kenzie's foot and smiled at her. "Kenzie, sometimes you need to have faith in something besides logic." She jumped up. "Bio break."

She zipped down the hall while Grace picked up the picture. "We all look more like Dad's family than Mom's. Don't you think?"

"Yeah, maybe because Dad is one hundred percent and Mom is a melting pot." Kenzie smiled. "I've often wondered if Mom has a little Scottish blood in her too."

"Maybe."

Jamie flopped into the chair and picked up the leather-bound book. "Ready for more?"

Grace nodded. "Absolutely."

It worked. I've met the most handsome man I've ever laid eyes on. Rory MacLellan.

Jamie said, "See, Kenzie, the dress worked. Gran met Granddad."

Snorting, Kenzie replied, "Well, she had to—otherwise there would never have been Dad or us."

Rory MacLellan has recently started to work for Dad. He's a sheep farmer by choice. His family lives in Glasgow, but he wanted a different life, so he hit the road and ended up in our fair village looking for work. After spending time with Father around the farm, he was hired. I'm smitten.

It's been two weeks since Rory started work and I've managed to bump into him almost daily. He is so strong but not much of a talker. A strong, silent man with a gentle heart. I catch his eye as I walk through the fields, and I do believe he is interested in me. When will he talk to me? Mother has caught me watching him, and she smiles. I think she has guessed my heart has begun to beat a different rhythm.

Today was the day. Rory asked if I'd like to go for a walk with him on Sunday after church. I hope this is the beginning of our future.

Jamie flipped several pages ahead and then back. "It looks

like she skips a lot of days based on the dates. It's been about a month when she writes again.

Rory MacLellan has confessed he is captivated by my charms. I still can't believe it. He asked if there is another who has expressed interest, which I take to mean he is wondering if there are men vying for my hand. I have given him my heart; there is no other for me. If he approaches my father and requests to become my husband, I will accept him gladly.

"How romantic," Grace gushed. "See, she fell in love."

"It would seem that lightning did strike twice in our family after putting the dress on." Kenzie got up off the couch and stretched her arms above her head. "But that doesn't mean it will work for Jamie."

"Or us." Grace yawned and got up too. "Jamie's potential beau went back to his old flame."

"But Caleb may be waiting in the wings." Kenzie bent over to give Jamie a one-armed hug. "I'm exhausted and going to head home. Wait to keep reading, okay? I love uncovering our family's past together."

The mantle clock struck midnight. Jamie said, "It's already Saturday. Who has what plans later today?"

Grace said, "I'm running errands and checking on Mom and Dad's house, and Kenzie has work."

"We'll regroup here later and keep reading the journals."

"Sounds like a plan." Grace followed Kenzie out the door. "I'll lock up."

"Thanks, Grace. Night, Kenz."

A muffled goodnight reached her ears. Jamie shut the book and laid one hand on the cover the other over her heart. "Goodnight, Gran."

20

Jamie walked through her living room more times in one day than she did in a normal week. The journals were like magnets pulling at her. Only two more hours until both sisters would arrive with pizza and salad. She made sure there was wine and beer in stock just in case someone wanted something stronger than iced tea.

She checked her cell phone. Nothing from Caleb since her text. Jamie fired up her computer and confirmed a few appointments via email for the coming week.

She heard a car door bang and glanced out the window. What was Steve's SUV doing in her driveway? She slipped her clogs on and hurried to open the front door.

She strolled down the walk and over to the driver's door, and the window slid down. "Steve. This is a surprise."

"Hi, Jamie." He was beaming. "We were out driving around and I thought it might be a good time for you to meet Yvette."

Jamie leaned forward and smiled at the lady sitting in the passenger seat. "Hello."

A petite blonde with deep brown eyes waved at her. "Hi,

Jamie, it is a pleasure to meet you. Sully's told me all about you." Yvette certainly was bubbly and her high-pitched voice was unexpected—Jamie expected a low purr, like a kitten.

She glanced at Steve. "I hope only the good things." Turning to Yvette, she said, "Would you like to come in for a cup of coffee?"

Yvette's hand hovered over her seatbelt. "Sully, it would be nice to talk to a friend of yours."

He hesitated. "Why not?"

He shut the car off and got out, then dashed around the other side to open Yvette's door. Steve took Yvette's hand, they walked behind Jamie and through the open door.

Yvette looked around the living room. "Your home is charming." She smiled. "It is a wonderful reflection of you."

"Thank you. When I bought it a couple of years ago the charm was missing, but with a lot of elbow grease and help from my family, I was able to transform it back to its original glory, right down to the flower gardens in the backyard."

"I'd love to see them."

Taken aback at Yvette's boldness, Jamie said, "Right this way." She led the way to the garden. Steve caressed Yvette's hand, which Jamie pretended she hadn't noticed. "My mom has a green thumb and my dad was raised on a sheep farm where they were excellent at growing everything. I guess you could say it's in my DNA."

"This stone work is lovely." Yvette pulled away from Steve and wandered down the crushed stone path.

Quietly, Jamie said, "I'm surprised to see you here with Yvette."

"She came up for the weekend and I told her what happened last Saturday. I didn't want there to be any secrets between us if we're really going to give ourselves a real chance. That's when she asked to meet you."

Jamie crossed her arms over her chest. One eyebrow arched. "I see. And you didn't think to call first?"

"I didn't want to make it awkward in case you said no, and it meant a lot to Yvette."

Jamie sighed. "Fine. But you need to work on friendship skills." She trailed after Yvette, explaining about what would be blooming soon and what was still dormant in the beds.

Yvette looked at Jamie, her head cocked to one side. "You know, he thinks very highly of you."

"He's a good lawyer and we've had some fun too."

"I know. You went riding and to the movies. But I really wanted to apologize to you. I'm responsible for you getting stood up last weekend. I had no idea he had plans when he agreed to meet me."

With a dismissive wave of her hand, Jamie said, "It wasn't a big deal. Caleb and I had a good time at the aquarium."

"Can I be frank?"

Caught off guard Jamie hesitated. "Um, sure. I guess so."

"They're very similar but different men, Sully and Caleb."

"Okay." The word was drawled out. "I'm not sure I understand what you're getting at."

"They're both one-woman men. I knew that the minute I met Sully, and then when I met Caleb I just knew. They don't go around breaking hearts. When they fall, they fall for keeps."

"I'm curious—then why did you break it off?"

"I was scared."

"What? I thought you broke it off because you wanted to live in Boston."

The look on Jamie's face must have caused Steve to grow concerned. He hurried over to the girls. "Is everything okay over here?"

Yvette said, "We're just getting to know each other. Girl talk."

"If you say so." He glanced at Jamie. "Mind if I go grab a glass of water?"

"Sure, there's a pitcher in the fridge." Jamie pointed to a small table and chairs. "Why don't we sit down?"

Yvette called after Steve, "Can you give us a few minutes?"

Steve said, "Yeah. Um, give me a high sign when you're ready to have male company."

Yvette settled on the wooden chair and smiled at Jamie. "I can see why Steve wants us all to be friends."

Jamie shifted uncomfortably in her chair. "Can I be blunt?"

"By all means." Yvette smoothed back her bangs.

"You broke up with Steve and then you called asking him to get back together?"

"I'm not a fan of change."

"And now? What is any different?"

"It's simple. I am a one-man woman. It took some time, but I realize my future is with Sully and if that means Vermont, then so be it. It's not like it's moving to the moon."

Jamie nodded, mildly surprised by her honesty. "You don't have any issue with Steve and me being friends, and you want us to be friends too?"

"Correct again." Yvette's smile warmed her eyes.

"Just to be crystal clear, Steve told you we dated a few times, and it doesn't bother you *at* all?"

Yvette leaned over and held her hand out to Jamie, who hesitated, not understanding what was going on. "Jamie, I am what some would call a little ditzy. However, despite my cold feet, I've always known Sully is the man I'll marry. We have been together since college. I'll admit I wasn't thrilled about leaving the city, but after coming up here I see now I can make a wonderful and happy life here with Sully. There are three relationships between two people. The ones where we are true to ourselves, and the other as a couple. I needed to make sure that both Sully and I were ready to share a life."

Jamie nodded. "I think I understand."

Yvette patted Jamie's hand. "When you met Sully, he was at this crossroads. Spending time with you showed him what he had lost with me, and I've known for several months that I wanted our relationship to work out. You can be honest—there wasn't any sparks between you, right?"

Jamie shook her head.

"It felt like he was a good friend or brother?"

"Yes. That's exactly what it was like. We had fun but no chemistry."

Yvette sat back in her chair. "I hope you won't think I'm being too forward, but is there something between you and Caleb?"

Jamie dropped her eyes. "I'm not sure what is or isn't between us."

"Did you know he went to see his parents this weekend?"

With a shake of her head, she looked away. "I haven't heard from him."

"According to Sully, he's trying to figure out what his next assignment will be for work."

She visibly wilted. "Does he plan on leaving soon?"

"You'll have to ask Caleb. Call him." Yvette's smile was genuine. She pointed to the house. "We need to put him out of his misery. He's dying to know what we're talking about."

Jamie relaxed, her brain spinning. "I'm glad you stopped over and next time you're in Vermont, give me a call. We can go shopping or out to lunch."

Yvette stood up. "I'd like that." She hugged Jamie. "I hope we'll become good friends. It'll make the transition to becoming a Vermonter that much easier."

"Steve's a lucky guy."

"Do you think I can get you to call him Sully?"

Jamie shook her head. With a laugh she said, "No, but you can try."

Yvette smiled. "I guess he's two different men for each of us. He's my love Sully, and your friend Steve."

Jamie locked arms with Yvette and strolled through the back door. She announced, "Steve, I like her."

He exhaled loudly. "So we're all good?"

Jamie hugged Steve and Yvette. "Better than good—we're going to be friends."

❦

"You're never going to believe who stopped by today," Jamie said as Grace set the pizza box on the counter.

"Who?"

"Steve and his girlfriend, Yvette." Jamie nodded and grinned.

Grace's hand flew to her mouth. "Here?"

"In the flesh." Jamie got plates from the cabinet.

"And what did you think about her?"

"I liked her—she does seem to love Steve. And she very casually told me that Caleb is visiting his parents for the weekend and making a decision about what comes next for his career."

"And what do you think she meant by that?" Grace flipped open the box top, picked off a mushroom from the pizza and popped it in her mouth.

"I'm going to assume it means he won't be hanging around much longer." Jamie put plates, napkins and silverware on the counter. She held up a bottle. "Wine?"

Grace shook her head. "I'll wait for Kenzie." She licked her fingers. "Did he say he was leaving?"

"I have no idea, it never came up." Jamie pulled the cork and poured herself a glass. "If he leaves, he leaves. I can't get all tied up in knots over something I can't control."

"I know, but…well, you know."

"Grace, the only thing I know for sure is we had fun together."

"Is that what you're calling it now, and what about how you feel?" Grace smirked. "I know you and something has changed dramatically."

Jamie traced her lips with her finger, remembering how *his* lips felt. "How could I deny it? I've never felt like this in my life. When he was kissing me so sweetly, tenderly and passionately that it rocked me to my core."

"Do you think it felt like that for him?" Grace's curiosity was evident.

"How would I know? It's not like we talked about it afterwards."

Kenzie appeared in the kitchen. She grabbed Jamie's glass. "Thanks, sis." She took a sip. "What are we talking about?"

"Caleb."

Kenzie mouthed formed a perfect circle as she said, "Oh?"

Jamie reached for her glass and then said, "Keep it, I'll get another."

"Before you got here, Jamie was telling me about Steve showing up with his girlfriend."

"That must have been interesting. What's she like?"

"She's very nice and beautiful."

"Was it awkward?" Kenzie opened the salad container and chomped on a slice of cucumber.

"Not really. When we started talking I thought she was going to be all territorial, but she reassured me she was happy Steve and I are friends."

"Do you think she was sincere?" Grace asked.

"I do, and you'll have a chance to meet her at some point and you can see for yourselves." Jamie handed out plates.

"The sooner we eat, the faster we can get back to Gran's journals and find out about the wedding." Grace plopped in front of the counter. "If you want, I can read a while?"

"Thanks, squirt, but I really want to keep reading. It feels like I'm supposed to read at least this one."

Kenzie joked, "After all, it's her future we're trying to unravel."

Jamie threw a balled-up paper napkin at her. "Just wait until you try the dress on and we'll see what your future holds."

Kenzie grinned and picked up a slice of pizza. "I'm never putting the dress on. I'm happy borrowing Robbie for a date as needed or when I'm looking for a little male companionship for hiking and rock climbing."

Jamie teased, "The poor guy. Does he know he's your someone borrowed?"

Kenzie munched on a slice, her eyes sparkling. "He doesn't seem to mind."

21

The MacLellan girls were settled into their favorite places in Jamie's living room. The pizza was forgotten and the room glowed with soft reading light and a fire flickered in the hearth. Jamie opened the journal to where they had left off, cleared her throat and said, "Are you ready?"

Grace and Kenzie said, "Yes."

I found a moment to talk with Mother today, alone. I've told her about my deepening feelings for Rory and she told me she's thrilled. She and Dad believe he is a good man. She asked me if I'd tried on the dress and I confessed that I had in the wee hours of a morning many weeks ago. She said the magic continues. I wonder if it will carry over to the next generation—that is, if I'm blessed with wee ones. I may be getting ahead of myself, but I believe I will become Rory's bride before the year has come to an end.

Jamie stopped reading and looked at Kenzie and Grace. "So, she tried the dress on and she is in love. I think the big moment might be on the next page…"

Grace urged, "Stop stalling for dramatic effect and start reading."

Jamie giggled and turned the page.

It's been several weeks since I wrote in this diary. But it has happened. Rory asked Dad for my hand in marriage. We're to be married in two short months. It will give his family time to receive the announcement and travel to our village, where the ceremony will take place. I will wear the dress that is stored in my hope chest, and once I'm officially a married woman it will be placed inside for my daughter and daughter's daughters. I believe this wedding dress is blessed with an enchantment of love. I won't have time to write in this journal while preparing for my new life, but I will return to it upon my marriage.

"They didn't have a long engagement," Grace stated. "Or was that typical back in the day?"

Kenzie pushed herself to a sitting position. "Who knows, but if memory serves me correctly, Mom and Dad didn't have a long engagement either. Maybe that's part of the family magic too."

Jamie placed the book on the cushion. She crossed to the mantel and took down a framed photo. Taking a moment before passing it to Grace, she said, "Have a look. Mom didn't wear Gran's wedding dress."

"Well, she wasn't a daughter. She was becoming a daughter-in-law."

Kenzie stuck out her hand. "Lemme see."

Grace sighed. "Dad looks very handsome in his kilt and jacket. If I ever decide to get married, I wonder if my future husband could be convinced to wear a kilt."

"Are you thinking about trying on the dress too, Grace?"

Very quietly, she said, "Maybe."

"You've always been the romantic." Normally one to tease her, Kenzie didn't, but handed the photo back to Jamie. "How many more pages do we have in the first journal?"

Jamie held it up. "Just a few." She settled back in the chair and adjusted the lamp.

I am officially Mrs. Rory MacLellan, although I told my dear husband that I was still Arabel Mackenzie MacLellan and not just a

Mrs. Thank the heavens he likes the fiery spirit I'm blessed with and never wants me to change. I was a little worried, as some women have become church mice upon taking marriage vows. I'm looking forward to be blessed with a bairn or two, and I pray they find the happiness Rory and I now share. If someday one of my children or grandchildren reads this, I'd like you to know I wish you love and happiness all the days on this earth.

Jamie closed the book. "Gran always told us marrying Granddad was the best decision she had made. It's nice to see she felt that way right from the very beginning of their life together."

Kenzie mused, "The two marriages we've grown up around were special."

"Maybe there is something in the magic of the dress that gives our family an edge, so that we intuitively understand what it takes to make a marriage work," Grace said.

Jamie set the book on the table. "I think marriage is different for each couple. Maybe what our family figured out was the art of compromise. Knowing when to give a little and how to graciously accept it when on the receiving end."

"Mom and Dad do seem to be able to do that really well," Kenzie said.

"I don't remember what it was like with Gran and Granddad. They were always happy when we were around."

Jamie chuckled. "You don't remember how she'd get after him? She'd shake her finger and scold him."

Grace shook her head. "Maybe I was too young to really remember. He died when I was six."

Kenzie agreed. "Those times are a little foggy for me too."

"She missed him 'til the day she died. Now that's love." Jamie wiped a tear from her face. "Enough of the sadness. We can change direction. Kenzie, what do you want to do with your future?"

"Like, do I want to get married?"

The expression on Kenzie's face made Jamie want to

laugh, but she held her smile in check. "That's exactly what I'm asking."

Kenzie pretended to shudder. "Well, I'm not going to run out the door and grab the first guy I see and marry him."

Grace giggled. "You could tackle someone. You're stronger than most guys around here. Well, except Robbie."

"Kenz, I'm not suggesting you go on the prowl, but I would like to know you're open to the possibility of love and a future." Jamie dropped on the couch between her sisters. Taking Grace's hand, she said to Kenzie, "Promise me you'll think about it, 'cause I think we've had this all wrong. We don't have to give up anything to find great love other than giving someone a chance."

Slowly Kenzie shook her head. "I'll think about it, but I'm not making any promises. Right now, my focus has to be on my gym."

Grace looked around Jamie. "You never know, you might meet someone at the gym who likes some of the same activities you do."

She snorted, "There's wishful thinking."

Jamie turned to Grace. "And you, kiddo—"

Grace held up her hand. "I'm going to wait and see how things work out for you two before I commit to any new ideas."

"Gracie, out of the three of us, you've always been the one with the most loving and kind heart. I think that's why you went into the medical field. Surely you want to find love."

"I don't know, maybe. The most immediate plan is to move out of the apartment and find a small house of my own. I want roots like you and Kenz have. For now, that's enough for me. Love can wait."

"What about you, Jamie?" Grace asked.

"I don't know where—or if—something might lead with Caleb, but I'm open to the possibility." Jamie stretched her arms over her head. "I'm glad we read Gran's journal together. It reminds me when we would spend each summer with her in Scotland, romping in the fields and going to the Bluebell Woods."

She grasped her sisters' hands. "Let's make a pledge to go back to Scotland this summer together. We haven't all been there at the same time in a few years."

"Get the calendar and let's pick a date. When Grace goes into work on Monday, she can request the time off and I'll ask Robbie to cover the gym for me."

Grace high-fived Kenzie. "Once again, it's time for sister-cation."

The clock striking the hour caused Kenzie to look up. "I'm going to head home. Grace, want to follow me?"

"Sure."

The sisters walked out the back door, and Jamie locked it behind them. She wandered into the kitchen and picked up her phone. No messages.

❦

Caleb scanned the contents of an email on his laptop. "Huh, looks like I can get back to work next month." He stared out the window. In his mind he could see Jamie's face. He could almost reach out and touch her. How could he leave her, but how could he give up a career he had worked for all his life?

"Caleb!" Mom called up the stairs.

He rose and headed down to the kitchen. He walked in and lifted the lid on the pot, inhaling the savory aroma. "Yum. Beef stew and biscuits."

She placed a hand on his shoulder. "There's nothing like stew on a cold, damp day."

He broke off a piece of a biscuit and dunked it into the rich brown gravy. Popping it in his mouth, he closed his eyes. "Mm, you've outdone yourself again."

Mom blushed. "Well, you introduced me to experimenting with spices, so I've kicked most of my recipes up a notch."

"And it shows." He glanced around the room. "Where's Dad?"

"He went to get firewood. I thought we could eat in the family room tonight. It's so cozy in there."

Caleb leaned against the refrigerator. "Hey, Mom, can I ask you something?" He hoped he sounded casual.

"Of course, honey."

"I met a girl."

She clasped her hands together. "That's wonderful news, Caleb. Is she someone special?"

"I think she could be, but here's the rub. Steve was dating her, sort of, before he and Yvette got back together..."

"Wait." Mom whipped her head around. "What did you say? They're a couple again?"

He held up his hands in mock surrender. "Don't get testy with me—I thought he called you."

"Well, he didn't, but go on. You were talking about a girl he dated and then broke it off with."

"Well, in full disclosure, he was supposed to take her to the aquarium but ended up spending the weekend with Yvette. Instead I took Jamie—that's her name—to the aquarium and we went to dinner on the wharf." His eyes grew bright remembering the way she smiled all day.

"Did something happen?" His mother's eyes sparkled. "I hear a little more in your voice than just a day filling in for your brother."

"You'd love her. She's smart, funny, the oldest of three sisters and not to be overly mushy," he confessed, "she makes me think about putting down roots."

Mom beamed. "Are you saying what I hope you're saying?"

Caleb chuckled. "She's totally wrong for Steve, but she's perfect for me. Well, in her imperfect way."

"Ah, honey, this is wonderful news. So, what's the issue?"

He was thrilled to see his mom so happy and hoped his next news wouldn't upset her too much. "I got an email today for a job in Europe for three months. Some hotshot wants to do it up right but doesn't want to trust the locals to cook."

Her face drooped. "When would you have to leave?"

"In about four weeks." He pulled open the fridge and grabbed a beer. Twisting off the top, he said, "I'm thinking of going and see if what I'm feeling is real or if it's just because she's the first girl who's captivated my attention for longer than a week or two."

"That should tell you something right there." Mom patted his cheek. Looking squarely into his eyes, she said, "Tomorrow you need to drive back to Vermont and spend time with your young lady. Take the job, and when you get back you should have some answers. If you find you can't or don't want to live without her in your life, tell her."

"Is it really that simple?" Somehow Caleb didn't think he would move that quickly.

"Love is never complicated unless we make it that way."

"Mom, you're the best." He wrapped her in a bear hug. "Do me a favor and don't say anything to Dad or Steve, at least until I know what I really want."

Mom put her finger up to her lips. "Your secret is safe with me."

"With that settled, can we eat?" Caleb grabbed a bowl. "I'm starving."

❦

Jamie was ready for the rush of the week ahead when her cell phone rang. She glanced at caller ID and a grin split her face. Caleb.

"Hello?" Her voice sounded a little breathless.

"Hi, Jamie. I was wondering—if you're not busy, would

you like to have dinner tomorrow night?" His voice was smooth as warm honey.

Without hesitation she said, "Yes!" She shook her head, silently admonishing herself for sounding too eager. "I'd love to."

"Great, I'll pick you up at six-thirty."

"I'm looking forward to it. See you tomorrow night."

"Bye, Jamie."

The line went silent and Jamie danced around the room. She was going on a dinner date with Caleb.

22

Jamie agonized over her outfit, everything from her earrings to tights. Piles of clothes were discarded in a heap on the bed. After settling on a simple print dress and heels, she took one last look at her makeup. Satisfied it was just right, she shut off the lights.

She pushed the curtain aside and peeked out, watching for his Jeep. Headlights swept over the early spring green of the lawn. She dropped the curtain and grabbed her coat off the chair. Slipping into the sleeves, she picked up her small clutch. She practically floated to the door. Opening it, she noticed Caleb's hand hovering over the doorbell. In his other hand was a pot of tulips.

Her heart sank.

He handed her the flowers, grinning. "I know you have a fondness for flowers."

She nodded and mumbled, "Thank you."

He stopped her as she turned to place the flowers on the side table. "Jamie, is something wrong?"

"No, it's fine." She was hoping her face didn't betray her feelings.

"It's obvious that something is bothering you. Tell me."

She glanced at the lovely blooms. "Well, I didn't expect you to copy Steve."

His eyes narrowed. "I'm not sure what you mean. I'm my own person."

She dropped her chin. "I'm sorry, I shouldn't have said anything. Let's just go to dinner."

"Not until I understand exactly what you mean." He hovered in the doorway.

She tapped her foot, debating if she was overreacting, but she decided she'd better just say what was on her mind. "When you came for dinner, the first night, your brother sent me lovely tulips and now you're bringing me the same ones."

"What? You think Steve sent them to you?"

She could see the flash of annoyance in his eyes. She was sorry she brought it up but continued, "Of course—who else could it have been?" Her hand grasped his. "Oh, Caleb. Were they from you?"

"It doesn't matter," he grumbled. "I'm glad you liked them."

Her voice softened. "It matters to me." She pecked his cheek "Thank you." She slipped her arms around his mid-section and held him tight. "Do you still want to have dinner with me?"

He loosened her hug and pushed her chin up with his finger to place a tender kiss on her lips. "More than anything."

Playfully she pushed him out the door. "I think Italian is in order tonight."

His forehead wrinkled and he asked, "Why Italian?"

"My family's favorite restaurant is the Pasta Bowl and I want to introduce you to the owner, Joey Romano. He's been a family friend for years and it's got the best fettuccine alfredo on the planet."

He held open the Jeep door. "You say that now because you haven't tasted mine." Closing the door behind her, he jogged around to the driver's side. "Is it that place on Main Street?"

"That's right, a few doors down from Kenzie's gym. We can park behind her place." Curious she asked, "Did you enjoy your visit with your parents?"

"I did. I'll fill you in over a glass of wine."

Caleb slowed and pulled into a parking spot on the street and turned the car off. Before Jamie could get out, he placed a hand on her arm. "Jamie, Steve's more of a roses guy."

Jamie tilted her head and smiled. "I wish you had told me sooner. However, I know now and there's no harm done." She patted his hand. "Ready to go inside?"

He chuckled. "I am so ready."

❧

Candlelight, wine and romantic music playing softly in the background added to the happiness that flowed over Jamie. She tried to concentrate on Caleb's funny stories, but she was lost in the depths of his penetrating eyes. *Is this what love feels like? I've never been so entranced with a man like this before.*

"Jamie, what do you recommend?" Caleb topped off her wineglass.

"Definitely the fettuccini—the pasta's made in-house and the sauce is to die for. It's my absolute favorite, but I only order it on special occasions since it will take hours of exercise to justify eating it."

His smile warmed his eyes. "That's all I needed to hear."

After placing their orders, Jamie picked up her glass and swirled the rich red wine. "I know you love to cook, so the chef part is easy to see. But what made you become a personal chef?"

"I wanted to see the world, and this way I'd get paid, my expenses are covered and I have the opportunity to travel."

"Practical." Jamie took a sip and set the glass on the table.

"Mom and Dad have always known I have a serious case of wanderlust. But they thought it wouldn't last as long as it has."

"Where did you go to culinary school?"

"In Cambridge. I attended a very intense course after high school. Received my degree and a professor recommended me for my first job. From there it was easy to get more gigs."

Trying to keep her voice light, she said, "How long are you gone—you know, when you're working?" Her heart constricted.

"It depends on the customer. Some are a couple of weeks, like an extended vacation, and they want me at the homes they rent. There are times where I've traveled to one location for several months. Like a movie set."

Softly, she said, "Oh, that's a long time."

"The nice part of my job is I can pick and choose which jobs I take. I have a few clients I enjoy working for, so I tend to take the repeaters. The financial rewards, plus bonuses, make it really hard to turn down."

"It sounds like you're in high demand." She refolded her napkin and avoided looking at Caleb. She didn't want to think of him being gone for months at a time.

The salad was delivered and Jamie nodded for fresh pepper. Caleb did the same before answering the question that hung heavy in the air.

"That's one way to put it." He picked up his fork. "I got an email from one of my better clients. They want me to go with them on a European holiday this summer."

Jamie's fork stopped midway to her mouth. "When would you leave?"

"In four weeks. Until September."

"That sounds exciting." Jamie's salad tasted like grass clippings in her mouth.

Caleb extended his hand across the table. Grazing her fingers, his voice was firm when he said, "Jamie. Look at me."

Her heart quickened and she got lost in the depths of his blue-green eyes.

"I don't leave for a month. I'd like to slow things down and spend time getting to know each other."

She swallowed the lump in her throat. "I'd like that too."

Still holding her hand, he said softly, "Did you think this date was a one and done?"

She shook her head. "I'm not sure what I thought. I knew you'd have to go back to work and it's not like going into an office."

Linking fingers, he said, "No, but as much as I travel, I also have a lot of free time."

She smiled and squeezed his hand. "This is actually perfect. We can date when you're around and have fun. Little Miss Independent will be fine when you're traveling. If we want, we can Skype and text to stay in touch."

"I'd really like that. Before we get too far ahead of ourselves and you have me hopping on a plane, can we enjoy tonight?"

"Oh, jeez, you must think I'm crazy. Already planning for when you're on the road." Jamie pulled her fingers back and focused on buttering a hot dinner roll.

Caleb chuckled. "You can't fool me, Mac."

Her eyes shot up. "Are you going to start calling me Mac instead of Jamie?"

"Until I can think of something else. It's a good attention-getter."

She giggled. "I like the way it rolls off your tongue." She looked over his shoulder and frowned. "Don't look now, but the spies are here."

Caleb swiveled around.

She groaned, "I told you not to look."

"Well, I had to know who was spying on us." He waved.

"No biggie—it's just your sisters and Robbie." He turned back to Jamie. "Should we ask them to join us?"

"No." She averted her eyes. "Well, if they're still here during dessert, maybe. But only for dessert."

Caleb caught the waiter's attention. He pulled out a piece of paper and jotted a note. Pointing to Robbie and the girls, he asked the waiter to deliver it. He picked up his wineglass and held it up in the spy's direction. Grinning, he raised it in toast to them.

"Caleb, what did you just do?" Jamie hissed.

He grinned. "I asked them to let us enjoy dinner and we could all have a quick dessert and then go our separate ways."

"That's not such a bad idea." Jamie brightened.

"Now let's forget about our audience and enjoy a romantic dinner for two."

Kenzie poked Grace. "Will you look at them? They're eating at a snail's pace to torture us."

Grace looked over her shoulder. "I don't think Jamie would do that—she knows we're dying to get over there."

"Exactly my point."

"Ladies." Robbie leaned into the bar. "They're on a date. Maybe we shouldn't have chosen to have drinks here, of all places."

Kenzie snorted. "Don't pretend like you're Mr. Innocent. I told you where they were going and you were into coming here."

"Maybe I'm thinking this wasn't such a great idea. If I was on a date, I wouldn't want all of you waiting to pounce once the dishes were cleared."

"When was the last time you went on a date? Like over a year ago."

Grace hissed, "Kenzie, don't be rude. Robbie's being selective and I admire him. It's easy to go out with just anyone when you have no intention of getting serious about them. He's waiting until he has a connection with someone."

"Thanks, Grace. Logic and beauty. Are you sure you're a MacLellan?"

Kenzie interrupted, "What does that mean?"

He twirled Kenzie's barstool to face him. "And when was the last time *you* went out on a real date, and not just hanging out with yours truly?"

"I don't have time for all that nonsense. I have a business to build and I can't be distracted with mushy stuff." Kenzie swiveled her stool so she could keep one eye on the couple and one eye on her companions. "Besides, I'm perfectly fine single."

Robbie held up his hands in defeat. "You didn't say happy, but I'm not going to say another word." He pretended to whisper in Grace's ear but was loud enough for Kenzie to hear him loud and clear. "The lady doth protest a bit too much."

Grace giggled. "That's one thing about Kenzie that will never change—she is the prickly one."

"It's okay. I've got her pegged. She's got a tough exterior, but underneath it all, she's a marshmallow."

Kenzie interrupted them. "Hey, look. They're done. Should we wait a minute or rush over?"

Robbie looked in Jamie and Caleb's direction. "It appears to me Caleb just asked for some extra chairs. Take a look."

The waiter was strategically putting extra chairs around the table, keeping the aisle clear. Without waiting for an agreement from Robbie or Grace, Kenzie hopped off the barstool and sauntered over to the table. "How was dinner?"

Jamie smirked at her sister. "It would have been better if we hadn't had eyes watching our every move."

Caleb stood up and took a chair closer to Jamie, leaving

Robbie to have his chair. Grace and Kenzie sat down and smiled sweetly at the waiter. He came over and offered dessert menus. The ladies ordered slices of cheesecake while Caleb and Robbie each ordered an after-dinner cocktail.

Grace shifted in her chair. "Well, you never did say—how was dinner?"

"Have we ever had a bad meal here?" Jamie asked.

Grace grinned. "No, but someone had to break the silence. It was killing me."

Caleb draped his arm around Jamie's shoulder and grinned. "Best meal I've had in a few weeks."

Kenzie's gaze roamed the group. "I don't get it."

Robbie said, "I'm guessing he's referring to the dinners at Jamie's."

Caleb said, "Robbie, I knew you were a smart man the minute I met you."

Stammering, Kenzie said, "But she was dating Steve at the time."

Robbie slung his arm around her shoulders. "Kenz, relax. Let's just say a man can have hope."

Kenzie's eyebrow shot up in amazement. "Have you had the hots for her since the dinner party?"

Caleb grinned and leaned into the group. "What would you say if I told you she intrigued me the moment I met her and she stalked off to the ladies room, her temper spiking and eyes shooting daggers?"

In mock protest Jamie said, "What are you talking about? I was gracious and let you have dinner with your brother."

Tenderly kissing her temple, he said, "If I'm going to be honest, I'd have rather he left and you stayed."

A satisfied smile spread over her face. "Hindsight is twenty-twenty."

23

Jamie rushed through her end-of-day routine and glanced at her watch one more time. Caleb was picking her up at five, and they were going out to Racing Brook Stables for a short ride.

"Oh, shoot, I forgot to call Jo." Grabbing her cell, she dialed. "Jo?"

Jamie could hear the smile in her greeting. "Hey, Jamie, what's going on?"

"I was hoping you could do me a favor. Caleb and I want to come out for a short ride. Would you mind if we took Chloe and Pirate out?"

"No problem. I'm headed out tonight, so I'll have them saddled and ready. All you need to do when you get back is do their tack, feed them and then lock the barn."

"That's great. You're the best."

"Anything for love, Jamie."

Sputtering, she said, "What do you mean?"

"Jamie, we live in a small town. Do you really think I haven't heard about the new hot guy in your life?"

"It's not what you're thinking. We've just started dating."

"Uh huh."

Jamie could tell she was amused. "Besides, he's leaving in a couple weeks. He has a job in Europe for the summer. So I'm not going to get too attached." She fought to keep her voice even.

"Hey, I'm sorry. I didn't know that very important detail. Are you doing okay?"

"Of course I am. I've known from our first official date this is his lifestyle. He loves his job and he's in high demand."

Jo let out a low whistle. "He must be a superb chef."

"Well, we know he makes great pork chops, and he cooked for me over the weekend and my taste buds wept."

"And...anything else you want to share about your man?"

Jamie face flushed hot. She sidestepped the implied question with grace. "He's not my man, as you put it. We're dating and enjoying each other's company, nothing more and nothing less."

"Let me ask you one question and then I'll let you go," Jo said.

"Shoot."

"Are you dating others or are you exclusive?"

"I'm not dating anyone else and I don't think he is either."

"That sounds like a serious relationship to me. But if you say it's casual, I'll believe you."

"If you're done grilling me, I need to run home and change. I have exactly fifteen minutes before Caleb picks me up."

"You go ahead and we'll talk soon."

"Thanks again."

Jamie disconnected and flipped off the overhead light switch. She paused. *Is Caleb my guy?* With a shake of her head, she raced down the walkway to her car. She now had fourteen minutes.

❧

"Oh, shoot." Jamie peered through the windshield. "He's early." She parked in front of the garage door and hopped from the driver's seat. Joy radiated out of her. "Hello, stranger."

In a few long strides, Caleb was holding her in his arms. His eyes searched hers. "I know I'm early."

She giggled. "Guess you can't wait to get to the stables?"

He pulled her close. "You've been on my mind all day."

"Slow day?" she teased.

"I need you to know, I'm crazy about you."

"Caleb, we agreed we aren't going to get serious." She laid her hand on his chest. "I can feel your heart beating." Looking into his eyes, her breath caught.

"It's too late."

"What is?"

"To be casual. You're in my every waking thought. I can't get you out of my mind or my heart, and I don't want to."

"But you're leaving soon. It will be hard on both of us..."

"In case you haven't noticed, we already are serious. It just hasn't been verbalized."

Jamie didn't know if she should put distance between them or succumb to her feelings. She whispered, "Caleb." She closed her eyes.

"Jamie."

Her eyelashes fluttered. She tilted her head back, inviting him in. His lips brushed hers. Letting go of her doubts, she took a step deeper in his arms. He continued to shower feather-light kisses on her mouth and face. She kissed him back tentatively, and then slower and deeper. Jamie slipped under the spell that wove them together. She felt as if she were drowning, happily taking what Caleb was willing to give her.

Time stood still. She never wanted this feeling to end. But he cleared his throat, his lips still touching hers. "Jamie."

"Um."

"You need to change."

She took a half a step back, reluctant to leave the warmth of his embrace. "Right." She shook her head. "Let's go inside."

Caleb took her handbag, briefcase and her keys. He opened the door for her and stepped aside so she could enter the house first.

"I'll need five minutes, tops."

"Take your time." Caleb dropped her bags on the kitchen counter and looked around the tidy room. "Do you want to have dinner here tonight?"

Jamie called from the bedroom, "Sure. I picked up some shrimp—quick and yummy."

She emerged from the other room in jeans, boots and a short-sleeve tee with a sweater draped over her shoulders, her hair bouncing in a ponytail. "Ready."

He whistled appreciatively. "How do you do it?"

She crinkled her nose. "Do what?"

"Change that fast and look this good."

She could feel the blush running up from the bottom of her neck to the top of her forehead.

His hand slid sensuously down her bare arm. She shivered with anticipation. She reached out lacing his fingers with her own, then brought them to her lips, lightly kissing his cool fingertips.

"I could stay right here, but we need to go. Jo saddled the horses for us."

He pulled her close. His voice was husky. "I'll remember where we left off."

Jamie swung her leg over the saddle and grabbed the reins. Sitting astride, she waited for Caleb to mount Pirate.

"How long has the farm been in Jo's family?" He clicked his heels against the horse and began to move toward the gate. Chloe ambled alongside of her stablemate.

Jamie pushed her sunglasses into place. "I think two hundred years or something like that. But like many farms in the county, it used to be filled with dairy cows. Over the years the herd dwindled, and when Jo took it over she transitioned it to a riding stable. They still have a few head on the property. She leases land to other farmers for crops."

"And Robbie doesn't have an interest in horses?"

Jamie's lip twitched with amusement. "What makes you think he doesn't?"

"He's not working the farm."

"True. He took a different path."

"How did he get involved in the fitness biz?"

She glanced at Caleb as Chloe broke into a light trot. Glancing over her shoulder, she said, "You haven't figured it out yet?"

"You mean that he's crazy about your sister and she has no clue?"

"You hit the nail on the head. Basically, Robbie would follow Kenzie to the moon if that's where she said she was headed."

Caleb urged Pirate into a slow trot. "Doesn't he realize a girl likes a guy to not be a puppy dog?"

Jamie drew back on the reins, bringing Chloe to a halt. A flash of irritation laced her words. "It's not like that."

"It seems like she won't give the guy the time of day. At least from the casual observer."

Jamie could feel her temper spike. "Well, you're wrong. Kenzie and Robbie have been best friends since they were babies. They grew up together and may have had a date or two years ago but I don't think either of them knows how the other really feels about them. There's a reason why Kenzie has never dated any one guy for long. They don't compare to Robbie, and vice versa."

Caleb nudged Pirate closer. He leaned over and brushed his lips to Jamie's. "Let's stop talking about your sister. I'm leaving in a couple of days and I don't want to waste a single moment of our time together."

Jamie's heart lurched when he mentioned leaving. "You're right. Let's not talk about anyone else." Her eyes twinkled.

Caleb's eyebrow arched. "What did you have in mind?"

"Caleb Sullivan." She could feel the color rise in her face. "I thought we'd head back to my place, make dinner and sit by the fire."

"That sounds like a perfect evening." Turning the horses back toward the barn, Jamie and Caleb let the horses set a meandering pace. Chloe pushed open the gate with her nose, and Jamie slid down and latched it behind them. Caleb dismounted and, taking Jamie's hand, strolled to the barn.

"Do you think you'll have time to talk when you're traveling?"

"Of course, and we'll text and Skype and maybe even do the old-fashioned letter thing."

Jamie squeezed his hand. "This will be good for us."

She swallowed the lump in her throat. All she wanted to say to was, *don't go.*

Quietly they took care of the horses, and Caleb pulled two apples from his pocket. After passing one to Jamie, he held out his hand to Pirate, who nickered and devoured the apple in a few quick bites. "Hopefully he'll remember me so when I get back we can ride again."

She slid her arms around his waist and leaned in, her lips hovering over his, and whispered, "You're a man no one could forget."

Caleb threw a hefty chunk of wood in the crackling fire. Turning his head, he watched Jamie through the window. A slow smile spread over his face while his heart constricted. Two days until he wouldn't see those sparkling baby blues on a regular basis. He squeezed his eyes shut, committing to memory the way her smile started in one corner and spread to the other side. The way her deep chestnut waves curled around her cheek and fell like silk down her back. He itched to twirl a lock around his finger.

He shook off the fantasy and opened his eyes, turning his attention to the fire. He caught a whiff of her perfume, a mixture of roses, peony and a hint of citrus, alluring and feminine and uniquely Jamie. He drank in her scent. He was going to miss all of this and more.

"Hey, you." Her voice was soft and the come-hither look made his mind go blank.

"Hey yourself. I pulled out the chaise and grabbed a blanket out of my car. I hope it's not going to be too cool to sit out."

Her head cocked to one side and she looked up through her lashes. "I'm never cold when I'm close to you."

Caleb pulled her close, nuzzling her neck. "Have I told you I love the perfume you wear? It's intoxicating."

Jamie giggled. "You smell pretty good yourself."

The fire cracked and popped. With arms locked, they moved to the double lounge chair. She scooched back, laying the blanket around her shoulders, and Caleb bent over her. Resting his forehead on hers, he said, "I wish I wasn't leaving."

"I'll be here when you get home."

A tear hovered on her bottom lash. Using his thumb, he wiped it away. "Don't."

She gave her head a fierce shake. "I won't."

He lowered himself down next to her and put an arm around her shoulders. Jamie snuggled deeper into the circle of his arms. Lifting her face, she beckoned him in. He knew she waited for his kiss and he wasn't going to keep her waiting.

He claimed her mouth. His kiss deepened and blood hummed. He had never felt this way about another girl.

They came up for air. Jamie's voice was husky as she whispered, "I can feel your heartbeat in your kiss."

He loved everything about this girl. Several times those three little words almost slipped out. But he wasn't going to be the first one to say it—he feared it would scare her away.

"Caleb."

"Hmm." His lips trailed down to the hollow at the base of her throat.

Jamie leaned back in the chair, and his lips never left her skin. The chaise was plenty wide enough for two, but they lay thigh to thigh and arm to arm. There wasn't room for a breath between them.

Her voice breathy, Jamie said, "The stars are amazing tonight."

Caleb pulled back. "They're nothing compared to your eyes."

He turned her hand over, palm up and placed a tender kiss in the center. She shivered.

"Jamie, I've wanted you from the moment I laid eyes on you. When you struggled with the door knob at Steve's all this"—he gestured around them—"is all I've wanted. To be with you."

"I feel the same way."

An alarm on Caleb's watch buzzed. He glanced at the time. Sorrow filled his eyes. She struggled to stand. "I know." He could hear the sadness in her voice. "You need to go. I'm pretty tired anyway."

"Okay." Rising, he grabbed a bucket of water and poured it on the fire pit. "I want to make sure this is out before I go."

Jamie pulled the blanket tighter. Smoke billowed off the wet wood. Caleb poked at it and poured on some more water. "I'm pretty sure it's out."

Caleb took her hand, and the couple walked side by side through the house to the front door. Jamie pulled it open.

He cupped her cheek. "Dinner tomorrow?"

Jamie stood on her tiptoes and brushed his lips. "Six?"

"It's a date." He pulled her close. "I'm counting the minutes."

Her voice had a hint of a tremble. "Good night, Caleb, drive safe."

"Sleep well, my darling Mac."

She waited while he walked to the car and then closed the front door, the outside light burning bright.

Caleb patted his pocket and started to open the Jeep door. He wanted to give Jamie something that would remind her of him, but not tonight. Tomorrow would be better.

24

"Our last night together for three months." Jamie wiped her eyes with a tissue. She was embarrassed about her emotions bubbling up last night and she intended to clear the air as soon as Caleb arrived.

Earlier she'd shot him a text saying she'd meet him if he'd just say where they were going for dinner. Checking her phone, she saw he still hadn't responded. Grabbing her handbag and a light shawl, she decided to wait in the car. She didn't need a man to pick her up. She was perfectly capable of getting anywhere she needed to go.

Backing down the driveway, she stopped short when she heard a horn blare. She slammed on the brakes and looked around. His Jeep was blocking the end of the driveway.

She put the car in park and waited. In the rearview mirror, she saw Caleb was jogging up the drive. She slid down the window. "Hey. I sent you a text saying we could meet."

"Jamie, I didn't get a text and when I say I'm picking you up, that's what I'm doing."

Sparks flashed from her eyes. "I'm perfectly capable of getting where I need to be."

He leaned in the window and kissed her cheek. "Did I do or say something to upset you?"

"Of course not, I just didn't see any reason for you to drive here and then have to backtrack to a restaurant."

"It gives me more time to spend with you." His finger slid down her bare arm. "Please shut your car off and let me drive you."

She debated for about thirty seconds and was happy to relent. "Since you're here, we might as well go together." She put the car in drive and parked in front of the garage. Before she could open the door, Caleb opened it and helped her out. Pulling her into his arms, he kissed her—a slow and tantalizing kiss.

"I've been looking forward to having you in my arms all day. You have no idea how slowly the hands turn on a clock."

Everything fell back into sync between them. Her heart soared with delight.

"I missed you too." Her eyes sparkled.

"Before we go, I have something for you."

Jamie tilted her head back. "You got me a present?"

He grinned. "I did, just a little something."

They strolled to the wrought-iron bench in the front yard and sat down. Her pulse raced. It was way too soon for an engagement ring.

Taking her hand, he said, "Jamie, for the first time in my adult life, I don't want to hit the road. I want to stay here, with you."

"Oh, Caleb. We have responsibilities, but when you're done with your trip I'll be here."

"I was hoping you'd say something like that." He reached into his shirt pocket and handed her a jewelry box.

She sucked in her breath. "Caleb, it's too…"

He laid a finger over her lips. "Jamie, in my family there's an Irish tradition. When you're dating and the relationship becomes exclusive, wearing a Claddagh...well, it signifies a promise."

She opened the box, and lying on the velvet lining was a Claddagh pendant. He took it from the box and opened the clasp. "I'm hoping you'll accept my promise of a future together."

She ran her finger across the raised gold and pulled up her hair. He reached around and clasped the chain. The pendant rested in the middle of her chest. "You want us to have a future?"

"I do." His words were thick with unspoken emotion.

She cupped his cheek. "I'm sorry about before."

"I understand there's some stress involved. I have one foot on a plane and the other here."

Her smile grew into a small grin. "I appreciate that you're not a love 'em and leave 'em kind of guy."

He snorted a laugh. "Sometimes I'm just a saint."

She cocked her head. "Are you excited to go?"

He took her hands in his and lifted them to his lips, tenderly kissing the top of each one. "The time will go by quickly, and before you know it I'll be knocking on your door." He'd avoided the direct question.

With a catch in her voice she said, "Promise?"

Crushing her to his chest, Caleb held her tight. He murmured in her hair, "Wild horses couldn't keep me away."

Clinging to him, Jamie giggled, "It's a good thing I don't own any wild horses."

Kissing the top of her head, he said, "Do you still want to go to dinner?"

She nodded. "Let's eat really slowly."

He slung his arm around her shoulders and steered her toward the end of the driveway. "And then after, let's come back here and wait for the sun to come up."

"I'd like that."

Jamie blinked the sleepiness from her eyes. She was covered with a blanket.

Shouting, "Caleb!" she leapt from the couch.

Frantically she dashed to the front window and let out a groan of relief. His Jeep was still parked in the driveway.

"Jamie?" Caleb stood in the archway of the kitchen his hair standing on end and looking fresh from sleep. "I was just putting on coffee."

She flew into his arms and, holding him tight, said, "I woke up and you were gone. I thought you left without saying goodbye."

He smoothed her hair off her face. "I wouldn't just disappear and miss a goodbye kiss from you. That would be a horrible way to start my day."

Jamie nodded against his chest and sniffed. "For both of us," she mumbled. She didn't want to let go, but the smell of coffee lured her to lift her head. "You really did make coffee."

He joked, "I know you can't start a day without at least two cups. I brewed a pot and thought we could have a light breakfast before I head out."

Jamie extracted herself from his arms and padded over to the cupboard. Taking two mugs off the lower shelf, she set them on the counter. Noticing the cream was already sitting on the counter, she said, "What can I fix you for breakfast?" Grinning, she added, "I'm cooking. Scrambled eggs?"

He leaned against the counter and gave her one of his heart-melting looks. "We can cook together, but a very important question—do you have cheese?"

She pulled a block of cheese from the fridge, held up a jar of salsa and gave him a lopsided grin. "Vermont cheddar, what could taste better?"

"Just one of the reasons why I'm over the moon about you, Miss MacLellan."

The jar thudded on the granite counter. "Oh, Caleb."

"Come here." He held out his arms, and Jamie stepped into them. She looked up into his blue-green eyes. He pecked her on the lips. "Jamie, I'm hooked on you."

With a hitch in her voice, she said, "Me too, and frankly it scares the crap out of me."

He chuckled. "And why is that?" He brushed back her hair from her eyes.

She stared deep into his eyes and murmured, "Now I have something to lose."

"I love your honesty, but I don't see our relationship as something to lose—we have everything to gain." He tweaked her nose. "I don't want you torturing yourself over the fact that you've admitted you have feelings for me."

"I'm not. I mean, I won't, but..."

"But nothing. Jamie, we're lucky. We have someone who makes our hearts skip and tumble in wild abandon."

"I hear what you're saying, but you're talking to the girl who said she'd never have these kinds of feelings for anyone, let alone for an Irishman."

"And what's wrong with a man of Irish descent?" he teased.

"I thought if I ever did really fall for a guy it would be with a Scot."

"Ah, like your dad." He kissed the tip of her nose. "I'll do my best to live up to your father's standards."

"That will be easy." Jamie stood on her tiptoes and claimed his mouth with hers, committing the feel of his lips and the taste of him in her memory. "You already do."

She pulled back, and there was a hairsbreadth between them. "Breakfast?"

"If you're going to keep kissing me like that, I might not get on that plane," he growled.

She giggled. "I'm not going to be the reason you get fired." She patted his chest. "Let's eat and get you on the road so I can get to the office." She glanced at the clock. "It's already eight. I guess I'll be late this morning."

She walked back to the other side of the counter and blinked away the tears that threatened to spill down her cheeks. She was not going to let Caleb see her cry.

Working quickly, she dropped a hunk of butter in the skillet, and the eggs and shredded cheese followed. With a few stirs, the eggs were ready. Handing Caleb two plates he scooped up the eggs, putting more on one than the other.

She pointed to the mound of steaming, creamy yellow eggs. "That one is yours."

Caleb laughed. "I hate airline food, so I like to have a good meal before I leave."

"So true. They look perfectly cooked."

"That is just one of the breakfast items I cook well."

She cocked an eyebrow. "Oh, really?"

Caleb winked. "I guess you'll just have to wait and see." He held up his mug. "Let's toast."

"With coffee?"

"Sure, I never heard it had to be with spirits." He waited for Jamie to lift her mug.

"What are we toasting to?"

His fingers brushed the Claddagh pendant she wore around her neck. "To the most unexpected and wonderful surprise I've discovered while visiting Vermont."

Jamie felt heat rush to her face and she knew it was a deep shade of pink.

"To unexpected surprises."

25

With Caleb gone, Jamie's days slipped back into their familiar rhythm. She wished it was still tax time or something to keep her busy, but as it was she filled her time looking for new clients and her evenings either at Kenzie's gym or taking her bike out for a spin. Often one or both sisters joined her, doing their best to fill the unexpected void Jamie felt.

Her computer dinged, signaling an incoming Skype call. She hit a few keys and Caleb's rakishly handsome face filled the twenty-five-inch screen.

"Bonjour, mademoiselle."

"Hey, you." Jamie's grin stretched from ear-to-ear. "I didn't expect to hear from you." Her gaze slipped to the corner of her screen. "It's really late in France." She drank in his face. "You look tired." He was sitting in what looked like a small semi-dark room. "Is the house nice?"

He rubbed a hand over the stubble on his chin. "It's gorgeous. However, the first few weeks with a client are always tough. I ask up front their likes and dislikes or if they have anything they absolutely must have on the menu, and it's still a learning curve every time. On top of that, sometimes the home kitchens are lacking basic essentials. So I've had to order supplies."

"It sounds stressful."

"It'll smooth out. It always does." His smile warmed her heart. "I've missed you—what have you been doing?"

Jamie leaned back and pointed to the piles of folders on her desk. "Work, work and more work."

A flash of concern flashed across his face. "I hope you're doing more than work. Have you been hanging out with your sisters?"

"Sure, we've taken a few bike rides, done some hiking and gotten together for dinner a few times."

Caleb leaned toward the screen. "How's the plans for the big Scotland trip?"

"Good, seven weeks and counting. Kenz is closing the gym for a week and Robbie will reopen it before we get back."

"I'm sure you ladies are looking forward to seeing your parents."

"Other than Skype, we haven't seen them in months. Dad is loving being home and Mom's happy if Dad's happy."

"What will you do while you're there?"

A tiny smile graced her face. "We'll fish, hike the hills and finally come to terms with Gran's passing."

He nodded, somber. "That's right, this is your first trip back."

"We were there for the funeral, but it was such a quick trip. I keep waiting for the phone to ring or a letter in the mailbox. She loved writing letters. I'm guessing it'll hit me the first time I walk into her kitchen and she's not there waiting with a cup of her special tea blend."

"At least you're not doing it alone. You'll have Kenzie and Grace and your parents too."

Jamie flashed to Gran's kitchen and the last time she was in it, and choked back the tears. "Let's change the subject. I don't want to waste our time talking about something that's not going to happen for several weeks."

"Have you heard from my brother or Yvette?"

She brightened. "Actually, Yvette and I have plans this weekend. We're going shopping."

"Has she been staying at Steve's?"

"I think so. The last we talked, she was setting up a studio and starting to paint."

"I'm happy things worked out for them." Caleb's smiled faded. "As much as I hate to say it, I should let you go. Breakfast is early and I have a dinner party for twelve tomorrow night." His fingertips touched the screen, and Jamie stretched her hand out.

She murmured, "Not quite the same as holding hands, is it?"

He chuckled softly. "Not even a little bit."

She brought her hand to her lips and blew him a kiss. "Talk to you in a few days?"

"You can count on it." He returned the gesture. "Take care."

"You too."

Caleb disconnected the call.

Shadows crept into the corners of the office. Jamie shut down her computer and straightened the folders on her desk. She tilted the blinds to almost closed; she was ready to head home.

She dug her cell phone from her handbag and hit a speed dial button.

"Pasta Bowl."

"Hi, I'd like to place an order to go."

"Your usual, Jamie?"

Jamie laughed. "Thanks, Joey. See you in ten?"

Caleb pulled up the calendar on his computer and checked one of Jamie's old emails. "She'll still be in Scotland after I wrap up this trip."

Clicking the keys, he sent an email to his brother. *Bro, can you get Kenzie's email for me?*

He closed the laptop and made himself a note to follow up with Steve if he didn't hear from him by end of day tomorrow.

Caleb checked his email one last time before going to bed. "Yes!"

As he read the email, he grinned. "You're always one step ahead of me." Steve's email contained not only Kenzie's but her father's email as well.

He sent an email thanking Steve and then zipped off a short email to Kenzie and a final one to James MacLellan.

"I might just be able to pull this off."

Before he lay down, he slid open the drawer in the bedside table. Resting on a swatch of velvet was a diamond-and-sapphire ring.

"I've waited my entire life for you, Jamie MacLellan. Seven weeks is going to feel like an eternity."

Jamie pulled the car up to the back door of Steve's rambling Victorian and honked twice. The back door opened and Steve strolled down the steps and leaned into the driver's side window.

With a sunny smile she said, "Good morning, I'm here to abscond your girlfriend for the day."

"So I hear. She's almost ready and asked me to let you know she needs five more minutes. Want to come in for a coffee?"

Jamie shook her head. "No thanks."

"Okay." He paused.

She looked up through her dark glasses. "Do you have something on your mind?"

Casually he asked, "I was wondering…have you talked to Caleb in the last few days?"

"We've been trying to Skype a couple of times a week, and in between we text."

"Good to know." He nodded and looked toward the house.

Jamie's eyebrow arched. "Are you checking up on me for him?"

He held up his hand. "Not at all, I was just wondering. I've had one email from him."

"Is that unusual?" she quizzed.

Steve shrugged. "No, I guess not. I was thinking since he stayed here for a while he might touch base a little more."

Yvette skipped down the steps, wearing a floral sundress, matching cardigan sweater and swinging a bright pink handbag that matched her wedge sandals. "Hey, Jamie, sorry to keep you waiting." She laid a hand on Steve's arm. Standing on her tiptoes, she lightly kissed his lips. "I'll see you later?"

"Sure, have fun." He walked around the front of the car and held open the passenger door. "Don't rush home. I have a ton of paperwork and research to do for a client."

Yvette looked at Jamie. "Do you think we'll be back in time for dinner?"

"We can be." Jamie thought they'd be gone longer and told her sisters she wasn't going to be back early. It was going to be a long, lonely night.

Steve bent down and looked at Jamie. "If you ladies would like to have dinner here, I'll pick up a couple of steaks. I'm not up to Caleb's caliber, but I can barbeque a good porterhouse and toss a salad."

Yvette giggled. "Don't forget dessert and wine." She blew

him a kiss and turned to Jamie. "Let's roll before he starts talking about his grilling prowess."

Jamie put the car in reverse and backed down the short driveway, pausing while a truck passed by and then pulled into traffic. She tooted the horn, and the girls waved to Steve.

The first part of the trip was Jamie telling Yvette interesting tidbits about Vermont. They chatted like old friends. As they neared their exit, Jamie's thoughts turned to Caleb's parents and decided Yvette could fill her in.

Jamie asked, "Tell me about Mr. and Mrs. Sullivan. Are they nice people?"

Yvette smiled. "They are really super people. The guys are a lot like their dad and their mom is such a sweet lady."

"You know, I would have guessed they were nice. When I met Steve I thought he was smart and nice."

Yvette gushed, "Isn't he the sweetest guy ever?"

"He is totally over the moon about you." She glanced at Yvette.

"Oh, Jamie. I'm sorry."

"For what?"

"Sometimes I speak before I think."

Jamie giggled. "Yvette, we had zero sparks. Lots of good conversation." She decided to tell a tiny fib, hoping Yvette would relax and enjoy the day. "It was clear to me that we weren't going to be anything more than friends."

"And then you met Caleb." Yvette fanned herself. "He is smokin' hot."

Jamie snorted. "In case you haven't noticed, they *are* brothers."

Shaking her head, Yvette said, "Steve is a good, solid guy and Caleb is the mysterious one, never in one place for long. But"—she tapped her brightly polished fingernail on the tip of her nose—"I've heard Caleb talk about you. Trust me, I've been around this family a long time, and I know things."

Jamie gripped the steering wheel tighter. "I don't know

what you're talking about. We're dating, but right now it's long distance. Nothing serious."

"Oh, Jamie, really, who are you trying to convince?" Yvette brushed her bangs out of her eyes.

"It's the truth." Jamie flicked on her blinker and slowed. "He travels for his work and I live here. There isn't going to be anything more than what we have right now."

"Are you saying you haven't fallen in love with him?"

Jamie thought about dodging the truth as she eased into traffic. "I do love him. But I can't live a vagabond lifestyle. My business is here. I own my home and I have no desire to follow a man around the world."

"Wait, what if things were different and he was willing to relocate to Vermont?"

Jamie's eyes flicked between the road and Yvette. "I would never ask him to make that choice."

"You're not answering the question. Would you want more if he was here?"

Her heart hammered in her chest. "Are you asking so that you can tell Steve how I feel about his brother?"

Yvette held up her pinky. "This is just between us. I would never share girl talk with Steve or anyone, for that matter."

Jamie picked up speed as she exited the highway. "If things were different, I might consider something more serious with Caleb." The sun danced off Jamie's necklace.

"What are you wearing?"

Jamie did a quick double take. She was confused. "What are you talking about?"

"The necklace—is that new?"

Jamie held out the pendant. "This?"

"Yes." Yvette's smile widened.

"Caleb gave it to me the night before he left."

Yvette shrieked, "I knew it!"

"Yvette, don't go getting ahead of yourself. It's just a necklace."

From under her sundress, Yvette pulled out a similar necklace. "This is a Sullivan family tradition and exactly my point. Caleb has *never* wanted to be exclusive with *any* girl."

Jamie frowned. "It doesn't matter. We don't have a future."

"Do you want one with Caleb?"

"Let's talk about you and Steve."

"Stop avoiding the topic."

Jamie pulled into a parking lot and eased into a vacant space. Shutting off the car, she unbuckled her seatbelt. "Here's the scoop. But don't judge me."

Yvette smiled. "Promise."

Jamie couldn't help but smile at Yvette's open and sweet nature. "My entire life I've watched my parents have a wonderful and committed marriage. My sisters and I decided a long time ago it would be impossible to find a man who would treat us the way our dad treats our mom, with respect, love, trust and a true partnership. When we started dating we discovered most of the guys were the exact opposite—clingy, needy, jealous, and they wanted to be the center of our lives and never really understood our sisterly bond. We made the decision that we'd date, enjoy life and stay independent single women."

Yvette shifted in her seat and listened closely as Jamie talked. "You must know there are good guys like your dad out there."

"It crossed my mind when I met Steve that I might be wrong. He's a good man, but he was already spoken for, although I didn't know that specifically at the time—he kept taking phone calls every time we were together, and I'm guessing he was talking to you."

Looking sheepish, Yvette said, "Guilty as charged."

"I was fine. When Caleb took me to the aquarium, I had the best time from the moment we left my house until we got home." A tiny smile tugged at the corner of her mouth.

"Is that when your feelings for him bubbled to the surface?"

"Yvette, you have such a way with words. But yes, I did see him in a different light. When he took me home, we kissed."

Yvette slapped the dashboard. "WHAT?"

A slow grin spread over Jamie's face. "It was a sweet but toe-curling, heart-racing, blood-humming kind of kiss."

"And?"

"And what?" Heat flushed her cheeks.

"You did more than kiss. Come on, you can tell me."

With a shake of her head Jamie grinned. "Use your imagination and fill in the blanks."

With a knowing look, Yvette said, "Caleb wouldn't have made you feel like that if you weren't open to a future with him."

Jamie pulled the keys out of the ignition and dropped them in her bag. "Yvette, I've thought about this a lot. You can't have a successful marriage when one half of the couple travels for several months, then comes home for a couple of weeks before hitting the road again."

Yvette's mouth dropped open. "Who said anything about marriage?"

26

Jamie blinked, her eyes wide. "Isn't that," she stammered, "isn't that what you were talking about?"

Yvette teased, "We were talking about a relationship, and a marriage certainly qualifies."

"Yvette, I've told you, I'm not planning on getting married."

Yvette's eyebrow arched. "That only means sometimes the best laid plan changes."

Jamie pushed open the car door. With one foot on the pavement, she stared out the windshield. "I never thought I would fall in love, the kind of love that would carry me through good and bad times, that would be strong enough to weather whatever storms come. The kind that deepens over time."

"Sounds like you've given this a lot of thought."

Jamie wilted. "I have, and maybe I'm being unrealistic, but I would rather avoid getting into a relationship with the hope of a lifetime and be disappointed he can't live up to my expectations."

Yvette grasped her hand. "I've known the Sullivan men

for a long time, and Caleb is a one-woman man. He's not a player, never has been."

"So you say. But his career takes him all over the world. What if I got pregnant? I don't want to be a single parent."

"Jamie, don't you think you're erecting roadblocks without cause?"

She shrugged. "For now, I'm going to enjoy what we have and not worry about what may or may not happen in the future." Her face brightened. "We came to shop, not dissect my love life. Are you ready for some retail therapy?"

Yvette pulled down the visor mirror and checked her hair and makeup. Wiping away a smudge under her lower lashes, she said, "I know, I know, I'm such a prissy chick."

"It doesn't bother me. We all have our own quirks."

Yvette snapped the visor up and announced, "I'm ready to shop until our feet can't walk one more step or we can't carry one more bag."

"Guess I've been forewarned." Jamie hit the lock button on the car fob. Hearing the *beep, beep,* she pointed down the street. "Let's start on the other side of Church Street and we can wind our way up and down the side streets. I have a perfect place for lunch."

"Lead the way." Yvette pushed her large oversized sunglasses up her long, elegant nose. "Eh, look at these bricks." She gingerly stepped along the walkway on her high-heeled sandals. "If I can walk through the North End in Boston, this will be a piece of cake." She giggled. "Is there a good bakery we can get something to nibble on later?"

Jamie couldn't help it—she laughed out loud. "A fashion plate with a sweet tooth."

Yvette smoothed down her dress and grinned. "You've only seen this side of me. You should see how I dress when I'm dabbling in my studio."

"I'm sure you dress to work, but I'll bet you don't go anywhere without, at the very least, a swish of mascara."

"Jeez. You haven't known me that long and you already guessed most of my secrets."

Jamie linked her arm through Yvette's. "Come on. I know just the place to start, and we'll end the day with a cup of coffee and a slice of the best chocolate cake with Vermont maple buttercream frosting."

Yvette laid the back of her hand across her forehead and pretended to swoon. "Can we start with cake and end with shopping?"

Jamie laughed and pointed Yvette down the street. "A girl who thinks like me."

Jamie pulled away from Steve's house after making two trips from the car to the house with Yvette's shopping bags. She declined dinner and got on the road. She wanted to get home to Skype with Caleb.

The radio on the car cut off with the ring of her cell phone. Pushing the hands-free button on the steering wheel, she said. "Hello?"

"Jamie. Hi." Caleb's voice was music to her ears.

"Hi." A slow grin spread over her face. "I was going to call you later."

"I wanted to check in and ask if you had fun shopping today?"

"How did you..." She laughed. "Oh, you must have talked to your brother."

"I did. He said you were going to show her Vermont isn't just farms and mountains."

"I'm happy to say she did her fair share to keep the economy humming."

"If there is one thing Yvette does really well, it's shop." He chuckled.

Jamie glanced at the dashboard like she was looking at

Caleb while they talked. "We had a lot of fun. She's not what I had expected."

"Oh?"

She could hear the surprise in his voice. "I guess after hearing some of what you and Steve said about the breakup, I wasn't quite sure I'd like her."

"And now?" The question hung in the air. Caleb waited for her to respond.

"We never stopped talking. She really loves Steve."

Caleb's voice was low and husky. "Jamie?"

Jamie's breath caught in her chest, and her heart hammered.

"I'm in love with you."

Tears sprang to her eyes, and she pulled over to the side of the road. "Caleb."

"Are you crying?"

Sniffles answered him.

"Sweetheart, are you still driving?"

"No." A soft hiccup escaped her lips.

"Talk to me. Why are you crying?"

"You. Said. You. Love. Me."

With a chuckle he said, "I did and I do."

"You're three thousand miles away," she said, her voice thick with happy tears.

"That doesn't mean I can't tell you how I feel, does it?" His voice was light and teasing.

"Well, no. But I wish you were here."

"It won't be long now before I'll be home."

"And sister-cation is just around the corner, and then you'll be here when I get back, right?"

"Absolutely. Three weeks isn't that long, especially when ten of those days you'll be having a ball running through the Highlands and sloshing through the cold rivers sporting top waders, a big floppy hat and carrying a fly-fishing pole."

She giggled. "There's miles of river and plenty of room for another fisherman."

He chuckled. "That's a sound I love to hear, you giggling."

Jamie wiped the dampness from her cheeks. "Do you like to fish?"

"Never really took the time to learn the art of fly fishing. But I do know how to cook them."

"Then I'll make you a deal. Everything I catch, you cook."

"Sounds fair."

"I wish we were on Skype. Talking is so much better when I can see your handsome face."

"I miss your beautiful smile, Jamie, but I close my eyes and I see you."

The ache of missing Caleb was more than she bargained for, but now was not the time to talk about it. She deliberately didn't say anything more and moved on to a generic topic.

She checked her side mirror and pulled back onto the two-lane road. Keeping her voice light and carefree she asked, "Tell me, how it's been going over there?"

"I'm in Ireland, and we'll be here until it's time to fly back to the States."

"So you did a month in each country—Italy, France and Ireland?"

"Yeah, a lot of dinner parties, a couple of brunches, but overall everything's run smoothly."

"Do you like one country better than the others?" Jamie pulled into her driveway and waited for the garage door to open.

"They all have high points, but there's only one place I really want to be."

Jamie held her breath and longed for Caleb to say Vermont. "Where's that?"

"Wherever my girl is."

Her heart melted just a little more. "Oh, Caleb. You say the sweetest things." She put the car in park, turning off the engine as the door softly closed.

"I try."

"Hold on while I get off Bluetooth."

Jamie stepped from the car with the phone glued to her ear. She strolled through the back door. She kicked off her shoes and dropped her bag on the counter, then flopped onto the couch. "You now have my undivided attention, so where were we?"

"Talking about my favorite place in the world."

Jamie smiled into the phone. "So, anything else going on?"

"Not really. Why don't you tell me about your family's home in Scotland?"

"It's been in our family for generations. Someday my sisters and I will take over the farm."

"Sheep, right?"

"It used to be a huge sheep farm, but now we have cottages to rent and there is even a wedding venue on the property. We have a manager for the animals and work with a local event planner for small weddings. Nothing big, but each wedding is special and intimate."

"Describe the farm to me. Paint me a picture with your words."

"It's heaven on earth." With a small laugh, Jamie said, "At least that's what I've always thought. The pastures are separated with tree-lined stone fences and the hills roll, flowing from the top to the lowlands. The little pavement there is intersects with the gravel road leading to the main house. There are six picture-perfect cottages dotting the landscape in the very heart of the farm. They were previously used for farmhands, but after Gran had a new main house built for the family she converted them to rental cottages."

"It sounds amazing." His voice was warm and encouraged her to keep talking.

"Oh, and the heather covers the hills in August—it's

simply breathtaking. We have some very rare white heather growing on the farm too."

"I thought it was just purple."

Jamie laughed softly. "Scots are a touch superstitious and they believe in magic. White heather is considered lucky, and brides often include it in their bouquets."

"Do you know why it's lucky?"

Her voice took on a touch of a brogue. "I wouldn't be part Scot if I didn't know. I'd suggest you settle in for a big dose of history."

"Consider me settled and all ears."

Her voice had an excited catch. "Supposedly, in the third century Malvina, the daughter of the legendary poet Ossian, was to marry a Celtic warrior, Oscar. As most things went in that time, he died in horrible battle. A messenger delivered a spray of heather to her at the time he delivered the news. When Malvina heard, she was brokenhearted. It was his final gift to her, eternal love. As she wept, her tears turned the heather from deep purple to pure white. It is written she proclaimed that despite her sorrow, this pure white flower would bring good luck to those who found it."

He said softly, "That's quite a story."

She looked at her parents' wedding photo on the side table. "My mom carried white heather when she and my dad got married. I think that's why they've been so lucky all these years."

"Is there anything else that you think is special about the farm?"

Her voice softened. "There aren't enough hours left in the day to tell you everything. Maybe someday I'll show you the views from the summit, or we'll stroll around the farm path. Oh, and the waterfalls and loch are not to be missed."

"You really love it there."

"The land has a part of my soul."

Caleb didn't speak for several long moments.

"Caleb, are you there?"

"I'm here." His voice was husky but subdued. "You've painted quite a vivid picture for me, and someday I hope you'll show me your Scotland."

"I'd love to and"—Jamie snorted—"I'll even teach you how to fish." She heard Caleb yawn. "I'm sorry, I've talked way too long. You should get some rest."

"It *is* late. Good night, Miss MacLellan."

"Sleep well, Caleb."

Jamie didn't want to move off the couch. She wanted to stay frozen in the sweet glow of sharing her beloved Scotland with Caleb.

"One day you'll see how magical a sheep farm can be." Jamie closed her eyes and pictured her and Caleb walking hand in hand through the fields of heather.

27

Crash.

"Damn it!" Jamie gave the shattered vase on the hallway floor a once-over. After rushing to the kitchen, she grabbed a small broom and dustpan. Sinking to her knees, she carefully swept larger chunks and tiny shards into a pile. *I'm sorry, Gran—this was one of your favorite vases.*

The doorknob turned and before whichever sister was on the other side could enter, Jamie called for them to stop.

Grace hovered in the doorway. "What happened here?"

"I was getting the large suitcase from the attic and it came tumbling down along with my duffel bag. Of course, it crashed into the table, and before I could stop it, the vase crashed into smithereens."

"Was that Gran's?"

Jamie's lips drooped as she said softly, "You know how much it meant to me."

"I'm sorry, sis." Grace bent over and held the dustpan as Jamie swept the last of the pile into the metal pan. "As Gran would say, it's just an object—it can't replace a memory."

"True, but it was hers."

"When we get over there, maybe you'll find another one to bring home. You know she had tons of them."

Jamie's head bobbed. "Yeah, that's a good idea."

Grace picked up the suitcase and set it on its wheels. "I'm going to take this outside and make sure there isn't any glass anywhere."

"Thanks." Jamie did one final sweep of the broom. "Have you heard from Kenzie?"

"No. I'm assuming she'll be over soon. She wanted to go over the last few details with Robbie before the end of the day."

Jamie sat back on her heels and pushed back the hair from her eyes. "You seem to be in the know."

"Kenzie felt the need to fill me in on every detail last night when we talked. You know how she is right before we go on sister-cation."

Jamie stood up. "I do. I suffer from the same compulsion to have everything sewn up before we get on the plane."

"The difference between you two is that Kenzie has a backup, and you know Robbie will do a great job of keeping everything running smoothly. You don't even have a receptionist."

"Robbie's a good guy, and for the record I don't need office help. I give my clients enough time to be prepared and I always pick the middle of the month for travel so nothing major is happening."

"It's easy for me. I put the vacation request in, it goes on the calendar. As of five o'clock on Friday, I'm free."

Jamie tossed the small broom at Grace. "Here, you might need this."

Grace ducked. "Take care of that dustpan before I'm plucking glass out of your hand."

She stepped outside and Jamie emptied the pan into the kitchen garbage, checking to make sure all the slivers were gone before putting it back in the closet.

"Hey, Jamie!"

"Coming." Jamie hurried out the door to see why Grace sounded so excited.

She was holding a letter. "I think this might be from Gran."

"What are you talking about?"

"It came out from under the bottom of the suitcase lining. When I turned it upside down to shake it out, this envelope fell on the ground."

Jamie turned the envelope over. "It does look like her handwriting."

Grace's voice dropped to just above a whisper. "How do you suppose it got there?"

"Let me think." Jamie tapped edge of the envelope in the palm of her hand. "I must have used this suitcase on the last trip before Gran died."

"Are you going to open it?"

"Don't you think I should wait for Kenzie?"

"It's addressed to you, not us. Open it."

"I need to sit down. Leave the suitcase and let's go out back."

Grace trailed behind her. Settling into the wicker loveseat, Jamie ripped open the top of the envelope and removed a piece of paper. Unfolding it, she glanced at the contents and smiled. "I'm going to wait for Kenzie."

"Here I am." Kenzie jogged across the patio and pulled up a chair. "What do you have there?"

"It's a letter from Gran that I found in Jamie's suitcase."

"Really?" Kenzie stretched out her hand. "Can I see it?"

With a touch of irritation in her voice, Jamie said, "I'm going to read it if you'll take a seat."

"Well, excuse me. I'm sure I speak for Grace when I say you're taking too long."

"Then be quiet," Jamie snapped. Kenzie and Grace sat back and waited while she cleared her throat.

Dearest Jamie,

I hope you don't mind that I went into your room so I could slip a wee little note into your suitcase as a surprise for later. When you find this, don't tell your sisters, as I did the same for them. On second thought, I'm sure they're with you now, so it's no longer going to be a surprise.

During our visit I wanted to tell you about a very special dress that you will receive after I'm gone. After giving it much thought, I've come to the conclusion that will be my last gift to you, my beautiful, strong and independent granddaughters. Each one of you reminds me of myself when I was a young woman. Oh, you're all individuals, but there is something that connects you to me: love and blood.

I hope your father has found my journals to pass on to you. There are so many stories untold and so much I still wanted to teach you. But time is dwindling. Now, don't cry, I've been blessed beyond my wildest dreams by growing up on this farm and then having the opportunity to meet and marry your grandfather, who understood why I could never leave this land. When my son James went to America I thought my heart would shatter like glass. I missed him so much. But instead of heartbreak, he met your mother, Olivia. She became the daughter I always longed to have. They went on to have the three of you. Jamie, Kenzie and Grace, you are my legacy.

Many times the four of us have talked into the wee hours of the morning about your desire to never marry. I'd like for you to keep your hearts open to the possibility of love and continuing the legacy of our family.

Jamie, this is for you specifically. Please don't read this aloud, but if you wish you can tell Kenzie and Grace what I wrote later.

Jamie fell silent and continued to read, smiling and nodding as if she could hear Gran's voice. She then looked at her sisters and began to read out-loud again.

My darlings, it's time for me to finish my letters and turn in for the night as tomorrow is our last day together, and what plans we have. A hike along the waterfall and the heather is in full bloom, and as a surprise I'm going to show you the secret place where my dear Rory picked white heather for me.

Until we meet again, all my love, Gran

Jamie wiped the tears from her cheeks and averted her eyes. She knew her sisters were doing the same.

"What did Gran say that she didn't want you to read to us?" Kenzie asked.

Jamie made a hasty decision and decided to keep Gran's real message to herself. "Basically, she asked me to always stay true to our bond. No matter the miles between us, sisters are forever."

Grace nodded. "I'm never going to live more than a short drive from either of you. So don't go making any plans to change zip codes."

Kenzie hopped up from the chair and slid it back into place. "Don't worry, squirt, I'm not going anywhere and I don't think Jamie is either—our businesses are tied to Easton. You're the one who could fly the coop since you can work anywhere."

Grace sniffed, her chin jutting up. "This is my home and I wouldn't want to live any place but here."

Jamie grinned and clicked her heels together. "You know the saying, there's no place like home."

"Ain't that the truth?" Kenzie patted her stomach. "Do you have anything to eat in that house? I had a tough workout and I'm starving."

Jamie frowned and said, "Who stocks up before vacation? Call in a takeout order to the Pasta Bowl and you can go pick it up on your way home."

Kenzie held her cell phone up. Prepared to dial.

"Hold up," Grace said, "I'd like to know what time we're leaving tomorrow."

Jamie got up and said, "We need plenty of time to get to

Logan, check in and grab lunch before we get to the gate. We board at seven."

"I know what that means—we're leaving at nine." Kenzie groaned. "Am I right?"

Jamie protested, "You never know about traffic and I'm not cutting it close."

Kenzie sat up. "Relax, I'm not picking on you. Well, not much." She grinned. "Are you taking fishing gear?"

"No. There's plenty at Gran's."

A cloud fell over Grace's face. "Do you think we'll ever stop thinking of it as Gran's house?"

Jamie's smiled faded.

"Maybe we should just call it the farm." Kenzie reached out for her sisters' hands and squeezed them tight. "After all, it *is* the MacLellan family farm, and last I checked my passport reads *MacLellan*."

Grace's eyes sparkled. "Hey, mine does too."

Jamie forced a smile. "You're funny. I guess that makes it unanimous."

She hauled her sisters up from the couch, eyes shining bright. "I have a Skype date with a handsome man, so you two need to go home and pack. In twenty-four hours we're going to be on our way to endless fields of heather and fish just waiting to be caught."

Jamie settled into her desk chair and fired up her computer. Checking her watch, she pulled up the chat box and pinged Caleb. His face appeared before her eyes.

"Hello, beautiful."

His smile made her ache to run her fingers over his face. Two more weeks. "Hi. It's good to see you."

He held up his hand so they were fingers to fingers. "Are you packed and ready for the big adventure?"

"I'm packed and my sisters stopped over. We're leaving early in the morning. I'm afraid we'll run into traffic and get delayed. You know the traffic around Logan can be tricky."

Smirking, he said, "I do, and missing an international flight wouldn't be a good way to start your sister-cation."

Laughing out loud, Jamie said, "That's an understatement, and my sisters would kill me if I was the reason we missed our flight." Propping her cheek on her fist, she said, "I'm always the planner, not just for vacations, but for everything we do."

"Good to know for future reference. Which airport are you flying into?"

"Glasgow. We'll rent a car and drive to the farm. It's about an hour or so north of the airport."

"Oh, I thought your dad might pick you up."

"It's easier if we have a car. Usually we take off while Dad is working around the farm. He likes to fix things for Gran." Her face fell and her gaze dropped.

"Jamie, what's wrong?"

"He used to spend a lot of time puttering around the house. Gran would make lists of projects for him, but I'm sure he's gotten everything done that needed to be fixed."

"So maybe there's not much to keep him busy. Hey, sweetie, look at me."

Jamie looked up.

"If you want your dad to pick you up, call and ask him."

In a shaky voice, she said, "No, I don't want anything to be, well, different." She took a deep breath, she rolled her shoulders. "There's nothing like leaving the bustle of the city and driving through the winding roads of Scotland."

"You're looking forward to the drive," he stated with simplicity.

"It's breathtaking—the land is so green and lush. We have

great memories. Kenzie, Grace and I have hiked over every hill and lowland on the farm. Danced in the cool, shallow stream that winds through the fields. Lain back in the heather and watched the clouds ebb and flow through the sparkling blue sky." She sighed. "It's a magical place, Caleb."

"It does sound idyllic. A great place to spend summers for the Sisters MacLellan."

"I don't do it justice. As kids we traveled with our parents all over Europe. Although many places were beautiful, nothing ever had that intangible feeling I get the minute I walk up the stone path to the house."

Caleb ran his hand through his hair. "If I didn't know better, I'd think you were born and raised there."

A mischievous gleam popped in her eye. "Aye, and I happen to have a kilt, the sassy version a lass might wear."

His eyebrow cocked. "Oh? Maybe you can answer a burning question for me—what does a man wear under that thing?"

Jamie threw back her head and laughed. "Maybe I'll get you one and you can find out for yourself."

"That sounds a little bit like a challenge, Ms. MacLellan."

"Only if you're man enough," she jested.

"I'll wear it if you wear your kilt. We can match."

She giggled. "Sure, and we'll go out to dinner?"

"Whatever you want, my love." Jamie's laughter was contagious. He leaned back in his chair and chuckled.

Jamie's laughter died and her eyes were bright. "I'll be glad when we're together again. I've really missed you."

"More than you thought?" Caleb teased.

"So much more."

"I'll be on your doorstep before you know it."

"I'm counting the days."

Caleb blew her a kiss. "Me too."

28

The plane's overhead lights dimmed and Jamie arranged her plaid pashmina to ward off the chill. She stared out the window at the inky, star-filled darkness, her thoughts drifting to the farm and Gran. How she wished Gran would be there, welcoming her with open arms.

Grace snored softly, body slumped against her shoulder. Jamie draped her shawl over Grace and glanced at Kenzie. She was sound asleep with her hood pulled up and hands tucked into the front pocket on her lavender sweatshirt.

Gran is smiling down on the MacLellan sisters. Even though she won't be there physically, her spirit will welcome us home.

Jamie closed her eyes and drifted to sleep.

"Jamie, wake up. We're going to be landing soon." Then Grace shook Kenzie and said virtually the same thing to her.

"How long have you been awake?" Jamie pushed her bangs out of her eyes.

"Not long enough to get up and use the restroom before

the fasten seatbelt sign came on." Grace squirmed in her seat. "I wish I hadn't had so much water."

Kenzie was grumbling about the same issue while Grace handed Jamie her shawl. The plane pitched forward, tires screeching as it bounced on the runway. It kept a steady speed to the terminal. The overhead speaker squawked with the standard *Welcome to Glasgow* before announcing the local time and temperature. Finally, the attendant reminded everyone to choose them again when they booked passage and safe travels.

The girls pulled their carryon bags from under the seat in front of them and unbuckled their seatbelts. Grace tapped her foot. "Can't the line move quicker?"

Kenzie snapped, "It's not going to get any faster with you doing that annoying tap, tap, tap."

"It's keeping my mind on something else other than what I really am thinking about."

"Girls, bickering about who needs to do what isn't going to speed things up, so be ready to get up when you see an opening."

"Ladies?" A deep male voice caught Grace's attention, and she looked up. He took a step back, creating a space in front of him.

She squeaked, "Hello."

Jamie poked her. "Get up. He's going to let us off first."

Kenzie draped the strap of her bag over her shoulder and mumbled thanks."

Grace slid out of the middle and looked into his deep green eyes; they reminded her of the Green Loch. "Thank you," she murmured.

"My pleasure." His brogue was light and musical.

Grace stepped aside to let Jamie go ahead of her and followed her sisters off the plane. The gentleman was one step behind her until a throng of people separated her from her sisters. Looking around, she wanted to thank the man, but he too was gone.

Jamie walked up and snapped her fingers in front of Grace's face. "Earth to Gracie."

"What? I'm coming." She hustled through the crush of travelers, keeping one eye on signs directing her to the restroom and the other looking for the green-eyed man. Giving up, she ducked in behind her sisters.

"We'll meet outside," Jamie called to them.

Grace used the facility and then splashed water on her face as she peered into the mirror. "Not your best look to impress any man."

Kenzie came out of a stall. "Did you say something?"

"Just talking to myself." She dried her hands and left.

Kenzie said, "I'm feeling a little antsy. It's weird, you know, being here."

Jamie tapped her chest. "Gran's with us, right here." She gave Kenzie a quick and hard hug. "You feel her too, right?"

Kenzie nodded, tears filled her eyes.

Jamie tugged on Kenzie's sweatshirt and said, "Let's go find Grace before she takes off with Mr. Green Eyes."

Kenzie laughed. "He *was* cute."

"She has good taste." Jamie bumped Kenzie's shoulder. "I wonder where she gets it from."

With a quick retort Kenzie said, "Me, of course."

Grace asked, "Feel better?"

"Good enough to get our bags and rental car, and then we can hit the open road."

Grace's eyes twinkled. "Shotgun!"

"No, you had shotgun on the way to the airport." Kenzie's lower lip jutted out as she plastered on her fake pout.

"You didn't call it." Grace wagged her finger in front of Kenzie's face.

"Girls, we're not children. Let's behave like the ladies we are and you can take turns. Which means, by default, it's Kenzie's turn to ride shotgun."

Grace couldn't quite pull off her sad face long enough to be effective before she burst into giggles. "It doesn't really matter—the car will get to the farm at the same time whether I'm in the front or back."

"If you feel that way, Grace, I'll take shotgun for the whole trip." Kenzie smirked.

"Nope, we'll switch." Grace pointed down the hall. "Baggage claim is that way."

Inching forward, Jamie eased the car into traffic and looked left and then right. The girls had decided to splurge and rent the luxury SUV, in baby blue, for their vacation. Kenzie, ever practical, pointed out with the split folding seat there was room for all their luggage.

At first traffic was typical of any city, cars driving too fast and bobbing and weaving in traffic. But soon Jamie spotted the exit she needed. Flicking the blinker on, she pulled off the highway and they were cruising down a two-lane road winding through the lush green hills.

"Oh, look." Jamie pointed out Kenzie's window. "There's the waterfalls Gran took us to every year."

Kenzie got a wistful look. "Remember, she'd always say we should look for the fairy hiding under the falls."

Jamie giggled. "I remember one time, when Grace was small, she decided she was going in to find the fairy and fell head-first into the water."

Grace laughed. "I don't remember that, but I learned the water around here is icy cold."

The mood in the car lightened as they reminisced. Grace leaned forward between the seats. "How old was I when Grandad died?"

Jamie looked at her in the rearview mirror. "Maybe four?"

Kenzie said, "We were here. Mom and Dad had gone into the city for dinner and Gran was putting us to bed when Grandad called to her. She told us she'd be back to finish our bedtime story, and then I can remember hearing her scream." She shuddered at the memory.

Jamie said, "She always said it was a blessing she was able to hold his hand in those last moments." In the rearview mirror, she saw Grace wipe away a tear. "Grace?"

"I wish I could remember him. I have a vague memory of him towering over me, and he smelled like the sunshine."

"We were all too young to really remember. But Gran said it was the best way for Granddad to pass on, to be surrounded by the people he loved most."

Kenzie watched the landscape drift by the window. "Do you think Dad is more like Grandad now that he's gotten older?"

"We should find some pictures and see if they looked alike." Jamie slowed the car. "Anyone want to stop and pick up some teacakes and cookies before we get to the farm?"

"Traditional Scottish tea? Count me in." Grace shook off the sadness and smiled. "And I'll even pick up the tab."

Jamie pulled the SUV up in front of a small pastry shop. She turned off the car and unbuckled her seatbelt. "Can you believe we're finally here?"

Kenzie pushed open her door. "I'm starving, so let's hurry and then get our butts out to the farm."

As soon as they stood on the curb, a truck horn tooted and someone waved.

Kenzie waved back. "We've been spotted. I think that was Gran's neighbor, Angus."

Grace held open the shop door. "Do you think he'll swing by and let Mom and Dad know he saw us?"

Jamie stepped into the shop with Kenzie behind her. "More than likely. We'd better not dillydally too long. I wouldn't want Mom to worry."

Kenzie said, "Mom will know exactly what we're doing. We can't drive through town without stopping at MacMeekin's."

A cry of happiness made them turn and greet the shop owner.

"Oh my goodness! The MacLellan girls have found their way home."

"Hello, Mrs. MacMeekin." Jamie gave her a warm hug. "It's been a while."

"Hello, dear, 'tis good to see you." Jamie was pleased to see that she still had a swirl of salt and pepper-colored hair swept into a bun tied with a jaunty pink ribbon. "What can I get for you today?" She gathered Kenzie and Grace to her ample bosom and tweaked Grace's nose.

"We were hoping you still had some cream buns, and of course a wee bit of shortbread?" Jamie peered into the case and pointed to the scones. "Are those oatmeal?"

Mrs. MacMeekin took a large white pastry box from the shelf behind the counter. "A bird told me you girls were arriving today, so I baked cream buns just for you."

Kenzie smiled at Gran's best friend. "Mrs. M. that is so sweet of you. But how did you know we'd stop by?"

"There isn't a time in all these years you've been coming for a summer holiday that you haven't stopped here before heading out to the farm. I can plan my day by your routine."

Kenzie chuckled. "You're saying we're predictable."

"Not at all, lass. I'm saying you're regular customers, and ones I treasure." She slid open the heavy glass door to the case. "Now, what can I put in the box?"

Before Mrs. MacMeekin was done, the girls had her fill the

box with all their favorites: shortbread, scones, empire biscuits, Scottish cookies with a raspberry filling, and of course the cream buns. After paying the bill, the girls walked to the car with promise to stop back soon.

On the sidewalk Grace pulled open the box and selected a piece of shortbread. "Can you believe she baked us cream buns?"

Kenzie peered in the box and teased, "You can't wait, can you?"

"Look who's talking?" Grace held open the top and then turned to Jamie after Kenzie took a cookie.

Jamie unlocked the car. "She's an amazing woman. We need to visit at least once more before we go home."

Kenzie groaned. "Why did you have to mention going home? We just got here."

"I want to make sure we make time for Mrs. M, that's all."

Grace brushed the crumbs from the front of her sweater. She mumbled with her mouth full, "And we will."

Jamie held open her door. "Ladies, hop in. It's time we finish our journey. You know Mom has looked out the window a hundred times." She slid in behind the wheel and waited for her sisters to buckle up.

Grace scrambled into the backseat. "I hope Mom has the kettle on."

29

Jamie slowly drove up the gravel driveway and drank in the sights and sounds of life on the farm. Sheep grazed on the sweet, emerald-green grass and the herding dogs lazed in the sun in front of the barn doors. Chickens pecked the ground inside their run. With the windows down, she took a deep breath and knew her sisters' thoughts mirrored hers. It was good to be back on MacLellan land.

Dad was standing tall on the walkway, sporting a jaunty cap and dark sunglasses that hid his sparkling blue eyes. Mom was standing on the top step, not in the doorway where Gran would have been waiting, but close enough to create a lump in Jamie's throat. She swallowed hard and parked. She turned the key, and as soon as she was unbuckled she flew into her father's arms with Kenzie and Grace with her. Dad beckoned for Mom to join them. How long they stood in the afternoon sun didn't matter—time stood still.

"My darling lasses, it's about time you stopped dawdling."

Jamie face shone with happiness. "Dad, Mom, it is so good to see you both. I think this is the longest we've been apart."

Mom brushed the hair back from Jamie's face, kissed her cheek, and did the same with Kenzie and Grace. "My beautiful daughters. You are a sight for sore eyes."

Dad began ushering them to the house and Grace ran back to the car. "Guess where we were?" She held up the white box.

"Ah, you saw the inside of the MacMeekin bakery before stepping foot in our home."

"Daddy, you know it's tradition. Besides, aren't you curious to see what's inside?"

"I'm hoping you bought enough cream buns so I can have at least two."

"James MacLellan," Mom admonished. "I think one for tea will be sufficient."

Dad smiled and took the box from Grace. "What else did you get?" Smacking his lips, he peeked under the top. "Let's go inside—your mother and I want to hear all the details of your life."

Kenzie tried to bite her tongue but blurted out, "Jamie should go first."

"Kenzie, you seem to be bursting with news," Mom said.

In a rush of words, Kenzie said, "Jamie's got a super-hot boyfriend."

"She does now?" Dad said. "Jamie, should that be the first topic of conversation?"

"Kenzie," she hissed through clenched teeth. "You can't keep anything quiet."

"If we waited for you to tell Mom and Dad, they might never know about Caleb."

"Caleb—is he Scottish?"

Jamie pushed open the door. "No, Dad, he's more Irish than anything. His name is Caleb Sullivan."

Jamie was unpacking her bag in her room. Gran had made sure each granddaughter had her own space when visiting. Special care had been taken to decorate them with her and her sisters in mind. Jamie's room had large windows to greet the morning sun with soft colors in shades of purple and cream. A plush carpet covered the dark wood floor, keeping toes cozy in the cool early morning air or on damp, rainy days. A full-sized bed was snuggle-worthy, draped in a down comforter, and it was piled high with handmade throw pillows. Everywhere Jamie looked, she could see Gran's special touches.

A soft knock on the door interrupted her thoughts. "Come in."

Mom poked her head in the door and looked at the stacks of folded clothes. "Can I help?"

"No, but I'd love some company."

Mom settled into the rocking chair next to the window. "Was the trip uneventful?"

"Yeah, you know overnight flights—settle in and sleep."

"And now how are you feeling, being back?"

Jamie sank to the floor. "I'm not going to say this was easy. But seeing you and Dad waiting for us helped."

"We've tried to change the routine, but everything falls back to how Gran handled life here."

With her head bowed, Jamie spoke softly, like she was in church. "She was a remarkable woman."

"When I look at you, I see some of her facial expressions, and you're strong, just like she was."

She took a deep, steadying breath. "Will it get easier, coming here?"

"It will, in time. Life goes on, and Gran wanted you and your sisters to think of this as your home. She had hoped someday you'd bring your children here."

"I don't know if children are in the cards for me."

"Sweetheart, why would you say such a thing? You're young, with plenty of time to have a family." Mom crossed the room and stood next to Jamie. She pushed a lock of auburn hair away and turned Jamie's face to look into her eyes. "Tell me about Caleb."

Jamie sighed. "He's sweet and generous in spirit, thoughtful and kind."

"Is that all?"

"No, he's so much more, and very handsome. Not stuck-up handsome—you know, the kind of guy that's comfortable in his skin."

"Grace told me he was Attorney Steve's brother."

"He is." Jamie laughed. "I think I told you about the dinner party where I had a plan to see if Steve and I had sparks. Well, the night before I received a bouquet of tulips, and of course I assumed they were from Steve. But then I found out Caleb sent them."

"Well, that's sweet."

"Oh, Mom, every time I saw Caleb, I had these feelings for him. I kept pushing them aside, determined to see if something was going to work out with Steve. The day he stood me up..."

"What? Who stood you up, Steve?"

Jamie nodded. "The week after I had had everyone for dinner Steve was supposed to take me to the aquarium, but he sent Caleb to pick me up and he spent the entire day with me, taking me out to dinner and when he drove me home, we kissed."

"Who, Steve or Caleb?"

Jamie smiled. "I'm not being clear. I spent the day with Caleb and he kissed me."

"How did you feel about that, being that you were dating his brother?"

"I wasn't really dating Steve." Jamie's gazed dropped to the floor. "In that moment, all my fears fell away. I knew I was wrong about everything. Of course, later they resurfaced. He travels extensively for work and I can't have a relationship where I would hardly ever see him."

"People change careers all the time." Mom pushed Jamie's chin up. "Have you asked him what he wants?"

Her eyes grew wide. "I would never ask him to give up his career for me. That wouldn't be fair."

"Have you been talking since he's been away?"

She beamed. "Of course—we Skype, text, and when I get home, we have plans. He's going to be in Vermont, waiting for me."

"Honey, as your mother, I'm going to give you some advice."

"Okay."

Mom spoke with simple sincerity. "Give Caleb a chance to tell you what he wants out of life. He might just surprise you. And one last observation—whether you know it or not, you've given him your heart."

Jamie nodded. "I love him and it scares the hell out of me."

Mom patted her leg. "Now put your stuff away. We have time for a walk before dinner."

"Is it the traditional first night dinner of lamb?"

Mom grinned. "Is there any other choice? Oh, and I'm assuming you and your sisters are planning on getting up early and heading out to your favorite fishing spot?"

"I've been dying to cast a line since we touched down."

Mom laughed. "Don't tell you father or he'll be begging you to go too."

"Girls' day first, then fishing with the parents."

❦

Jamie woke as the first streaks of sunlight warmed her face. She sat up and stretched, and then leapt from the covers. She dressed in a flash, and in stocking-feet tiptoed into the hall and tapped on her sisters' doors. Then she crept down the stairs and entered the spacious kitchen. After turning on the coffeepot, she set out three insulated travel mugs, rummaged in the refrigerator and filled the cooler with premade sandwiches, fruit and cookies for lunch.

She snapped her fingers. "Water."

She pulled everything out and repacked it with the bottles on the bottom. Closing the lid firmly, she placed it by the door.

Kenzie and Grace bounced into the kitchen. "Coffee ready?" Kenzie asked.

"Almost. Grace, do you want to put the cooler in the car?"

"Sure. I'm glad we loaded all the gear last night." Grace slipped out the back door as the coffeepot sputtered its last bit of dark brew into the carafe.

Kenzie grabbed the cream and sugar bowl. While Jamie filled each mug, Kenzie added cream and sugar to each one. Securing the lids, she passed one to Jamie. "Here's yours."

Jamie slid open the top and took a tentative sip. "Hot." She waved a hand in front of her mouth.

"I should hope so." Kenzie took the two remaining mugs and slipped sunglasses in place. "Let's hit it before all the beautiful trout swim away."

"Ha, that won't happen." Jamie grabbed her keys and followed Kenzie to the car, where Grace was sitting in the passenger seat.

Kenzie remained silent and slid into the backseat for the short drive to their favorite stream. Jamie pulled the car off the road and parked. Quietly the girls stepped into their top waders, pulled on their fishing vests and floppy hats, each lost in her own memories. With poles in hand, they made their way to the water's edge.

Jamie looked up and down the river. The crisp morning

air caressed her face. The heaviness she had been carrying in her heart slipped away with the current.

They fanned out in the riverbed. Jamie had the first cast of the day. It sailed over the water's surface before slipping into the pool, and then she jerked the line skyward.

The cadence of the cast, back and forth, as the line glided on the air, presenting the fly to the fish was therapeutic. The rhythm of casting was second nature to Jamie, as she had been fly-fishing since she could hold a rod.

The birds sang in the trees and the water gurgled as it flowed around her legs, the sun warming her shoulders—it was pure heaven. She stole a glance toward her sisters, and the look of serenity on their faces mirrored how she felt. This wasn't about catching fish for dinner; today was about reconnecting with Gran.

A few hours later, Grace gestured toward the bank. She began to pick her way over the slick stones. Kenzie followed, and Jamie was the last to reach the grassy bank.

"Lunch?" Grace flopped back on the grass and massaged the bicep in her casting arm. "My muscles forgot how to do this."

Kenzie laughed. "Maybe I should add a casting session to our workouts to keep us in shape."

Jamie attempted to sit cross-legged and gave up, as her waders didn't bend. She didn't want to take her top waders off only to put them back on. "This is pure bliss."

"Do you think Mom and Dad were disappointed we wanted to come out today, just the three of us?" Grace asked.

"No," Jamie said. "They get it."

"Did you fill her in about your romance?" Kenzie's voice had a hint of teasing.

"Yeah, we talked, and I've decided to just let go and enjoy whatever comes." Her eyes followed a bird in flight. "I really love him."

Kenzie gave her a sidelong smile and said, "You're just figuring that out?"

Jamie flopped back in the grass. "He's a good man, and even if things don't work out in the long run, I don't want to miss out on any time I can spend with him."

Grace peered at Kenzie over her sunglasses and winked. "It's about time you came to your senses."

Jamie rolled over to her side and propped her head up in her hand. "What do you mean?"

"It's as plain as the nose on your face how you both feel about the other. Why keep fighting it?"

"I get the feeling everyone can see what has been right in front of me."

Kenzie snorted. "I saw it the night we had the dinner at your place."

"I was sort of dating Steve."

"Yeah, but he was too perfect for you."

"Hmmm. You're right. I need someone who challenges me."

Kenzie turned to Grace. "Since you're younger, take pity and help me up."

"Let's just lay here a little longer and then we'll head home," Jamie said. "I'm not ready to leave."

Kenzie tossed her a wrapped sandwich. "Then eat something and soak up the sun. Rain is in the forecast for later today.

30

Jamie's nose twitched. She flicked open her eyes and sat up. Kenzie and Grace were sound asleep in the grass as the lazy river gurgled next to them. Kenzie was snoring softly and Grace was lying on her back, face tilted toward the sun.

"Hey, Sleeping Beauties. Wake up."

Grace yawned and stretched her arms overhead.

Kenzie grunted and opened her eyes. "What's going on?"

"Looks like it was nappy time." Jamie glanced at her watch. "It's almost three. We need to get going before Mom and Dad send out a search party for us."

Grace jumped up. "I feel great. We should go fishing more often."

The girls stowed their gear in the back of the car and made the short drive back to the house. As they came around the last corner, Jamie leaned forward. "I don't remember Mom saying we were expecting guests for the weekend, do you?"

"Nope." Grace leaned forward and poked Kenzie's arm.

"I wonder who's here," Jamie mused.

Grace suppressed a grin. "Guess we'll find out soon."

"Do you guys know what's going on?" Jamie stopped the

car before getting to the house and looked at her sisters. "Well, do you have any ideas?"

Grace shook her head. "No, we have no idea. Right, Kenz?"

Jamie dropped the car in drive. Pulling up to the back door, she said, "I don't know why I've got butterflies."

"Jamie," Kenzie admonished. "We've had guests at the farm before. Stop overreacting."

"You're right." She flashed her sister a smile and said, "I'm just being silly."

The girls hauled the fishing gear to the garage and put it back where it belonged. Grace grabbed the cooler and headed toward the kitchen. Kenzie and Jamie followed her.

A low whistle stopped Jamie mid-step. She turned toward the tree line. Someone was standing in the shadows. She took a slow step forward and then broke into a run.

Racing across the gravel driveway, she threw herself into Caleb's arms. Tears streaming down her face, she covered him with kisses.

"You're here!" she cried.

He chuckled. "I am. Are you surprised?"

"Oh, Caleb, I can't believe it. I didn't expect to see you for two more weeks."

"How could I wait when a mere five-hour drive separated us?"

She cried, "When did you get here?"

He held her in his arms and said, "About noon. I must admit, I thought you'd be back a bit sooner."

Not wanting to let go, Jamie looped her arm through his and grasped his other hand. "We fell asleep on the riverbank."

"How was the fishing?"

"We didn't catch anything, but that doesn't matter. We had a blast." Jamie looked at him from the corner of her eye. "Did my parents know you were coming?"

With a sly smile, he said, "Who do you think gave me directions away from where you'd be fishing? I didn't want to risk any chance you might see me."

"Then come and we'll have tea, the Scots way. Hopefully there are still some cookies leftover from yesterday."

"I stopped at this bakery in town on my way here."

Giggling, Jamie asked, "MacMeekin's?"

"How did you know?"

"It's the only and best bakery in town." She glanced at her clothes. "I'm a mess."

He kissed her forehead. "You're beautiful." Arm in arm, they strolled toward the house. "Do you think after we have tea we could go for a walk and you can show me the farm?"

"Sure, but we might need raincoats." She pointed to the dark clouds rolling toward them. "It's going to rain."

He glanced up and said, "I don't have one. Maybe we can go later."

"You can borrow my dad's." They arrived at the house and Jamie held open the door. "Ready?"

His eyes held hers. "Yes."

Mom had the kettle on and cookies were arranged on a plate along with a few other pastries Caleb had brought with him. "I thought we'd sit out back, but it looks like we might get damp, so your sisters have set out cups and plates in the living room and Dad lit a small fire."

Jamie noticed Caleb's puzzled look. "When it rains this late in the summer, a fire takes the chill off."

He kissed her forehead. "Maybe I should see if your father needs any help."

Caleb left the room and Jamie twirled around the center island. "Mom!" she squealed. "What do you think? Isn't he adorable?"

Mom patted her hand and smiled. "He's a sweetheart."

"When did he call to see if he could surprise me?"

Casually Mom said, "A few weeks ago," as she poured boiling water over the tea leaves.

Jamie's mouth formed into a large O. "You've known all this time what he was planning and you never said a word?"

With a small laugh, Mom said, "When I'm asked to keep a secret, I do."

Jamie gave her mom a quick hug. "Thank you. This is the best surprise ever."

"Why don't you go into the living room and I'll be right in?"

Jamie hesitated, torn between staying to help her mom and going to see Caleb. "Are you sure?"

"You haven't seen Caleb in months and you want to hang with me? I think not." Mom shooed her from the kitchen.

Jamie hovered in the doorway and watched her father and Caleb leaning against the mantle chatting like old friends. She wanted to sing and dance a jig. "Are you two getting acquainted?"

"Caleb is a fine man." Dad pulled her into a one-arm hug. "I hear the fish weren't biting today."

Jamie kissed Dad's cheek. "To be honest, they didn't have a chance to bite—we fell asleep on the bank."

He chuckled. "Sounds like a nap under the Scotland sky was just what you needed."

Her eyes got dreamy. "Being on the river is so relaxing."

"Caleb, do you fish?" Dad's voice boomed.

"No, sir, I've never had the opportunity to fly-fish, but I'm hoping I can convince Jamie to take me out."

Dad's smile went from ear to ear. "Caleb, call me James, and tomorrow we'll go with Olivia and the girls."

Caleb grinned. "Excellent. I look forward to it."

Mom came in carrying a tray with two pots of tea. Kenzie and Grace weren't anywhere to be seen, so Jamie excused herself to find them. She called up the stairs, "Tea's ready!"

A muffled, "Coming," drifted down.

She went back to the living room. "Where are your sisters?" Mom asked.

"They're coming. Caleb, sit next to me." Jamie ushered him to the sofa.

Mom poured tea and offered a steaming cup to Caleb and then Jamie. Dad helped himself from the other pot. Kenzie and Grace joined them just as Mom settled on the sofa.

Caleb cleared his throat, and his voice trembled slightly. "James, Olivia, I want to thank you for welcoming me into your home."

Dad slipped his arm around Mom. "We're happy to have you here."

Caleb turned to Jamie and took her hand. "Jamie, seeing you today was like my heart started beating again. I didn't realize until the moment our eyes met just how much I love you."

"Caleb—"

He laid his fingers on her lips. "Hold on there. I'm not done."

Her eyes became saucers, and she remained quiet.

Caleb slid from the sofa and landed on one knee.

Taking her hand and looking deep into her eyes, he continued, "I've thought about this moment since you stormed out of the restaurant. The flash in your eye burned my soul and I knew there would never be another woman for me."

He put his hand in his shirt pocket.

Jamie's hand flew up and covered her open mouth.

"I know how much your family and this farm means to you. I knew this was the only place I could ask you the most important question of our lives."

He took her left hand and held an engagement ring at the tip of her finger.

"Jamie MacLellan, will you do me the honor and say yes? Marry me and spend the rest of our lives together."

The tears trickled down her cheeks, a sob escaped her throat and she ran from the room.

❦

Caleb looked around at the family. Shock and confusion paralyzed him.

"Go after her!" Kenzie and Grace shouted in unison.

He raced from the room. Franticly he searched the grounds. Relief poured over him when he found her perched on a fence watching the heavy clouds. "Jamie?"

She turned her tear-stained face away from him. "I'm sorry, Caleb. I can't marry you."

"But why?" he croaked. "I know you love me, and I'm crazy about you."

She sniffed and blinked away her tears.

"Jamie." His voice was stern. "I'm not leaving until you tell me why you won't marry me."

"No. It's not fair to you." Her voice was filled with anguish. This was not how she expected her day to end.

He took her hand. Softly he said, "Why don't you let me be the judge of what is or isn't fair?"

"Promise you won't change your life based on what I'm about to say," she pleaded.

His eyes clouded with concern. "Go on."

Her voice cracked. "I can't marry you and watch you leave for three or four months, be home for a few weeks and then leave again. It would shortchange both of us."

"Oh, sweetheart," he cooed. "I haven't told you my other news." He gathered her in his arms and, using his thumb, wiped away her tears. "I'm done traveling. This was my last personal chef gig. Steve's been checking out locations between Easton and Rutland, and he's found a place where I can set up a cooking school."

She perked up. "You're going to live in Vermont? Full time?" She dried her face on her sleeve.

Caleb smiled. "I don't want to live anywhere else. Jamie, where you live is where I want to call home."

She pushed Caleb from the fence. "Will you do something for me?"

"Anything for you." He pecked her lips.

"Will you ask me again?"

He pressed his lips to her and kissed her properly.

For his ears alone, she whispered, "I have a different answer."

Caleb reached into this pocket and dropped to one knee. He took her hand in his, in a deep and crystal-clear voice, he said, "Marry me, have a life with me and love me for the rest of our days."

Jamie perched on his bent knee. Wrapping her arms around his neck, she said, "I do, I will and I'll love you with all my heart for the rest of our days."

31

Jamie wandered down the long gravel road. She told Caleb she wanted to see her Gran before they left for Glasgow. On the way, she picked a bunch of heather to place on the grave.

She passed the small church and went through the open gate, then gingerly picked her way among the old headstones until she found the Mackenzie and MacLellan plots.

"Hi, Gran. It's almost time to go home to Vermont. Kenzie and Grace are packing, and Caleb—remember, I introduced you to him—he's spending some time with Dad so I can hang with you for a bit."

Jamie brushed away a few stray leaves from the marker that read *Arabel Mackenzie MacLellan*.

"Two weeks hasn't been long enough to show Caleb all the special sights and sounds of Scotland. We'll be back, but until then we have so many decisions to make, a wedding to plan, where we're going to live, and of course Caleb needs to set up his business."

She sat down on the cool, damp grass. "I'm going to ask Dad if we can put a small stone bench here so when I come to visit I don't have to sit on the grass."

She wiped away a tear that slipped down her cheek. "You know, Gran, you pointed me in a new direction, sending the wedding dress and letter from Great-gran, and then reading your journals. Trying on the dress opened my eyes to the possibilities of a different kind of life. You wanted more for me, Kenzie and Grace."

Jamie looked toward the heavens. "I wish you could be here for my big day. I'm going to wear your dress."

She pulled herself up from the ground. Kissing her fingertips, she placed them on the marker. "I love you, Gran. Until next time."

Jamie strolled back to the farm. This was an even better trip to Scotland than she had imagined.

The bags were loaded in both cars. Caleb was waiting by his when Jamie ran back into the house to double check one last time.

When she bounced down the stairs, she could see through the window Caleb looked toward the house and her heart flipped. He was going to be her husband.

Pulling open the cabinet where Gran's vases were stored, she selected one. Turning around the kitchen one final time, Jamie whispered, "Bye, Gran, and thanks for looking out for me."

She and her sisters hugged their parents tight. "I'll call when we land in Boston and then when we get home."

Mom said, "And we'll be home in time for Thanksgiving and stay through the holidays. Maybe by then you and Caleb will have set a date for your wedding."

Dad shook Caleb's hand. "It was a pleasure meeting you, and look after my girls."

The MacLellan sisters said in unison, "Dad, really?"

"All right, well, off with you." He held open car doors and

shut them after giving each daughter one last hug and kiss. "We'll talk soon."

Jamie was in Caleb's rental car. She turned in the passenger seat and waved until she couldn't see them anymore. Caleb picked up speed as he turned onto the road with Kenzie and Grace following in their rental.

She leaned over to kiss Caleb's cheek. "Thank you for making this trip unforgettable."

He grasped her hand and, bringing it to his lips, kissed her engagement ring. "Every day is memorable when I'm with you."

She smiled at him with love in her eyes. "Let's go home."

The End

Order **Borrowed, Book 2 in The MacLellan Sister Trilogy**.

BORROWED: BOOK 2

CHAPTER 1

Kenzie bumped the hallway table and dropped her luggage, scattering mail over the entryway. She caught the jar of wild-flowers midair. With a tired smile, she murmured, "Robbie Burns, you always know what I need after a long trip."

She buried her nose in the blooms, drinking in the fresh scent of sweet pea, lavender and daisies. Carrying the jar into the living room, she placed it on the table where she could see it and flopped on the soft leather couch. Her cell buzzed. It was Robbie.

Putting a smile in her voice, she said, "Hello there." She closed her eyes and pictured his easy, crooked smile.

"Welcome home, Kenz. Good trip?" His voice was smooth, like aged whiskey.

"It was. You'll never guess what happened." Not waiting for him to ask, she shrieked, "Jamie and Caleb got engaged!"

With a low whistle, he said, "Wow, that's a shocker. The first MacLellan sister to tie the knot."

Kenzie propped her feet up and sighed. "I'm going to finally have a brother. He showed up in Scotland our second day there and popped the question."

"How did he ask her?" Kenzie could picture Robbie slouched in his comfy chair.

"It was so sweet. We were having tea and he dropped to one knee. Jamie freaked out, said no and ran from the house. Of course, Caleb went after her, and when they came back from the field an engagement ring was on her left hand and a smile as bright as the sun shining over the Highlands in our beloved Scotland."

"That sounds special for the both of them."

Kenzie laughed softly. "Right out of a romance movie."

"When are your parents coming home?"

"Sometime before the holidays." She twirled a short strand of chestnut-brown hair. "You know, one of these days we need to stop talking about you coming with me and make some definite plans. Scotland's like no place else on earth. After all, you do have Scottish blood in your veins."

His deep, rich laugh made her smile. She had missed him, and said, "Before we do that, I'll need to hire someone to keep the gym open while we're trip-tropping through the Highlands." She stood up and stretched one arm overhead, changed the phone to the other hand and worked out the kinks on the opposite side. "Or we'll shut down for ten days."

"Whoa," he chuckled. "Am I talking to Kenzie MacLellan?"

With a small laugh, she said, "Chalk it up to me being overtired, but I'm serious we need to hire someone." Kenzie tousled her hair. "I'll open tomorrow."

"Sleep in—I've got everything covered. I didn't expect you until late."

She grinned. "Robbie Burns, you really are one in a million." She thought, *I could use a man like you around all the time.*

"Oh, and I put a few essentials in your fridge so you don't need to go to the store, at least not today."

"Hey, did you go hiking?"

"I came back early it wasn't as much fun without you." Kenzie could almost hear the shrug in his voice.

Teasing him affectionately, she said, "Well, in that case, I won't forget your present. You deserve something extra special."

He chuckled. "Until tomorrow, Kenz."

She noticed a layer of dust on the glass table. Padding into the kitchen, she grabbed a bottle of vinegar and water. She polished every surface in the condo until it gleamed. Feeling more light-hearted than when she walked through the door, she made her way around her ultra-modern digs opening windows to freshen the air.

Curious to see what Robbie had bought, she wandered back into the kitchen and peered in the refrigerator. Greens, cooked shrimp and some fresh fruit. On the counter was an avocado. Dinner. Silently she thanked him again.

After adding some shrimp to her tossed salad, Kenzie carried her plate into the living room. After being with family for the last two weeks, the silence was deafening. She grabbed her phone and started to dial Jamie but stopped. She was with Caleb, in Boston.

I'll call Grace. One sister is just as good as two for an impromptu dinner.

On the second ring, she heard, "Hello?"

"Hey, Gracie, I was wondering what's for supper."

"Takeout, I guess. You?"

She toyed with her salad. "Robbie stocked the fridge."

Grace sighed and said, "He's a sweetie."

"I know, right? Do you want to come over? I have plenty."

"Absolutely! See you in twenty." Grace disconnected, but not before Kenzie heard a faint "*YES.*"

Kenzie set her plate on the coffee table and went into the kitchen to fix one for her younger sister. After it was ready, she slipped it in the fridge.

I wonder what will happen now that Jamie's getting married.

She kicked back on the couch and closed her eyes, drifting off. The door banging jarred her out of her tired stupor.

Grace stuck her head into the living room. "Hey, long time no see, sis. It's been, what, three hours since we got home?"

Grace as well as Jamie looked very similar to Kenzie. Their heart-shaped faces were just the start. They had the same coloring; crystal-blue eyes and auburn hair. Except Kenzie's was short and spikey, Grace wore her hair long with tough-to-tame curls and Jamie's was long and sleek.

Grace's eyes twinkled mischievously as she held aloft a pink-and-white striped paper bag. "Technically we're still on vacation, so I picked up sundaes."

Kenzie joked, "Good to know you're upholding the long-standing tradition—vacation ends when we go back to work." She peeked inside the bag. "Did you get me hot fudge on peppermint stick with extra sprinkles and whipped cream?"

"But of course," Grace chuckled. "Sans the cherry."

Kenzie wrinkled her nose. "What a way to ruin a sundae. At this very moment, you're my favorite sister."

Grace snorted. "Only until Jamie does something extra nice for you."

Kenzie dug in the bag and pulled out a container. She handed it to Grace. Grace's eyebrow spiked.

Salad forgotten, Kenzie licked whipped cream from the edge of the sundae cup.

Frowning, Grace said, "Don't you think we should put these in the freezer?"

With a lopsided smirk Kenzie replied, "No. The fudge is never the same after it freezes."

Grace furrowed her brows. "Kenz…" She dragged out her name. "Do you believe Gran's wedding dress is enchanted?"

"Maybe." Kenzie looked at her from under long eyelashes. "Do you want to try it on?"

Grace smirked, "You should be next."

"I don't want to jinx it."

Ignoring her response, Grace dropped her face. "Will Jamie have time for us after she's married?"

Kenzie closed her eyes and basked in the decadence of the fudge sauce. "Ah, this hits the spot."

Sharply, Grace said, "Kenz, did you hear me?"

"Gracie, of course she will. Jamie's getting married, not going to the moon. We may need to knock before just walking into her place after Caleb moves in."

Grace stirred the ice cream. "I'm happy for her. Caleb's a great guy."

"Me too."

"Who knew Jamie could smile all the time?"

Kenzie laughed. "Love does seem to bring out the best in a person."

The girls' phones buzzed and they looked down. "It's Jamie," Grace announced.

Hey—we'll be home tomorrow. Let me know you got home okay.

Grinning at Grace, Kenzie said, "I guess we have our answer—she's always going to be our big sister."

Grace took a picture of her sundae and texted Jamie, adding a caption: *Dinner. Yum!*

Moments later, their phones chirped. *Peppermint stick? Save me some.*

Grace's face perked up and she put her phone on the table. "I don't know about you, but I'm feeling better."

Kenzie beamed. "Me too. Now let's finish our dessert so we can eat our salads."

Jamie held up her cell so Caleb could see the picture. "Guess what my sisters are having for dinner?"

Caleb studied the small screen. "Ice cream?"

Jamie chuckled. "Technically we're still on vacation, so we can have ice cream too."

He pulled her into his arms. "Is this a MacLellan tradition?"

Jamie's bright blue eyes batted in his direction. Feigning innocence, she said, "And if I said yes?"

He pecked her lips and said, "I'll be right back." Caleb hurried from the room. While he was gone, Jamie unzipped her travel bag. Before she had time to decide if she should completely unpack, Caleb opened the door. "Good news. I told Mom we were going to miss dinner."

Jamie's brow wrinkled. "Huh?"

He flashed a flyer in front of her face. "We're going out for ice cream."

In two short steps, she flung her arms around his neck, showering his face with kisses. "I promise, you're going to love this tradition."

He chuckled. "I can't wait to discover more family traditions."

She stopped kissing him and looked in his eyes. "Can I ask you something?"

Caleb searched her face. "Of course."

Jamie chewed her lower lip and pulled him down on the bed next to her. "I can't wait to marry you, but I can't lose my sisters. We're not just related to each other, we've chosen to be best friends too." She unconsciously picked at a loose thread on the bedspread. "We have keys to the other's homes." Her voice dropped. "Do I need to ask them to return theirs?"

Caleb smoothed back her hair. His eyes held hers. "Absolutely not. The only thing I ask is the master bedroom and bath are off limits."

Jamie let go of the breath she was holding. Laughing she said, "Thank you for understanding."

"Sweetheart, they're going to be my sisters too, and you

need to realize I don't want to change your life just become a part of it."

Jamie's lips hovering over his. "When I think I can't love you any more, you do or say something so sweet." She kissed him lightly. "Now you said something about ice cream?"

Caleb said with a laugh, "Absolutely. I'm not breaking a MacLellan tradition."

Robbie prowled around his apartment. Kenzie was home and tomorrow couldn't come soon enough. The last two weeks dragged on forever.

He'd attempted, many times over the years, to pry her from his heart. She'd never see him as more than her best friend and coworker, but he loved her. For better or worse, she'd captured his heart a long time ago. She was in his blood. Maybe now that Jamie was engaged, there was hope Kenzie would let go of her foolish idea that a long-term relationship would take something away from her.

He leaned his head against the cool glass of the window, his body unmoving but his mind racing. *How can I make her see I'm the man who will love her for a lifetime but never ask her to change?*

Order **Borrowed, Book 2**
in The MacLellan Sister Trilogy.

THANK YOU

Thank you to everyone who was in my corner during the writing process of this series. Without you it wouldn't have been possible.

Suzanne

Jade

Mackenzie

GF1

Blondie

My girls Meg and Em

Thank you for reading *The MacLellan Sisters – Old and New.*

I hope you enjoyed the story.

If you did, please help other readers find this book:

1. This book is lendable. Send it to a friend you think might like it so she can discover me too.
2. Help other people find this book by writing a review.
3. Sign up for my newsletter by contacting me at http://www.lucindarace.com

4. Like my Facebook page, https://facebook.com/lucindaraceauthor
5. Join the Friends who like Lucinda Race group on Facebook at https://www.facebook.com/groups/1659098381010817/?ref=br_rs
6. Twitter @lucindarace
7. Instagram @lucindraceauthor
8. Book + Main Bites @LucindaRace

ABOUT THE AUTHOR

Lucinda Race is a life-long fan of romantic fiction. As a girl, she spent hours reading novels and dreaming of one day becoming a writer. As life twisted and turned, she found herself writing nonfiction articles but still longed to turn to her true passion, romance. After developing the storyline for the Loudon Series, it was time to start living her dream. Clicking computer keys, she has published seven books in the series.

Lucinda lives with her husband Rick and two little pups, Jasper and Griffin, in the rolling hills of Western Massachusetts. Her writing is fresh and engaging.

Visit her on:

www.facebook.com/lucindaraceauthor
Twitter @lucindarace
Instagram @lucindaraceauthor
www.lucindarace.com
Lucinda@lucindarace.com

MORE BOOKS BY LUCINDA RACE:

The MacLellan Sisters Trilogy

Old and New

Borrowed

Blue

The Crescent Lake Winery Series 2021

Blends

Breathe

Crush

Blush

Vintage

Bouquet

It's Just Coffee Series 2020

The Matchmaker and The Marine

The Loudon Series

The Loudon Series Box Set

Between Here and Heaven

Lost and Found

The Journey Home

The Last First Kiss

Ready to Soar

Love in the Looking Glass

Magic in the Rain

Made in the USA
Middletown, DE
16 July 2021

44263906R00172